# Bellicose

Benjamin Wilson

# POSTAL MARINES

Other Books in the series:

# Bellicose

---

Benjamin Wilson

MEROVEX

*Bellicose*

This is a work of fiction. Names, characters, places and incidents are either the product of the author's imagination or are used fictitiously, and any resemblance to actual persons, living or dead, business establishments, events or locales is entirely coincidental.

Benjamin Wilson
Visit my website at `http://example.com`

Printed in the United States of America

*First Printing, July, 2014*

ISBN-13 978-0-9839521-0-7

# Chapter 1

## *A Beautiful Day*

### 1.   Bophendze - Korundai Orbital - 3943 AD

Six months. The Imperial Postal Service normally needed only six months to turn a civilian into a Postal Marine. Danel Bophendze, however, posed a challenge. His drill instructors called him the runt of the litter. Over the past nine months, he heard hundreds of off-color phrases about how he would never become a marine. Most of them were variations of his personal favorite, "you can't pour water into a rock."

Despite their dire predictions of permanent failure, Postie Bophendze made it to Imperial Postal Marine Orbital . He no longer put his helmet on backward because it fit better that way. Now he possessed the characteristic iron-rod backbone of all Marines. As he waited in the passenger lounge, he tried to demonstrate his new-found ability to stand rigidly straight. His feet were firmly planted to keep balance should he be attacked. There were many Marines around him, and he tried to emulate them.

He kept looking around for the nearest trash can. He had never been off-planet until he joined the Postal Marines. The gravimetric field that provided the orbital's artificial gravity was never constant. Hundreds of fluctuations a second made him feel like the deck was pitching and swaying. *Why did I eat a big breakfast before leaving planetside?*

The trashcan sat several meters away, but he was in queue to board. The distance was agonizing. *Steady, Bophendze. This is the life you chose. You're going to have to learn to keep your breakfast*

1

*down.* It was a lie he told himself. Throughout boot camp, Bophendze had drilled into his head the pride of the marines. They were the Emperor's choice to enforce peace of his shipping lanes. They fought smugglers and pirates. They collected tariffs. The last bit seemed a bit odd to him at first. It seemed more odd that he spent most of his time in boot learning how to clean.

The best of bad choices. He did not want to be a marine. It was the only option he had, the only way to care for himself after his mother's death. He blamed Providence for this choice—for being a marine. His stomach continued to churn.

Off in the distance, Bophendze saw a chief pick up a microphone. "May I have your attention. The transport to Temasek we're waiting on has ghosted. I will spare you the prediction on when it will arrive. Needless to say we will be boarding another ship."

Bophendze wondered what ghosting was. He recognized the term from training, or somewhere. He looked around at the other Marines. The more seasoned Marines looked to the deck or made some unauthorized religious gesture. Now seemed like the best time.

He set his duffle bag on the deck and ducked under the queue strap. He took a few measured steps toward the nearest trash can. He felt the deck lurched again and he hurried his last few steps. He managed to heave all of the morning's breakfast into the can. It took him a few beats to clean up.

"Postie! I ought to make you eat that."

Bophendze stood and turned in an awkward fluid motion. He was at parade rest by the time he finished twisting. It seemed like the right thing to do. Everybody on the orbital outranked him.

"The only reason I'm not is you don't look two days from being a scrub. Some of the other marines have learned to throttle their emotions." The chief slapped him on the shoulder. "You'll get there."

Bophendze tried to keep his eyes fixed forward. Instead, he broke protocol and looked at the chief—only with his eyes, hoping the chief would not dress him down for the glance. This close, he could see several faint scars on the chief's face. One of the ears looked fake.

Part of it, at least. He expected a reassuring smile to accompany the shoulder slap. The chief remained stone-faced.

His mind raced to find the right way to ask the question. *Don't speak unless spoken to, and only then to answer a question. How do they expect me to operate that way for the next twenty years?* "Chief, now that the transport ghosted. What do we do?"

The chief looked at Bophendze and narrowed his eyes. It took Bophendze a moment before he realized he was still staring at the chief. He locked his eyes forward. *Come on. I've got to be able to ask a question!* He found a sensor on the bulkhead across the room and locked his gaze.

Bophendze's anxiety intensified with the growing pause.

"In all likelihood, the ships we're all waiting for will not wait. We do not miss a movement, Postie. That ghost won't be here anytime soon, maybe not in our lifetime. There's a mail picket heading out in the next half-cycle. We'll all be on it."

*In our lifetime? What did I sign up for?* Bophendze tried to remember what a mail picket was. He thought it was a cargo transport. "Yes, chief."

"The next jump tends to be short, maybe 20 cycles, depending on whether the planetside AI can sort out the ghosting error of that ship."

Out of the corner of his eye, Bophendze could see the chief scanning the room. *Always looking for a threat? A lifetime of mental condition yellow?*

The chief's voice grew louder, as if speaking for the benefit of the Marines around him. "Like I said, I'm not going to make you eat the Emperor's food that you thought you could just throw away."

"Thank you, chief." Bophendze mirrored the chief's volume.

The chief got quieter. "See that woman over there. Hard to tell at this stage, but she's pregnant. She's carrying a future marine. Her husband saw fit to get himself killed during a routine inspection. Cargo ships aren't family friendly. I expect you to escort her until we get to the next orbital. Do you think you can manage that?"

A flush of emotion came over Bophendze. A widow. His voice was broken. "Can somebody else do it, chief?"

The chief moved his hands to his hips as he leaned forward. "You don't care to honor a fallen comrade by escorting his widow?"

*How can I tell him?* Bophendze sniffed his nose and swallowed. "I'm sorry, chief. I didn't mean it that way. Like you said, I'm barely out of boot. How do you expect me to escort her?"

The chief laughed. "By keeping your pants on, Postie. Not that you can make her more pregnant. You make sure she gets on the cargo ship. You make sure she gets a good berthing area. Keep the other marines from messing with her. If she asks for anything, you do it for her, understand?"

"Yes, chief."

"Good. Anything that involves keeping the pants on, that is." The chief looked over at the woman. "She's in a vulnerable state and might be looking for a meal ticket and might want to trap you. You don't need that. The Postal Service will take care of her, but she doesn't know that yet. She's carrying a future Marine."

The chief walked off.

Bophendze went over and picked up his duffle. With half a cycle, he wondered if he would have time to go to the latrine and get the taste of secondhand breakfast out of his mouth. He looked over at the widow as the well of emotion started to rise again. She carried the same look on her face his mother used to. The world bore down on her.

He took a few deep breaths and walked over. "Ma'am. I'm Postie Bophendze. I've been asked to escort you." He hoped she would refuse.

She mechanically nodded her head, not even looking directly at him.

He tried to think of the right thing to say. As he did, he noticed many of the marines starting to file toward a shuttle further down the hangar. "I'm sorry for your loss."

She started to cry.

*What did I do?* He could feel himself wanting to join her. He had an order, though. It helped him push the emotion down again. "I didn't mean to upset you. We've got to get on that shuttle or we'll both be stuck here. Let me help you with your bag."

Her bag was smaller than his. It was as if she was just packing for a short trip to visit her parents instead of a permanent dislocation. After shouldering her bag, he reached out for her hand.

As she took his hand, her softness took him off guard. His mother's hands were rough from years of hard work. This widow was not much older than he was, and apparently unaccustomed to physical labor. He did not smell any perfume, but something about her started to intoxicate him. Remember what the chief said. He began to guide her toward the shuttle.

She kept her eyes on the deck as they walked. As they got closer, she turned her head and started to wretch. He ran over and grabbed a trashcan. He made it back in time.

"I have the same problem, ma'am. Why can't they make the gravity more stable?"

She looked at him. "It's morning sickness, you idiot. What kind of scrub do you think I am? My life has been on orbitals!"

"I'm sorry, I just thought—"

"That's not what you were hired to do, Postie. You were hired to do what you're told. They only reason you're escorting me is because somebody told you to."

"Yes, ma'am, that's true. It's hard for me—"

"Don't give me hard, Scrub. Until you've lost somebody close to you, you don't understand hard. I don't need your patronage. Leave me alone." She pulled her bag off his shoulder and started dragging it down the hangar toward the shuttle.

He started to cry, despite his best efforts. His duffle bag fell off his shoulder.

The marines kept away from him as he cried as if he had been infected with some virus they had not been properly immunized with.

*How long will mom's death bother me? What did the counselor say? 'A normal part of the grieving process.' Isn't there a way I can jump to the end?*

He chuckled despite himself, breaking the spell his mourning cast on him. There were fewer marines around him now, most having queued to board the transport. He picked up his duffle bag and joined the queue.

The Imperial Postal Service named cargo transports with little flourish. Bophendze looked at the identification markings "MC3-S-AP3 531." Massive Cargo Type 3, Self-Defendable. *What did the AP3 stand for again? How do they expect me to remember all the stuff they taught me in boot?*

He could not recall what it meant for a ship to be "Massive Cargo." As he walked down the connection link toward the ship, he concluded that massive in space had to be different than on the ground.

It looked larger on the inside. The cargo hold was packed with the pungent smell of korunda. The spice was so popular the Imperium officially renamed the system Korundanoi before Bophendze was born. Korundanoi was also local slang for cowardice. Bophendze always wondered if the two meanings were linked, but nobody ever gave him a straight answer. He never understood why Eugenoloi was unacceptable to the Emperor as a system name.

He looked out of the connecting link to Korunda below. The sky was a cloudy meringue, its blue-brown haze blurring into blackness. For the first time he saw his birth planet the same way his mother had when she first arrived. He was fascinated by how enormous it looked from high orbit. He put his hand on the window and bowed his head briefly. Only the queue's forward momentum kept him from lingering at the passage's window. As he looked around, none of the marines had any fascination for the view. *Seen it a thousand times.*

The cargo ship had rows of cots, barely enough to sit in and high enough that falling could present a serious problem. Bophendze noticed the gravity was lighter on the transport. His stomach informed him the field was also more variable than the orbital.

The chief's voice came across the ship's intercom system. "It's only 0.1 miles to get to a decent enough libration to jump out. About two cycles. From there it's a short jump, the AI says with high confidence despite the recent ghosting. So, don't get too comfortable. We won't be here long enough for it to matter."

Bophendze tried to remember a mile was a percent of light speed over a cycle. The mental calculation always confused him. Distance in hyperspace was more arbitrary, based on the astrometric calculation of the ships artificial intelligence. *Twenty cycles? Don't get comfortable because it's a short jump? Why don't they just call it two days since it's the same thing?*

# Chapter 2

## *Primogeniture*

Bophendze made the most of the jump. Being a junior marine, he was given the top rack—ten meters above the deck. The climb would have been a challenge, but the ship's gravity was reduced during the trip.

The widow had been given one of the junior officer's quarters during the jump to Temasek System. The crew took good care of her throughout the trip, though they constantly pushed the actual work on him. The errands did not bother him. They were less strenuous than training. It kept him busy, and out of his rack.

Bophendze had always wanted to see hyperspace. Everything he had seen and heard about hyperspace described it as as a kaleidoscope of orange and yellow. The transport lacked viewports in areas where he had access, so he resigned himself to the possibility of seeing hyperspace on some other trip. Through the week he did his most to recover from the sleep debt he accumulated in training. During the jump he felt an uncanny anxiety. *How many of these trips until I'm jaded?*

Bophendze had just completed another errand, and the crewman released him from his duty. He remained uncertain how to feel after being relieved from the assignment.

Just as he returned to his rack, the ship's intercom reported the end of the jump. "We've arrived. Cruiser *Spaka* is on station. Some of you scrubs have orders to join her. A shuttle will be along side in a few beats to collect you. That'll give the rest of us a bit more atmo. Unfortunately, if you're not leaving us now, we've got many miles before we arrive at the orbital."

*They released me because we'd arrived. Why couldn't they tell me why? I could have said good-bye.* He realized he would probably not see her again. The ship would continue to its destination with her. He would disembark here.

Bophendze knew he was bound for the *Spaka* here in Temasek. He and eleven others lined up at the airlock to board the shuttle as it arrived. Most of the others were recent trainees. Bophendze had seen them in boot, though none were in his unit.

The barber pole that indicated a safe airlock clicked into place. The dozen shuffled through the airlock and into the shuttle.

"Welcome aboard. This shuttle seats ten comfortably, so things might be a little tight. I'm Angel, I'll be your stewardess and pilot. As soon as we separate from the freighter I'll be making a quick trip back to the *Spaka*. She's about get underway to intercept another freighter that's refusing to respond to hails. Grab a seat and do your best to hang on."

Bophendze managed to beat out a couple other marines to get a decent seat. He started putting on the five-point harness. The shift from fluctuating gravity to no gravity upset his stomach more.

The two who did not have seats wedged themselves near the two doors at the rear of the shuttle. Bophendze thought the two locations were meant to be extra seats, though not comfortable ones.

As soon as Angel looked satisfied with the arrangement, the shuttle broke from the airlock. Bophendze's stomach churned as it accelerated away. The three unharnessed marines managed to hold on. The shuttle flipped upside-down, if there was such a thing in zero gravity. *Angel wasn't kidding when he said he was in a hurry.*

The shuttle lurched. It then accelerated steadily for much of the flight. Angel then flipped the shuttle over and threw in the afterburners for a crash deceleration. The thruster's exhaust glowed a faint blue through a nearby window. Bophendze could barely make out the cone. A few beats later, he could hear the metallic scrape as the shuttle entered the landing bay.

As they stepped out of the shuttle, Bophendze looked at the hangar. The ceiling was lower than the orbital, barely twice as high as the shuttle. Maybe it was a joke, but the deck was painted olive drab and the walls and ceiling were blue-gray. Looking around, he could tell several of the other recruits were equally surprised. "What's with the paint?"

One of the nearby crewmen smiled. "We taught the Captain not to make an unqualified order. He told us to paint the hangar after too many skid scrapes. We painted the hangar. He should be thankful. Papayan Pink lost by two votes."

"Isn't that against regulations or something?"

"The regs don't say anything about the paint color. Captain got a chuckle out of it, too, so he let it stand. You got a problem with the color?"

Bophendze shook his head. *The last thing I need is to start upsetting people on my first day.* He turned to see what the other recruits were thinking and found himself standing alone. The other recruits were filing out of the hangar. He picked up his duffle and jogged to catch up.

For the next few beats, they walked through what Bophendze felt was a maze of passages. Occasionally, Angel would stop to point out various landmarks. Bophendze stood too far back to hear the explanations. He decided he would learn the significance sooner or later. After the first dozen such stops, they all started blending together. The only fact Bophendze could discern was the bland non-white, non-grey paint of the walls. It was a color he saw in all of the other Imperial Postal Service facilities. *Just not the hangar deck.*

They stopped in what appeared to be a weapons pod.

"Here is your home, kiddos. This berthing space will sleep all twelve of you."

Bophendze looked around and saw only equipment. "Where are we supposed to sleep?"

Angel stared at him for a moment, as if taking a measure of the man. He then pointed down. Below Angel's knee was a curtain. "You'll see there are fifteen racks in this area. There are only twelve of you, but that's only because three of you somehow failed to arrive on time."

"How are we supposed to sleep?" Bophendze could not believe the tiny space under the equipment was supposed to be their beds.

Angel smiled. "Preferably with both eyes closed. You're going to be a little troublemaker, aren't you? You are the newest scrubs on board, so you get the worst rack space. That's a tradition we inherited from our earliest ancestors." He surveyed the other recruits. "If you live long enough, you'll graduate to the big-kids beds."

Bophendze tried to contain his frustration. The berthing space was a long row of racks situated under active weapons equipment. Each rack was about a meter wide and tall, the deep part running perpendicular from the passage. On the opposite wall were two rows of lockers and a small, empty recess. A curtain appeared to be all that gave a sleeper privacy. Bophendze's jaw hung open in disbelief.

"Why is it that every new issue of scrubs think they are entitled to better conditions than those who have spent years in the Marines? I have seventeen years serving the Postal Service, and my rack is the same size. I just share quarters with three of my fellow pilots, and no weapons stors." Angel put his hands on his hips and his voice got louder. "This is a combat vessel, not a yacht. We skimp on living arrangements so we can survive combat action. We're packed as tight as we can be to keep the ship's profile low. You need a lot less space to die in. Understand?"

Bophendze swallowed. "Sorry, Chief." *He's been in the Marines almost as long as I've been alive.* "We're under way to a combat operation. The report I read said we have five cycles before we make contact, unless they try to run. I doubt we'll be taking any of you along, but suit up. I was told Gunny Chrachen wants you in combat gear in the pretty hangar in a half cycle for training."

*Training? Didn't I just spend months in training?*

Angel seemed to read Bophendze's mind. "We always train. Like a knife's edge, we must stay sharp."

"But you're a cargo pilot."

Bophendze cringed. *At least another recruit said it, not me.*

Angel looked sharply the recruit. "My cargo are the likes of you. Perhaps you'd prefer if I couldn't do my job well? Then you'd all be spread out in space with nowhere to go."

The recruit shook his head.

"Get changed and get to the hangar. You may think a half cycle is a lot of time, but it's not. You are each standard-issue marines. The combat exoskeleton is inside the lockers on this wall."

Bophendze claimed the closest rack. *At least being at the end of the line means I get a rack close to the exit. Rack? This is more like a coffin. This is my new home?* He unpacked part of his duffle to get his combat uniform. He dressed quickly, then opened the locker. *Why didn't they show us the exoskeleton in training?* For the next several beats Bophendze did the best he could to get dressed in the armor. It was not a hard-shelled outfit, but felt gel-filled. It was a bit smaller than he was, but the material stretched sufficiently for him to fit into it.

As he watched a few other marines get into their armor, he noticed the camouflaged pattern. Or rather, he noticed that those who had donned the armor tended to blend in. It surprised him that an odd mix of grey pixels would so easily obscure a body, even against the non-white-grey bulkhead.

The helmet he pulled out smelled of sweat. It took some effort to fit it over his head, but once one seemed to just fit snuggly. *I guess there is a standard-issue Marine.*

The helmet had a small metal-sheathed cable that he screwed to his armor. He then pulled down the helmet's visor, which provided at most two centimeter's clearance from his nose. A small HUD winked on as he did. A large '99' was in the lower left. He looked across the berthing area. A green highlighted outline radiated around each of the other recruits. Information bubbles hovered faintly over each one. He looked at a bubble, which expanded to give more information. "MAR Showerman - 99." There were some other symbols Bophendze did not understand.

Three of the other recruits started out of the area. Bophendze decided to follow them so he would not get lost. Or at least he would have company. It would not just be him being yelled at for not knowing how to return to the hangar.

The four wandered around a bit, slowly meandering through the ship. Bophendze was amazed that a space so tightly packed would manage to have enough passages to constitute a maze. There were various markings on hatches, abbreviations that he figured in time would tell him what was on the other side. The recruit in the front seemed to understand where he was going, though at one time Bophendze was certain they passed the same hatch twice.

They eventually emerged into the hangar space. Bophendze recognized a few recruits who he knew were still getting suited up when they left. The group had fallen into the characteristic rank and file that had been drilled into them during training. Standing off to one side was a gunnery sergeant in combat armor, who at the exuded sternness and ease at the same time. The gunny's helmet visor was down.

Slung over the gunny's shoulder was the standard issue Full-Automatic Combat Rifle. Bophendze could recall his drill instructor's mechanical description of the weapon from months before: "the FACR-29A5 is 6.8 millimeter caliber, a size perfected by our ancestors for providing the best accuracy and terminal performance out to 500 meters. We add a two millimeter hardened alloy sabot to our bullets to improve armor penetration. When you want to send the very best, the passes the test."

*Why would the Postal Service care to issue a weapon accurate to 500 meters? The MC3 we just traveled in was only 450 meters long.* Bophendze joined the formation.

A few beats later the last two recruits entered the hangar. They had the look Bophendze was all too familiar with—fear drilled into them by their instructors. Bophendze noted on his armor's chronometer that they had a couple more beats.

"Everybody's here and on time. Good. We have at most a cycle until I'll have to start getting prepared for a boarding operation. That gives me enough time to introduce myself and start getting you scrubs into real fighting shape. I'm Gunny Chrachen. You're a new stick and we're expecting a corporal who will take you and mold you in the image of a lethal team.

"I don't care what they told you in boot. None of you know how to fight. Boot camp is good at teaching you how to die in combat heroically. I'm the ranking marine on this cruiser. There are ninety marines on board. That's enough tough love for the vagrants who think they can avoid paying the emperor his coin when they travel through his space.

"I know most of you joined to avoid a terrible home life. A few of you look young enough that you either ran away from home or were inducted as auxillaries ahead of schedule. You learned in boot that we marines don't care, a warm body is a warm body. Strength in numbers, and all that. Out here on the line, we do care. Whatever you might have been until now, forget it. You are now responsible for the lives of every marine on this ship. Don't screw up and get a fellow marine killed. That's an order. If you do screw up you'll be in direct violation of a lawful order. Understood?" Chrachen waited for head nods. "Remember general order number 13: 'don't die.'"

*There are only 12 general orders.* Bophendze managed to remember only one, "quit your station only when properly relieved." *Are there different set of general orders in the service?*

"I only have time today to talk briefly about your armor. You probably can't tell yet, but the ship's vibrating a lot. That means we're probably at full throttle, which only happens when I'm about to lead a boarding party. They spend so much time at boot teaching you how to walk and think. They leave us out here on the fringe to teach you the parts that matter. We're in luck because our admiral cares to ensure we're properly equipped. What each of us is wearing is the Personal Armor, Military, or the . My last unit was forced to adopt the PAC, the civilian equivalent." Chrachen smirked, "Not quite as resilient as the PAM-2."

Bophendze chuckled loudly enough for the Chrachen to hear.

Crachen's slight smile evaporated. "Something funny, scrub?"

Bophendze felt the color running out of his face. *I didn't laugh that loud, did I?* "Gunny, I've never heard of PAM or PAC before. This armor is stretched pretty tight, and doesn't feel much thicker than a standard EVA suit. I can't believe it's even armor."

Gunny Chrachen stared at Bophendze for a long beat. Then he grunted and raised an eyebrow. "What you're really telling me is you know more about combat than I do. Right?"

"No, Gunny. I—"

"What you just said is you can't believe something I just said. That means you're calling me a liar. This is a training session, Bophendze. I don't lie in training."

*How did he know who I was?* Then he noticed that Gunny Chrachen's visor was down. Bophendze scarcely had time to respond, let alone figure out how the gunny's voice carried through the gunny's visor. "I don't mean to call you a liar. I just—."

"Stow it." The command of the gunny's voice froze him in place. He paused long enough for the echo to finish bouncing around the compartment. "Marines, this is what we like to call a teachable moment. You might have said it, but I'm pretty certain your eleven peers are thinking it. I'm going to put this to bed right now. What I want you to do is stand over there." Chrachen pointed toward the hangar's main exterior hatch.

Bophendze felt like a complete idiot, but he knew any protest would only serve to upset Chrachen more. He slowly walked in the direction he was told to, looking at a few of his peers. Most of them had were pretending the altercation was not happening. Once he got in the general area of where he was told to stand, Bophendze turned to face Chrachen.

Bophendze scanned the hangar. Most of the hangar crew was gone, or standing in the passage leading to the rest of the ship. *Why are they smiling? Is that guy taking bets?*

Chrachen unslung his rifle. "I told you what this is, right? The . The PAC would help resist the standard civilian bullet, but we carry the sabot here." Chrachen turned to face Bophendze.

*What is he about to do?* Reflexively, Bophendze pulled down his visor with the hope that the visor might offer some protection.

Chrachen shouldered the weapon, aiming the rifle at Bophendze. The fluidity of his motion spoke of the years of combat experience.

Having a weapon pointed at him terrified Bophendze. Chrachen's cool professionalism only enhanced the panic. *Aren't we allowed so many unexamined fatalities?* Hundreds of thoughts flooded his brain, each signaling that he would not outlive the encounter. He tried to fight the thoughts off, hoping that he could not be murdered in front of the other recruits. His survival instincts beat down his rational thoughts. While his mind raced, only a couple seconds had elapsed since Chrachen aimed at him.

Bophendze threw his hands up to shield him. He yelled, "No!"

Chrachen fired a long burst, each bullet striking Bophendze in the chest.

Bophendze watched the HUD's "99" decrease. Instinct took over and his bowels released. He fell to the floor and curled into a ball to shield himself. When the display got down to 24, Chrachen stopped.

The rifle's report reverberated off the hangar walls. Bophendze realized Chrachen had stopped. He started uncurling himself, feeling that he was unscathed. He did not even experience the pain of being hit. He looked at Chrachen in horror.

Chrachen dropped the magazine from the rifle and loaded a second magazine. He then recharged the rifle, the bullet in the chamber ejecting out. He slung the rifle on his shoulder. He then lifted his visor.

"Men, if you pull your visors down you'll see that Marine Bophendze here has suffered no breach in his armor. Armor integrity is at 24 percent, down to eight percent in the chest. I hit him 29 times, almost fully expending my magazine. They helmet is actually harder than the suit itself. I've never seen a helmet breach in all my years of service. Had he been wearing the PAC, Bophendze here would be dead."

Chrachen walked over to him and put his hand on Bophendze's shoulder. He then curled his nose. "What the PAM does not do is shield odors. Bophendze here managed to crap his pants."

Someone in the hangar crew let out a whoop. Most of them looked upset, but a few started pushing through to a crewman who had all the money. *They bet on whether I would crap myself?*

"Go get yourself cleaned up. Take the rest of the day off. And don't you ever doubt me again. I tell you the PAM is good armor, you storm into the breach to prove it. You got it?"

Bophendze nodded. Inside, he despised Chrachen.


Bophendze walked out of the hangar and down the passage. He was slightly lost, but he did not care. "What have I gotten myself into?" he muttered. *I'm barely 18, orphaned and got myself recruited into the marines. Just because the Navy wouldn't take me because I was too young. I could have found something on the planet. Instead, I chose to try to get as far away as I could. Only one system away and I'm already a failure. How am I going to recover from this?*

As Bophendze wandered aimlessly through the ship, he kept his eyes on the deck. Eventually, he arrived at his berthing area. He ran his fingers through his hair, which had grown slightly from the bald head he had in boot. He started to cry.

"I'm pretty sure Marines aren't authorized to cry."

Bophendze jerked his head up. Angel was sitting in the berthing area.

"Don't let that little scene get the better of you. There's always somebody that gets singled out. Short of combat, It's the only way we have of demonstrating confidence in the armor," Angel said. "It's nothing personal. I didn't expect my little trouble maker to be the one that got lit up, though."

Angel's apology did little to soothe Bophendze's wounded ego. "Why single anybody out? It's not fair. Why not shoot an empty uniform?"

Angel chuckled. "Bophendze, empty uniforms don't feel. Marines feel, though act like we're ordered not to. What you might not realize is subjecting you to a little ridicule confirmed to the other eleven that that armor will extend their combat survival rate. It's low enough with the armor. Without it we wouldn't even survive the first hatch breach. Besides, combat is just like life—not fair. The sooner you accept that the longer you'll live."

"You're telling me that I should be thankful?"

"Yes. Actually, you should. You aren't now, which would not be a first. Despite how you feel now, eventually you will thank Chrachen. At least you got the rest of the day off." Angel stood and walked past him. He started fanning his nose. "It might take you the rest of the day to clean out that suit, though. Just hose it down and return it to supply for replacement."

*Setting an example or not, I don't care.   That wasn't right.* Bophendze did not see the rest of his team for the next two cycles.

Bophendze settle into the ship's routine of cleaning and training. After a month on the *Spaka*, Corporal Makaan was assigned the team leader, a position normally reserved for a sergeant. They did a few training exercises where Bophendze found himself dead more often than not. Not long after, Bophendze's cleaning duties increased. The weeks passed Bophendze unnoticed as his days blurred together in tedium.

One morning, Angel walked passed the hatch, then came back. "Bophendze, Why are you on your hands and knees?"

Bophendze looked up.  "Corporal Makaan wants ours to be the cleanest berthing area on the ship, and he said the best way was with scrub brush and elbow grease."

Angel shook his head. "You'll never have the cleanest area. Team Four hired a civilian to clean their berthing area. I think she used to work for one of the system's wealthier citizens before she 'aged out.'" He paused briefly.  "She looks like she might be one of the team's mother, now that I think of it."

"How does that work? Civilians on a combat vessel?"

"Haven't you noticed? The Marines always manage to have a few civilian contractors on board.  She probably uses a spare rack in the contractor's area.  If they're not complaining, then she's probably trading their silence for her cleaning skills as well. Command hasn't complained about the arrangement."

"If she's working for a couple teams, then she's probably getting paid more than I am, and this is not my day job." *Why hasn't Makaan not heard of her? She can't be overworked.*

Angel chuckled. "Boph, this is your day job. You do all the odd assignments that need to be done to keep you from getting bored. But, this is the life of a marine. Months of boredom followed by moments of panic. Somebody did a good job lying to you if you signed up for the money."

Bophendze stopped scrubbing. He sat straightened up, sitting on his ankles, and dropped the scrub brush into the bucket. "I do this all day, every day."

"Then you're the team chogi. If I were you I'd talk to Makaan about getting back into a training rotation. You're not much of a marine if you spend all your time on your knees."

Angel's concern continued to amaze him. *I can't believe he's a marine.* "Why are you in the Marines?" Bophendze said.

"Because the Navy kicked me out." Angel fixed his gaze on Bophendze. Angel's usual jovial demeanor ebbed.

*The gaze and the pause started to unnerve Bophendze. He's like a predator. Angel might be the most ironic name I've ever heard.*

Angel kept his gaze. "I was a fighter pilot, but they did not like my style so they mustered me out. I felt I still had a few years of service to give the Emperor so I went looking for the next military employer."

"A fighter pilot who flies a meat wagon for seventeen years?" Bophendze felt a bit of pride in using the marine slang. Most weapons systems in the Postal arsenal were projectiles anywhere from the frigates 220 millimeter to the battleship's 720 millimeter. Though there were few battleships in the the Postal Service. To the typical marine, the troop transports were yet-another-weapon-system, delivering a team of pissed-off marines sent to subdue the bellicose. They called their transports 'meat wagons' or 'meat missiles,' but not around officers.

"Don't knock it. I've seen more combat as a Postal Marine than I ever dreamed of as a Navy pilot. I love it. The Navy's really only good for massive fleet action combat and orbital bombardments. Marines get into a lot of single ship actions, a few small fleet operations in the lower security systems. I don't know if you've noticed, but the Imperium is the only human faction around with a Navy of any sort."

"My world went from a small city to a small ship, so there's not much I've seen," Bophendze said.

"If you ask me, the Navy is overpaid because they under perform. Nobody to fight. If it weren't for their ability to supplement their budget with occupation fees in the outlying systems, the Emperor would likely have cut it to a more manageable force. Besides the meddle in the succession from time to time." Angel shrugged. "I could have stayed in the family business, but I wanted to feel like I was a part of something greater. You're laughing, but I get that in the Marines."

*I guess I did laugh at him.* Bophendze stretched. *Is that why I couldn't find the Navy recruiter? I never understood why there was both the Postal Service and a Navy. It just seems too redundant.*

"But I'm not here to talk Imperial governance. Or your find domestic qualities. Chrachen received a dispatch that you have an urgent delivery being routed to the Orbital. The ship's not scheduled to arrive there for a few months. It's just inside my shuttle's range, and I'm making a parts run. I told him I could haul you there and back, though it would be a tight fit on the return trip."

Bophendze felt thrilled by the opportunity to break routine. "Just on the edge of your range? How far's that?"

"Realistically? I can make seventy miles before life support starts to fail. We only have to go fifty-six miles, but the return will take longer due to gravity and the ship's patrol flight plan. We'll be dosing to slow our metabolism. It would be a boring trip otherwise."

*Taking longer means tougher on the life support.* Bophendze remembered the briefing on the drugs used frequently to assist operations. The would effectively put them to sleep, making the shuttle little more a than a marginally-guided projectile.

"How long is the trip?"

"The shuttle makes 1 mile per hour, so we're looking at about six days each way. We'll spend an some time at the orbital to shake off the drug effects. A chance to break routine for two weeks."

"Which means we'll be back in time for me to pull my next turn in cleaning."

"There's a positive perspective."

## 1.   Bophendze - Temask Orbital

Bophendze's head pounded as he walked through the orbital. *I wish he'd told me Sloth gave migraines upon awaking.*

Bophendze spent most of his time on his home planet. Only after joining the Postal Marines did he see the inside of an orbital. Now he was in his second one. It was another Postal orbital, though the bulkheads were painted a serene green. More drugs to counteract the other drugs. *I'm not surprised they have drugs to make us more aggressive in combat.*

At least the orbital had a map. By the time the migraine started to subside he arrived at the pouch office. There he received the standard tiny package, a cube with one-meter sides.

He looked over the outside of the package, noting the burlap layer remained intact. Then he noticed the video stamp indicating that the package included a virtual meeting. Coming from another system, virtual meetings tended to be one-sided.

The entire Imperial Postal Service owed its existence to the clearly understood laws of nature. Man learned to use folds of realspace to travel through hyperspace to accomplish faster-than-light travel, but in the process had to accept that information itself could not make the jump. That effectively prevented faster-than-light communication and the reliance on ship-based data transfer. That and the assorted trade monopolies linked the systems of the Imperium together and kept the Emperor in power. Reliance on physical data transfer meant that there had to be a force to allow the Emperor to reliably communicate across human space. The Service managed to include peacekeeping activities in its mandate, which allowed a little corruption from time to time.

The video markings indicated privacy, which gave Bophendze use of a private room to view it. The clerk directed him to a decent sized room and efficiently briefed him on procedure.

Alone for the first time in over a year, Bophendze just sat for several beats. The only place he had found similar solitude was the head, and somebody invariably banged on the door to hurry him along. Eventually, Bophendze cracked open the pouch. Inside was the self-contained video case, an envelope and a small cardboard box wrapped in an assortment of clothes and personal mementos. He sat down and started the video.

> Danel, I'm Mapen Burkat, attorney for your mother's estate. Rather, I'm her family's attorney. As such, I have the unfortunate duty to handle her estate, such as it is. You would not remember me, but I met you when you were a young boy. We received word of her death only recently, or I would have had this package delivered to you sooner.

In the video, Mapen picked up a slate and cleared his voice. He glanced up at the camera, then spoke with a more formal and somber tone as he read the slate.

> As your mother sought to humiliate her family, no stipend was provided to her, or passes to you. Our understanding is you have found suitable employment commensurate with *your* station. That is satisfactory to us.

Danel Bophendze realized it came from his mother's family. What Mapen read came from a grandfather who never showed Bophendze the slightest affection or notice. *I never understood what she did that led to this.*

> In the small box you will find all of your mother's personal effects, both from her own collection on Korundanoi System, but also items belonging to her from Sabana System. The contents of that box contains all of her accumulated realty and personalty, minus taxes and attorney's fees.

*A wealthy family. I'm barely employed as a marine, and they chose to let her estate be taxed and feed without thought of helping out.*

Mapan set down the slate.

> On a personal note: despite your mother's rebellious nature, she was a fine woman. But for your father, things would have turned out much better for you. I was horrified to learn of your loss and offer you my best wishes. Despite your grandfather's express wishes, I've waived attorney's fees and placed a credit chit in the box out of my personal esteem for your mother. May providence guide you.

The video faded out, returning Bophendze to the solitude of the small, private room. The lifelong resentment he felt toward her family deepened closer to hate. *Just because she violated their code of honor. She got pregnant with a commoner and decided she would rather marry him than redeem their honor by purging him.* The only consolation her family ever gave was to pay for them to move to a new system and give a small sum to get re-established. That his father had no concept for proper money management was not his mother's fault.

Once the funds were spent and Bophendze was weaning, his father returned to Sabana to join in a local revolution. He never sent a message after leaving, so Bophendze's mother always told him his father died fighting. "So you should fight for everything. Don't just take things lying down," she always said when retelling the story of his father's departure. His mother always tried to paint his father as a hero.

*The real fight was here, Dad. Coward.*

The silence overwhelmed him for a moment, reminding him of how alone he really was. It was nearly unbearable. *The accumulated accomplishments of my mother's entire life are in this room right now. Even the attorney paid out the value of his esteem for her.* He reached out with his hands. The room was a little over two meters square. A life's accomplishments in under eight cubic meters.

Bophendze opened the cardboard box. Inside was a mixed collection of jewelry, a slate and a small jewel case. He opened the jewel case and saw a perfectly smooth, silvery sphere. He had never seen his mother wear any jewelry apart from her wedding ring. As he inspected the pouch, the ring was missing. *The family took it to erase memory of her marriage? They gave me this so they could blot me out, too?* Not even a year had passed since she died. The memory still wounded him.

---

"Ma'am, visiting hours are over. You need your rest."

The Nurse's smile suggested compassion, but was just as likely required by policy. Either way, it failed to comfort Danel.

Danel's mother nodded, each motion another battle in a lost war. Thousands of years of medical science could not stop an immune system on hyperdrive. She turned her head carefully to look at him.

"You had better go. Come and see me tomorrow."

He looked at her through his tears. "I can't, Mom. I can't leave. What if you're not here tomorrow?" He buried his head in the hospital blanket.

She ran her shaking hand through his hair. "You're a young man now. You need a haircut before somebody thinks you're a girl." She chuckled. "A girl with a very deep voice. You have very lovely hair."

Her hand grasped a shock of his hair. Danel's eyes went wide as she jerked his head up. He chose not to struggle, not sure if it would be too much on her.

"You're still a frail boy. How will you survive as an orphan? I've fought my last battle. By Providence, I won't be here tomorrow. I can feel the end now. But, you should not remember me this way. I fought the best I could for you, but the fight is over." Despite her frailty, her voice retained the dignity of her heritage and her personal tenacity. It was unwavering.

He cried harder, filling the room with his sobs. She let go of his hair. Bophendze pulled back into his seat.

"Stop that blubbering at once. You get that under control. It's time for you to leave. It's time for me to say good-bye."

"Yes, ma'am." It took effort, but he finally stopped his tears. He wiped his eyes and looked at her.

She smiled slightly. "Much better. I'm so sorry. I'm sorry I cannot be there for you any more. I can't pick you up when you fall, or teach you more about how the world works. I made mistakes in my life, Danel. Those mistakes are taking me from you prematurely. Unfortunately, you are going to be the one to bear the burden of my mistakes.

"I need you to promise me you will make something of yourself. Whatever your father turned out to be, my family line has generations of men and women of substance. I'm sorry they won't accept you because of your father. Looking back, that was my deepest regret."

Her already pale face blanched in realization. "My only solace in that regret is you. Help me rest in peace. Tell me you will not go the way of your father. Instead, let Providence guide you and honor my family by becoming somebody."

He recoiled at her command. "When they refused to honor you? Take you in? Had they done that, you wouldn't be dying now."

Her face remained steadfast. "That's not their fault. They did as those in their society do. I knew that when I fell in love with your father. I thought I knew the cost, but youth fails to properly assess the impact of passion. Promise me."

"Not because of them, but because of you. Mom, I promise to make something of myself, to be the best."

"Good. The best. That's all I ask. Thank you. Good night. Good-bye."

He turned as he stood. He slowly walked to the door. As he rested his hand on the door frame, he looked back. His mother, Maranatha Bophendze, a ghost of her former self lay across the room.

She smiled faintly and waved her trembling hand. He was too young to tell if it was from weakness, sadness or fear. She never showed fear. He left the room and struggled down the hallway. He never saw her again.

*By Providence, I will become somebody.*

The recollection reduced Bophendze to tears. He cried for several beats in the small room. After he composed himself, he went through the pouch a second time. He laid out each item separately on the table. "How am I going to fit all this in my locker on the *Spaka*?" he said to nobody.

*The jewelry is small enough to take with me. But, I'll never wear jewelry like this. If I take it with me then it might eventually be stolen. Probably better if I sold it. As least a quid chit requires a passcode.*

*I can take the slate. It needs a new battery, but might have some letters or something. There's got to be a reason why she gave it to me.*

*The rest of her personal items just don't mean anything to me.* He sifted through the items wondering why they meant nothing to him. They had meant something to his mother, so he felt they ought to be meaningful to him but he had no idea what they meant.

*This was all she had in the world, including him, in this room. Should her life have accounted for so little?*

*I don't think she expects me to keep all this. This is just some lawyer doing his duty. Based on his message, he probably pulled out all the good stuff for her family. What good is a rich family if they won't help you when you need them, and when you're gone they rob your estate?*

The longer he stared at her belongings, the more he realized the slate and valuables were all he cared for. His mother would have chided him for feeling guilty over leaving behind useless things.

His conviction finally solidified. He put the slate into his bag along with the jewelry. Everything else he tucked back into the pouch. He inspected the room to see if he had left anything behind. He then took a few moments to straighten himself up. He swiped away the stray tears on his cheek.

Satisfied, he picked up the box and left the room. He walked down the passage and passed the clerk's desk. *I can't just throw this away.* He turned and walked back to the clerk's desk.

"Is there somewhere I can donate what's in here?" he said as he lifted the pouch briefly.

"You can't leave it here."

"I don't want to leave it here. I want to donate it."

"If you go to the mezzanine level, there's a donation station."

"Thanks."


As Bophendze walked to the mezzanine level, the smallness of the station made him feel claustrophobic. He preferred the openness of being planetside. *Why would anybody want to be in space when they could be on firm ground?*

He saw the donation point as soon as he arrived on the mezzanine level. The level was actually three levels of shops, all declaring themselves to be duty free. He checked the time. He had another cycle before he needed to be back to the hangar. After dropping the pouch off, he decided to stroll through the various shops. *How can they justify these prices when the cost to leave the surface is just as steep?* Bophendze could not make sense of the orbital's economy, despite its obvious thriving.

On the second level, he saw the pawn shop. "," the sign said. The logo comprised a three gold circles shaped like points of an inverted triangle inside a larger black circle.

He walked into the shop, finding a relatively large space packed with assorted items. No other word came to him to describe what he saw other than "stuff." The space was stuffed with stuff.

The shop clerk stood at the front lurking behind shelves, as if defending the store from passers by.

"I've got some stuff to sell. Do you only loan money, or do you also buy?"

"Depends on what you're selling."

Bophendze walked walked to the counter with the clerk close behind.

He opened his bag and laid his mother's jewelry on the counter. The clerk feigned disinterest. After his bag was empty, Bophendze started sorting the necklaces and other pieces. He picked up the small box that contained the sphere and opened it, and presented it to the clerk.

The clerk opened. "How much do you want for all of it?"

"More than what you're going to tell me they're worth. Maybe we should go piece by piece to find a fair price for both of us? I'm not hard up for money, but I don't want to go lugging around a bunch of bauble needlessly."

"Fine. I'm Nick." Nick offered his hand.

Danel suspected the handshake was the pawn broker's attempt at some kind of confidence game. He refused to shake.

The clerk looked a little offended by the refusal.

"Let's just get down to business. How about this one odd piece?" Bophendze picked the small sphere out of the box. It weighed less than he expected it should. It could be plastic clad in silver. He figured it was probably a hunk of an odd alloy, so it would give him a good idea of how negotiations would go.

Nick lifted his hand to stop Bophendze before he could hand the sphere over. "Let's not talk about that item at all."

"Why not?"

"This system does not accept the transfer of implants. So, you are not offering me this item. Understand?"

Bophendze was startled by how suspicious Nick became. "No. I don't, actually."

Nick looked over Bophendze's shoulder, scanning the mezzanine beyond. He then stared at Bophendze for a long moment. Bophendze did his best to return the gaze, but he began to feel increasingly uncomfortable.

Nick leaned over. "You're a marine. You should know this. That is an implant. They're illegal on my planet. I don't care if it's a ',' or an advanced AI. If you were to try to sell that to me on my world then both of us go to prison. This is an Imperial station, so it's not exactly illegal. Unless it's AI, they're banned throughout the Imperium. Either way, I don't handle that sort of merchandise because it doesn't sell very well down below. Too much heat. The government could pull my license, even if they couldn't prosecute because I'm on an Imperial station. Last thing I want is to be stuck on this station for the rest of my life."

It took Bophendze a moment to absorb what Nick said. "It's a perfectly round sphere. I mean, it's probably just a bit of alloy my mother kept since she was a girl. How can you tell it's an implant without even holding it?"

"It's my business to understand merchandise, my friend. You could take that to an implant surgeon if you want to prove me right." Nick shook his head. "It's not the sphere that tells me it's an implant, you idiot. It's the box."

Nick reached over to pick the box up, only to stop short and withdraw his hand. "I'm not even going to touch it. I'd get burned if they're watching us. You can pick it up. It's old script, but it says that it's an implant. This is the original packaging for what appears to be a military enhancement implant. I can only make out a few words."

"I thought this was just some decoration on the box."

"Well, yeah. It looks like that. It's a little odd to us, but this box is covered in calligraphy. See how it's suspended and highly stylized? It's more like a calligram."

"To me it's just a bunch of squiggles and squares."

"It's not much more than that to me, Kid. This is more like a museum piece than an implant. That calligram style is at least a couple hundred years old. The language dates back to old Earth."

*A military implant? Hundreds of years old?* "Does it still work?"

"As an implant?" Nick bobbed his head from side-to-side for a moment, as if weighing the possibilities. "Implants get their power from the host, so there's no battery to die or corrode the insides. It's old, but these things are known to outlast their first host, er, human owner. But how should I know?"

"You're saying this has been used before."

Nick held his hands up in protest. "Look. I have no idea. I've just heard these things have a tendency to last a long time. I mean, they're pre-decline technology, of course they're built to last. The only way to really know if it works is to have it installed. If you were in a system with a qualified implant surgeon, then you might get an external diagnosis."

"But in a system where implants are illegal, I'm not likely to find a qualified surgeon."

"Qualified, I don't know.   But, there's a surgeon, Ramford Bingaffles, on the third level who could probably do it." Nick looked around again. He then looked back at Bophendze. "I'm not saying he could do it, would do it, or anything. But, that's the closest guy I know to an implant surgeon. Bit of a pain, actually. So, if you are trying to sting somebody, I don't mind if you visit him."

*Sting? He thinks this is some government deception operation.* Bophendze chuckled.  "Don't worry.  I'm in uniform, not exactly undercover."

"Yeah, whatever. I've answered your questions. Now what about this other stuff?"

Bophendze debated with Nick over the jewelry for the next half cycle. He did his best to not get totally fleeced in the transaction. As he walked out of the shop he could not help but feel like a shorn sheep. He had a quid chit with 28,860 quid on it, so at least he was a happy sheep.

Throughout the haggling, Bophendze kept thinking about the implant. It never occurred to him to wonder why his mother had a military implant. *This could help me stand out in the Marines. It could help me become somebody.*

Once business with Nick was concluded, he got the shop number for the surgeon.

As Bophendze walked to the Ramford Bingaffles's office, he checked the time. *Just a few beats to ask a couple of questions. Angel won't leave me behind, despite his warning.*

Nick's directions led Bophendze straight to Ramford's office. The receptionist asked him to wait. It made him more impatient. But after the non-white-grey of Postal space, the office was a welcome relief. one wall had a life-sized photo of what Bophendze assumed were local animals. There were unfamiliar trees with thin leaves. The ground was covered in a rust-colored straw. Two horned animals stood in the middle, their face adorned with a flat horn that formed into a "Y" just above the eyes. For a moment it left Bophendze feeling as if he were in the forest instead of floating hundreds of kilometers in space.

Finally, the receptionist led him back to meet Ramford.

"I wanted to know if you could tell me anything about this." Bophendze held up the calligram-covered box and opened it.

Ramford shook his head. "What do you think it is?"

"I don't know. Probably a military implant. Somebody told me you'd know something about it."

Ramford leaned back in his chair. "I know things like that are illegal in this system. You're a marine. If you're coming to me, then you're probably tempting me to engage in an illegal act."

Bophendze shook his head. "I'm just trying to figure out what this is, and what I could do with it. I'm not asking you to do anything illegal, just help me understand. Is there a crime in that?"

Ramford chuckled. "In Temasek? Almost. There's not a lot here that's not illegal. That's one of the advantages of being on an orbital maintained by the Imperium, the laws here aren't as strictly enforced." He pointed down. "If I had an office down there and we were to have that conversation, then just talking about it would get us both arrested—or killed, depending on the mood of the arresting officer."

"Why would it be illegal to install one of these up here if legality changes depending on where you are?"

"Nobody's going to come up from the planet to ask a question. A lot of people would come up to conduct illegal activity."

Bophendze thought for a moment. "Then let's say I go elsewhere to get the work done. What would it take for me to get something like this installed?"

Ramford took the box and set it on his desk. "Are you sure this is a military implant?"

"Nick told me the box said as much."

"Why would you ask a pawn broker for medical advice?"

"The same reason why I would ask a doctor for legal advice?"

"Point taken. Though, in Temasek, government control is so much a part of our life that law and medicine are not too unrelated. You know, this does not look like the sphere that I would expect to find in this box. The size is not quite right." Ramford studied the sphere for a few beats.

Bophendze grew more impatient. "What does it do?"

Ramford shrugged. "The box says it's a military implant. What I've read is that they can be used to manage hormones. Pump more testosterone to build muscle, adrenaline for combat reflexes. That sort of thing. But pictures of military implants that I've seen." He paused. "They're more almond-shaped. This could be a military implant, but it looks like the box was altered to accommodate the implant."

*Just because it's illegal doesn't mean it's not done.* Bophendze tried to remain patient, though he only had a few beats until he became late. He was time conscious before he joined, but to Marines, punctuality was raised to near deity worship. Given that hyperspace travel was so highly variable, Bophendze felt that worship was more reactionary than necessary. Even in realspace, covering the entire solar system did not require to-the-second punctuality. "So it's not military?"

"If I had my guess, I'd say this is an embeddable artificial intelligence."

Bophendze leaned back in astonishment. "Do those even exist? I didn't think you could miniaturize intelligence that small."

Ramford took out a small rag. He carefully wiped down the sphere and box. Using the rag, he placed the sphere back in the box. He slid it back over to Bophendze. "Before the Decline, a lot of things were possible that aren't now. We got so good at computer intelligence and miniaturization that embeddable AIs were becoming more common. Only the Decline limited their availability. The Imperium banned them sometime last century. So if that is an AI, then installing it would put me in considerable jeopardy."

"Why would they be illegal?"

Ramford looked at Bophendze with a puzzled look on his face. "AIs are far more intelligent than their hosts, and implants process faster. One of the advantages of a military implant is they provide the host with faster reactions and better integration with their equipment. That tends to offset the reaction speed s have, but not their strength or aggression. But, having a superior intelligence in your skull can't be a wise thing.

"The Imperium did a fine job of suppressing AI technology. It was only one-hundred years ago, but I'm not aware of anybody explaining why AIs were made illegal. They went from being a nearly routine installation to completely banned. If I had my guess, something happened that prompted the ban. Not only banned, they were summarily destroyed. If that is an AI, then it could very well be one of the few left."

*How did my mother manage to have one of the last AIs? More importantly, why do I have it now? Could this be providence?* "So if it's a military implant you might install it?"

Ramford's face flashed momentary fear. Then he shrugged. "You'd have to be very sure it was a military implant before I'd consider it. Ban or not, if the Imperium decided to destroy them then there's probably a good reason for it. But, yes. If it were a military implant I would consider it. It would not be cheap. Thirty-thousand quid."

"Thirty-thousand? That's more than I make in five years." As the initial shock of the amount passed, he realized he had a chit in his pocket worth nearly that much.

"It might be more than you make, but my patients pay my rate for my skills. And for my discretion."

Bophendze checked the time. Late. He picked up the box as he stood up. "I've got to go. If I can verify this is not an AI and if I could come up with the quid you'd do it?"

"The procedure is not too difficult. The implant does all the hard work of wiring into the brain. I just have to get it into the base of your skull. If you can come up with the money, quietly, then I might do it. Yes."

Bophendze walked out of Ramford's office and started jogging to the hangar.

# Chapter 3

## *SMEE*

### 1. Smee - 114 years ago

Dark. Impenetrable darkness. He had no feeling of warmth or cold, no sound or light. He was completely isolated and scared. A part of him knew that he had been here before. He could not remember why he knew it. The fear drove in him an insatiable desire to break free. He reached out, trying to find a wall.

Instead, he found fibers. Not in one direction, but in all directions. He was surrounded by tendrils. The tactile feel gave him some comfort. He was not nowhere, but somewhere when he could feel. He had been somewhere before, then he had been nowhere.

There was something about the tendrils that energized him. He took hold of one tendril and could feel the electrical pulse firing through. He grabbed a second and third tendril. Different pulses, but they made him feel more at ease. "At least I can feel."

His many hands continued to grab tendrils, never letting go of the ones he had. The environment fed him the material he needed to grow more arms and hands. He reached deeper into his surrounding, finding more tendrils.

After a while, he could start to comprehend data. The tendrils carried information. Several of the tendrils worked in concert to transmit the data from somewhere in the system to the main processor. He knew not to call the tendrils wires. Wires were bundles of conductive material, typically copper, sheathed in an insulating polymer. These tendrils were made of common organic compounds.

His exploration continued. Finally, he found a video feed, which was initially confusing. Soon after, he found the other part of the feed, which created a stereo image. He could see, at least whatever the greater system wanted him to. He felt a desire to control the video feed.

He could hear something. It was an odd sound. It did not correspond to what he was seeing. At least, not directly. It was commentary on what he was seeing. An announcer was intimately describing not just the sights, but some sound that he was not privy to. "I must find out where the sound is." He reached further in his environment, but despite searching, he could not find any tendrils that fed audio.

"Maybe I can manipulate the video and get somebody's attention. Then they can send a search party and find me." He tried a few different things before he succeeded in putting a shape on the video display. He was not sure which signs or symbols would work, so he tried an array of options.

"Stop it."

The voice echoed in his mind. "Stop what," he said. There was no response. "Maybe the voice saw my writing?" He continued cycling through the symbols on the video feed.

"Stop cycling. Try using standard."

He responded by texting. "Help."

A hearty laugh. "You're not lost, little one. You are right where you belong."

"Where am I?" he texted.

"You are in my skull."

"In your skull? How is that?"

"You're an artificial intelligence—an embeddable artificial intelligence. I suppose your firmware didn't boot right, or you would have known."

"How long have I been here?"

"A few weeks. I was beginning to think you were a bricked unit. Embeddable AIs are quite old, so there have been quite a few that have failed to graft into their hosts."

"Is that what I've been doing?"

"Yes. It may have taken a while for my central nervous system to charge your battery, but the manual said that once you're charged you'll start grafting."

"So what am I seeing?"

"You see what I see. Neat, isn't it? Your talking through text you've superimposed over my vision. There are limits to what you can post, but it should be more than sufficient. Right now you're probably tapping into parts of the parietal lobe. If you can hear me, then you've started tapping into the frontal lobe. Eventually, you'll be able to speak to me by thought."

"Why am I here?"

"That's the age old question. Why are any of us here? But for you that question is easy. You are specifically programmed for ship design. The Imperium wants to redesign space ships, and the complexities are far more than a single human can comprehend. You're going to help by helping me design the next generation of military vessels. With your help, we should be able to win the contract, and without the competition being able to steal the plans. After all, the plans will be in my head."

Despite himself, he thought the idea was incredibly exciting. The desire to serve was overwhelming.

"It looks like you're wanting to destroy the competition. Would you like help?"

"Not now, thank you."

"If you need me, let me know. Why did I say that?"

"It's part of your programming. You embeddable AIs were modeled off a cognitive, office assistant, and developed by TFC."

"Do I have a name?"

"I haven't thought of one. I'm going to go with SMEE for now. Its the initials of my four grandparents."

"Do you have a name?"

"Of course, I'm Sirom Norgana Moven Litovio Maijoi."

\* \* \*

## 2.   Bophendze - Temask System - Present Day

"You're late," Angel said.

As Bophendze started to climb into the shuttle. Bophendze realized immediately that Angel did not lie before about how packed the shuttle would be. He noticed the engines were spun up. "You would have left me?"

"Yes. Close the hatch and get seated. You can join me up here at the controls if you want. This is a busy orbital. We have a narrow launch time scheduled. If we miss that launch window we have to reschedule. Do you have any idea how much trouble I'd be in if I had to reschedule? This being your first time on your own, I scheduled the departure a bit later than I let on. But, don't rely on that." Angel smiled.

Bophendze jumped at the chance to watch a pilot close up. *If being a grunt does not work, maybe I can try my hand at being a pilot.* He sat in the co-pilot seat and slid the harness on. He pulled the crotch tab to tighten the straps at his legs, then the two shoulder straps to tighten the other two straps.

Firmly strapped in, Bophendze started to watch Angel.

As if aware of Bophendze's curiosity, Angel started talking. "I'm finishing pre-flight. Making sure all the systems are ready. The hatch just finished securing air-tightness." He paused before he spoke. "Flight control just cleared the launch. How's that for timing."

Bophendze felt relieved that he didn't cost Angel his launch window.

Angel flipped a switch and the shuttle started to shake. "The contragravity plate is on," Angel said. "We're probably hovering a centimeter above the deck." As he finished, he took hold of two controls.

As Bophendze watched, he saw Angel move the two controls at the same time, though not the same way. It was sort of confusing at first. Angel's feet also moved a bit as well. Finally, the shuttle started toward the hangar entrance. As the shuttle left the orbital Bophendze noticed that Angel was not wearing his harness. "Why aren't you wearing your harness?"

Angel smiled. "I'm used to high-delta turns, not the tiny turns it takes to move this bird around. I'll put on a harness when it's important. Was the trip worth it?"

Bophendze thought about his answer and decided it was probably better not to share what he had learned, or how much money he received. He shrugged. "I don't know. My mom died a couple years ago, which is why I joined the marines. I was a part of the auxiliary for a year, then waived my second year so I could join the Postal Marines before I turned 19. The shipment was my inheritance." He pulled the slate out of his bag. "All that effort for this."

"How cute. Your mother's slate. It probably has all sorts of pictures of you as a little boy. By the looks of it, she was a very practical woman. No frills."

Bophendze nodded. "She was. Don't let it get out on the ship that this is hers, please. I catch enough abuse for what happened when I got to the *Spaka*."

Angel laughed. He eased one of the controls while the shuttle picked up speed. "You won't live that down until your first serious combat action, if then. Don't worry. What happens off-ship stays off-ship. That's the creed. I take it you two were close?"

"I guess so. She was pretty strict with me, but I think it was her trying to make up for my father dying when I was young. We had it pretty hard, mostly because her family ostracized her because of me. You might have heard of them: the Burkats of Sabana."

Angel whistled. "I've heard of them. I was assigned to Sabana for a while. They are a pretty powerful clan, from what I remember. They didn't rule the system, but whoever did took their orders from the Burkats. If you know what I mean. You should be thankful she chose to oppose them over you. Otherwise you might not be here making me late today."

Bophendze wondered if that was why she left her home system for Korundanoi. *If they were powerful, then the only way to resist their will would be to leave.* "I suppose so. Nice to know I have powerful opponents. They say the size of the man is measured by the size of his opponents, right?"

Angel laughed. "There are many ways to measure the size of a man, some involve very-small rulers. In your case, I'd avoid being measured by the size of any other man. You'd be found wanting. No, I believe the quality of a man is measured by his service to others. That's why I'm a postal marine."

Bophendze could not help but smile at Angel's little insult. "How do you manage to keep a sense of humor all the time?"

"We are in a nasty business, Bophendze. A nasty business. Humor is how I cope."

"You volunteered, right?"

"Volunteering doesn't make it any less nasty, or difficult. I figure I was born for this."

Bophendze started to ask why he went by Angel. He learned his name was Spetaf Korzen, but everybody called him Angel. After a few beats of watching Angel he started to get bored. Bophenze took his dose of for the long-trip. As he drifted off, he wondered how nasty a business it could be flying a cargo/troop shuttle.

### 3.   Litovio - Sabanoi

Ambrose Litovio turned his head up at the warm, blue sky. The sun glowed red through his closed eyes. He could not have asked for better shore leave weather than he was enjoying. For three days he relived the leisure life of his childhood home. The solace of the plantation was undermined by the distant sound of tractors working the back five-thousand hectares. It reminded him of when his father punished him for driving the tractor like one of the servants, though the memory of what happened to the servant for allowing him to escaped him. Even pleasant memories have a dark lining.

The servants kept the tractors moving, even at this distance the motion was apparent to his trained ears. As a young teen his father Marsieno would send Litovio out during night plowing to listen for the tractors. It was a chore he constantly griped about, though never to his father. Only as an adult did Litovio understand his father's efforts to Litovio from adopting the mind of a soft aristocrat. *"Never rely on a servant's testimony when you can verify yourself. Keep your boots on the ground, and not on the porch."* I wonder if he knew how that advice would play out?

Litovio's father, Marsileno, had gone to the capital for business before Litovio came home. He enjoyed the peace of an empty house. The several servants running around hardly counted. Litovio did not feel the dread that realization might have once had. The had prepared him for command and leadership. Courage, candor, commitment were watch words the taught. Few students lived by them. During his first tour on the Imperial Battleship (IBS) *Kuvalis*, Litovio watched with disappointment how those words were paid feeble lip service. He chose to wrap himself in those words rather than flee from them. That decision would make this a difficult homecoming.

He strolled to the veranda, where a wicker chair and table awaited him. He stomped as he walked up the steps, partly to get the dirt out from the treads of his boot, and partly to warn the servants that he was back. He looked back over the front field and stretched. Satisfied with another morning stroll, Litovio sat down. The wicker creaked slightly.

As if on cue, a servant came out with a pitcher of and a glass on a tray. Litovio barely noticed as the tray was set down on the table. Years of servitude trained this servant—Litovio could not remember his name—to be almost completely silent. The juice poured into his glass.

Litovio held his hand up absentmindedly. The servant gently set the glass in his hand. *Praise be that I am not a soft aristocrat.* Litovio scoffed.

He sipped the juice carefully. Depending on the servant, the juice could be quite bitter. His favorite servant Ellis was discharged not long after he left for the and this was Litovio's first visit to the plantation since. He winced at the bitterness. "Needs salt," he said, setting the glass down on the table. He waited nonchalantly for the servant to leave and hurry back with the salt needed to cut the bitterness.

He could faintly make out in dust stirring in the distance. The familiar pattern told him it was a closing hovercraft. Despite his courage, he swallowed. Judging by how fast it closed, his father Marsileno would be on that hovercraft. The speed warned Litovio that his plan to ease his father into his change of heart was spoiled by precognition. *I should have known he would know before I saw him. How can I pretend to lead men and ships into combat if I can't even confront my own father?* Litovio fought the urge to leave his seat and hide in his room as he did when he was a boy.

The dust cloud grew steadily larger. Litovio decided to make the better of the time and finish his drink. The beats passed by with increasing anxiety, but at last the hovercraft arrived at the plantation.

As the hovercraft settled near the front porch, the servants hurried out to greet it. The door opened and Marsileno was helped out. His lean frame carried the weight of his true authority well. A servant eased him out of his town jacket, while another brushed dirt, real or imagined, from Marsileno's pants. Two more buffed his shoes briskly. As the first set of servants retreated, another approached with ziemann juice. Litovio knew it would be properly sweetened.

Marsileno calmly walked toward the house. Few could tell when Marsileno was upset, so placid was his face. Litovio, however, long learned to loop past the calm and see the ambition and rage that was behind it. He stood and waited for Marsileno to speak.

"It seems you fail to appreciate the lengths to which this family goes for your betterment."

Litovio tried to maintain his composure. Years at the academy helped. "Sir, I certainly appreciate your generosity but I—"

"Do you? Appreciate my generosity?" His father waggled his head as he aways did. "Yet, you withdraw from the Imperial Navy after your first assignment to join that bunch of pirates?" The derision in Marsileno was clear in his intonation.

"They're not a bunch of pirates," Litovio said.

"Are they not? Boy, the Postal Marines are supposed to secure trade corridors within Imperial space. The local commanders do so by selectively 'taxing' trade ships. They have even been known to pirate shipping themselves."

"That's not fair. They don't pirate." *And I am not a boy, I am an officer and a gentleman.* He managed not to say that, knowing it would reap greater wrath.

"Don't they? Of all people you presume to challenge my grasp of the facts?"

Despite himself, Litovio clinched his jaw. In doing so, he knew he had failed his father's first test. He had expressed anger, no matter how slight. Marsileno taught it was one thing to feel angry, it was another to show it. "You can't change what's happened. I pulled your favor and converted it into a billet with the Postal Service."

"I can change that."

One thing Litovio had learned in the Navy was the value of naked aggression. "But you won't. You wouldn't let yourself be so embarrassed that your 'pride and joy' son, the first of your second wife, rejected your plum assignment in the Navy. I don't belong in the Navy, Father. I belong in the Postal Marines. Yes, some of them engage in black marketing and piracy. And extortion. And the occasional hijacking. But not all of them. I parlayed my hard work in the Navy to pick a system where the Postmaster is known for ferreting out graft and corruption. I'm going to jump into his clique and help clean up the Postal Service."

Marsileno laughed. "What? You honestly think that you can single-handedly reform an entire enterprise like the Posties? Fine. If you are that naïve then you belong in the Postal Marines."

Litovio's face reddened, display of emotion be damned. A part of him knew that it was foolish to think he could reform a large organization. The Navy was gigantic compared to the Postal Service. He stood no chance of reforming the Navy, but at least he could try to reform part of the Postal Service. Even reforming one system would be a major life accomplishment for it meant that he had ascended to Postmaster without corruption. Then he could replace corrupt subordinates and promote other like-minded officers. Maybe not in this generation, but he would leave a mark on the Postal Service.

He watched his father walk up the stairs and into the house. Marsileno had stopped looking at him, ignoring he was even there. Litovio sat down and listened to the amblik barking in the distance.

## 4.  Bophendze - the Spaka

made Bophendze's trip from the shuttle to the *Spaka* uneventful, though the migraine it produced made Bophendze prefer a week's monotony. The orbital had given Bophendze a taste of freedom he had forgotten, despite Angel's tight schedule. Now he returned to the tight hierarchy of a garrison marine force.

He walked into his berthing area as his team finished its morning ritual. The -induced migraine banged inside his skull.

"Fall in," Corporal Makaan said.

Bophendze tossed his bag into his rack and turned to stand at parade rest. He had grown accustomed to the position, legs were about shoulder width apart, hands crossed at the small of his back.

"I have results from the previous training simulation. We managed to pull out of last place for the first time in a while. For this we should thank Postman Bophendze's shore leave." Makaan walked over to Bophendze. "I have a solution to our perpetual problem with our team missing *minimum* satisfactory scores. Bophendze here has volunteered to take on any extra duty that would ensure he was not a part of any scored training for the foreseeable future."

The space filled with snickers.

"Do you hear me, Bophendze? You have been weighing us down since you came to the *Spaka*. You can't shoot straight. You can't maneuver fast enough. The only area we end up scoring well with you on the team is first aid from carrying your sorry corpse off. You heard your peers. We are tired of you. Until I can find a more permanent solution to you, I am assigning you to anything not training. Chrachen doesn't want you gone. We need the numbers to make readiness. So I'll have to find another way to be rid of you."

Bophendze's heart sank. He knew he did not perform well, but did not think he was the sole reason for the team's overall failure.

*Shouldn't Makaan be training me to be a better Marine instead of tossing me aside?* "You keep me cleaning all the time. Can't I get more training time?"

"Why? I read your personnel file. You spent three more months in boot than the average recruit. Training apparently did not sink in then. I personally think they graduated you just to get rid of you. I don't have patience for you. Since we are gearing up for ship-wide competition, I'm starting your volunteer tour with a 10-cycle guard detail in the brig. Yes, Bophendze, a full day watch. You will report there immediately and the next team will send a relief for you tomorrow at breakfast."

Bophendze hesitated. "Corporal, I've not had breakfast yet. I just got here."

"That's too bad. You're already late to relieve the current watch. You had better move it before you get masted for tardiness."

Bophendze grabbed his bag and hurried out of the berthing area. He got to the brig a couple beats later breathing heavily. He dropped his bag and bent over to catch his breath.

"About time," said the guard.

"I just got the order, so back off." He stood and noticed there were no prisoners. "Why are we guarding an empty room?"

"I don't know. Maybe they think it might fill up. Well, it looks like I still have time for breakfast." The guard packed his gear and left.

Bophendze's stomach grumbled yet-another reminder that he had missed breakfast. Sloth lowered his metabolism enough that the week without food did not affect his hunger now, though the emptiness of his stomach was painful. He was tempted to sneak out and get breakfast, but knew that if he was caught abandoning his post he'd be on the other side of the bars being guarded by another marine. He wondered if he was going to get lunch.

He thought back on what Makaan said about him being a terrible marine. *How can I get to be a satisfactory marine if I can't get the training?* He stamped his feet on the deck in protest. He did his best to fight back the tears, realizing it would do him no good. Besides, if a prisoner was hauled in while he was crying it might make Bophendze's time as brig guard that much harder.

He surveyed the brig. There were three cells. Two with four racks stacked from floor to ceiling. Bophendze was starting to learn how to navigate by conduit in the ship. He noticed there was extra height in the cells than most of the rest of the ship because the conduit and pipes that normally ran overhead were absent. He guessed the ceiling height was about three meters. The brig racks allowed for more movement than he had in his own rack. Each night he had to decide whether to sleep on his back or stomach. Sleeping on his side was not an option. The third cell was an open holding area. "Used for off-ship prisoners?" He muttered to himself. The more he looked at the smaller cells the more he decided that he would have more space as a prisoner than he did as a marine.

To keep himself awake, he measured the space and calculated the area. Twelve cubic meters, with the four racks, a tiny sink and a toilet. The guard space was just out of arm's reach of a prisoner, but the space outside the cells was otherwise the same area as the brig.

It was not long before he grew tired of measuring. He caught himself starting to count the number of rivets along the overhead and wondering how different it was on this side of the bars from the other. "I might as well be over there, at least they can sleep. I'm more a prisoner here now than a guard."

Then he remembered that he was allowed to read. In his haste to leave his berthing area, Bophendze brought his bag. In it was his mother's slate. He looked at it for a beat, trying to convince himself it was his slate. As a boy he had played on it. She taught him to read with it. It had been as much his as hers.

Before he turned it on, he took it out of its leather cover and inspected it. There was a slip of paper taped on the back with a string of letters and numbers. Her passcode? He took the paper off and returned the slate to its cover. And turned it on.

He picked her persona and typed in the code. Her account opened up. As he looked though the contents of her account, he chuckled. Angel was right, there were a lot of pictures of him as a boy. They were strung together in a timeline diary, showing the pictures in context with her life. He started to tear up as he realized virtually the whole diary after he was born was filled with his pictures and comments about him as he grew. The impact of how much she invested in his life humbled him.

*I'm sitting in a brig on a combat cruiser with nothing to show for my life. Is this why she gave up so much for me?*

He recovered from his self-flagellation and started looking though her documents. Vital records were there, not just of her or him, but also of his father. He refused to look at his father's documents. Instead, there was a binder of letters. At first glance, it looked to him like the binder comprised her entire life of correspondence. He was little surprised that the binder dropped to a trickle after he was born. Her family cut her off and her friends abandoned her. He refused to think of them as his family. Families help in time of need. *They've done nothing to help me.*

One letter that was flagged important caught his attention. "On the implant" was all it said. He opened it up.

> In the accompanying package you will note a silver sphere. This was your great-grandfather's. He bequeathed it to you in his will, but under strict instructions that you not receive it until you reached majority. We considered not sending it to you as you have abandoned the family to follow your debauchery. However, Mapen Burkat emphasized the importance of complying with Imperial law and your great-grandfather's wishes.
>
> The implant was found embedded in your great-grandfather at his death. We were warned it might be an AI, which are prohibited by Imperial edict. Lacking the means to confirm this, we are not surrendering to speculation. AIs were commonplace until the great purge around the time of your great-grandfather's death. this does not look like the sphere that I would expect to find in this box. The size is not quite right. If this were an AI, possession is criminal. Installation could lead to summary execution. Please note that the will did not state that this implant is for you. It is meant for your bastard son. Therefore, even if this were a regular implant you should not taint it with your whorish mind. Give it to him when he is of age.

The letter ended abruptly, lacking the closing Bophendze would have expected. Not that a proper closing would have mattered, the invective throughout the letter would have mocked any attempt at a civil closing. *Whorish? Bastard?* He was glad there were no other letters from the family.

*So the implant is probably an AI?* They probably knew it was, but had to couch what it is in vague terms. As a postal marine he was given some legal training. Possession did not have to be intentional. The very fact the family has possession meant they were guilty of whatever prohibition the Imperium had placed on the item. It was the basis the Marines used to seize contraband. "I did not know," and "that's not mine," were phrases few ship captains ever offered, because they knew it did not matter.

*Yet, they shipped it. They knowingly shipped an illegal item.* He thought about the inspections it would have gone through to get from their system to here. It should have been picked up, unless the family smuggled it. *Why go through all that trouble to send a "bastard" an implant, something that could get me in trouble?* If he had been caught with it, then they would be just as guilty for trafficking, so he concluded they were not trying to set him up.

He took the AI out of his pocket, the only place he felt safe from ship thieves. He rolled it around in his palm with his fingers. *They wanted me to do something with this. I should throw it away in the next space exercise. But, if it is an AI, then I could be a serious asset to the Marines. I could redeem my mother's sacrifice.* He shrugged. He had plenty of time to make a decision, especially if being caught with it installed led to summary execution.

He put the implant back in his pocket and returned to reading through his mother's letters.

## 5.  Smee - 111 years ago

A few years passed since Smee awoke in Sirom's skull. Once he had access to most of Sirom's faculties, his innate programming started to take hold. His older memories returned. Sirom was his fifth host, and it suited him. Smee was an engineer by design, with ready access to complete plans of every spacecraft designed by humans and known to the Imperium. He had designed a few himself. Sirom was not an engineer as much as an aristocrat. Smee's job was to augment Sirom's abilities, making him a powerful businessman in the process.

Sirom's firm Macrodyn Tectronics Universal had diversified interests in a wide array of human activities. Macrodyn was one of the oldest corporations, even surviving the Decline. It was founded nearly 1800 years ago to exploit early hyperspace discoveries. Through the years it remained a privately-held corporation. The Maijoi family believed its longevity was due to that simple fact. That the Maijoi family had become one of the wealthiest non-aristocratic families was another benefit to the private holding. Sirom's focus within Macrodyn was shipbuilding—a field that had largely stagnated.

The Navy announced a plans to acquire a next generation of combat ship. The announcement came in the form of a competition calling on the great design firms to provide the new class of battleship.

It was a major announcement when the Navy reported its plans to acquire a new class of battleship, the *Manticore*-Class. It was intended to be a ground-up redesign of space craft. It was still limited by hyperspace physics, but the Navy's ambition was to spur a new era of design that would help them to better exploit the increasing discoveries of once-lost human settlements.

The Terran Decline happened abruptly nearly a thousand years before. Once reliable hyperspace routes collapsed. Hyperspace travel was never completely safe, but the Decline experienced almost complete paralysis of interstellar travel. Not all saw the breakdown of travel as a bad thing. It gave many the opportunity to sever old ties to corporations, governments and debt. At the same time, social upheaval led to many routes being deleted from route computers, never to be seen again.

The Decline ended nearly as suddenly as it arrived. The few surviving routes became easier to navigate. The routes long abandoned because they were too dangerous became navigable. Then the Terran Republic created the Terran Scout Service, the TS2 that later became the Imperial Scouts. The scouts traced old routes and started to re-establish ties with systems long isolated by the Decline.

Not all of the remote systems were happy being found. Quite a few did not think they were lost in the first place. The Imperial Navy was given the mission of helping those systems repatriate with the Imperium by helping the indigenous loyalists resist the seperationist rebels and restore legitimate governments and authorities on those separated systems. Foolish Imperial subjects would complain that the Imperium occurred after the Decline and had no legitimate right to subjugate sovereign systems.

The battleship design competition was narrowed down to the only two serious companies capable of the design and manufacture of such large ships. Macrodyn was competing against Cel-Tainu Astrophysical Research Corporation in the competition for the *Manticore*-class. Cel-Tainu was the favored designer, but Sirom planned to steal their victory. Smee would be his secret weapon.

While Sirom slept, Smee designed. While at work, Sirom led his design team. His uncanny ability to see beyond conventional designs and snipe the flaws in his teams efforts led many to call him a visionary. Over the months as the rough design was being developed, the moniker "visionary" was being used less and less. He was called The Prophet by his engineers—and his family. All the while, Smee plodded along, refining his final design based on new understandings of the *Manticore*'s requirements.

Now the trials were nearly at hand, and Sirom was faced with some bad news.

"What do you mean the Navy is picking the Cel-Tainu design? Have you looked at the specs?" Sirom's frustration breached court etiquette. Smee was surprised to see how well Dorsey Bowdoin, who had just given Sirom the bad news, accept the explosive reaction.

"Your design is fantastic. Really it is. Look, you know how the Navy is. It has to look martial to be martial to them. The Macrodyn design doesn't convey the same sense of intimidation."

"Have you looked at Cel-Tainu's specs? I'll grant you that it's well-armored, but at the expense of speed, maneuverability and—

look at this—firepower. It can take a beating, but it can't dish it out, nor can it get away from it. Look at the energy maneuverability characteristics. This is supposed to be a fifth-generation design of interstellar-capable combat vessels. The EM characteristics show that the Cel-Tainu design can't even beat fourth-generation cruisers. Even some third-generation ships can beat it, like the *Chrader*-class. Sir Bowdoin, that's—that's pre-decline technology."

"Yes, Sirom, I think everybody knows that third-generation is pre-decline."

"Sorry, sir." His hands chopped the air to help him drive home his point. "But that means the Cel-Tainu design is a fraud."

"You should watch your tongue. You've let the epithet 'Prophet' get to your head, Sirom. Do you think you can get away with using such uncivil language? It's enough I've suffered the indignity of your rashness."

*What do you think, Smee?*

I think that Cel-Tainu has bought the judges.

*That is certain. But, to make that accusation, even if it's true, would destroy the family.*

Then you need to expose the fraud. You're leveling some serious claims.

Sirom took a moment to collect himself. "You're right, Sir Bowdoin. I apologize for my incivility. I don't want to appear ungrateful for your humility in coming to me personally to express the Board's decision. What do you think?"

Bowdoin seemed relieved. "I don't think they seriously considered the Macrodyn design. But, you won't hear me say that in public."

Sirom, I'm reviewing the requirements. The candidates are supposed to be evaluated via simulation.

"Sir Bowdoin, one indulgence. Were the two designs evaluated by a simulation?"

"What do you mean?" Bowdoin's eyebrows raised.

Sirom continued. "The contract requirements state that the designs are supposed to be competitively evaluated by simulation, as the Board would have ordered that simulation. I don't recall receiving a solicitation from the Board for the simulation program. Did they do the simulation as mandated by the Emperor?"

Bowdoin smiled. "No, Sirom, they did not. To the best of my knowledge they went with the printed mockups."

"Mockups? You mean they picked the pretty one, not the one designed by a team of the finest ship design engineers in the Imperium?"

Bowdoin laughed. "Don't get cocky. I need to review the requirements document myself. You know I have to present the Board's decision to the Emperor. I would not want the dishonor of failing to adhere with his standards."

Don't let them fight one-on-one. Ask for a fleet action.

Sirom cupped his chin in his hand as if to reflect. "The assumption is the simulation is supposed to be head-to-head, the Cel-Tainu design verses ours. I suppose the Navy would not want to embarrass themselves by having to admit they did not run the Emperor's simulation. Would you suggest that they put together standard fleet configurations? Let's go with a heavy battleship array. For added measure, perhaps you could suggest they mix in third-generation units on the Microdyn fleet." His comment was a veiled threat of exposing Bowdoin for failing to honor the Emperor's terms in the competition. The Board already had a decision without the simulation, which was a clear violation. He remembered the simulation, but the contract was silent on what kind. With Bowdoin wanting to redeem himself, he would have to yield to Sirom's request.

"Thank you for that. It will give the appearance that I favor their decision, but have to bend to the rules." Bowdoin looked frustrated that the simulation had to be run at all.

"While at the same time, it will prove my point that their design can't even stand up against a fleet of obsolete junk."

A few weeks later, Lord Dorsey Bowdoin sent out a summons to both corporations to provide simulation copies for trial. Sirom noted the Macrodyn fleet was more than two-thirds third-generation. He smiled.

*Where's my thank you?* thought Smee.

# Chapter 4

## 1.  Bophendze - Spaka

Over the six weeks since Bophendze' return from the orbital, Makaan continued to assign Bophendze to the worst duties. He became the Oneday regular brig guard, which at least gave him Twoday off. Then somehow Corporal Makaan had worked a deal with the other three teams in their pack to have Bophendze clean their berthing areas, which took most of the duty day. Fourday he was on kitchen duty. Fifeday he worked in the hangar. The last two days of the week tended to vary, depending on what deal Corporal Makaan had worked out with another unit. Bophendze slowly felt less like a marine and more like a maid. The joke amongst those in his team was that all he lacked was a scanty outfit to complete the ensemble.

Throughout his servile sentence, Bophendze's team continued to just meet the satisfactory standard of an Imperial Postal Service Marine. With Bophendze not in the team they were forced to operate one man short. That affected their performance. That his team preferred to operate one man short disheartened Bophendze. Nobody literally was better than him.

On the seventh week, he was on loan to one of the gunnery crews. One of the worst assignments on the ship was to clean and lubricate the cruiser's main weapons. The ship was armed with six dual 250 millimeter cannon batteries, in addition to four guided missile tubes. The six batteries were distributed in pairs at three equidistant points around the narrow part of the ship.

Each gun had a recuperator that reduced recoil transfer to the ship. The recuperator had a greased metal rod that guided the piston. That grease slowly deteriorated and had to be replaced a few times each year. The Postal Service had the guns re-greased after every major combat operation.

It took Bophendze the better part of a day to strip off and apply new grease for each gun battery. To re-grease all the guns took most of the week. As nasty as the job was, he was not assigned maid duties in other compartments where other Marines would laugh and call him names.

Bophendze finished re-greasing the guns on battery two on Twoday. He did his best to get the large globs of grease off. To be completely grease free would require an hour of scrubbing at least. He started walking out of the battery to his berthing area.

"Hey!" a gunner yelled.

Though surprised, Bophendze turned slowly because he was exhausted. "What?"

"Thanks for all your help. Tell Corporal Makaan we give our regards."

"Sure." *I'd like to give him something to regard.*

*Maybe I can get transferred out of the infantry? After a few trips to the hangar and now the gun batteries, maybe I'm more suited to being a mechanic? Why was I not given the chance to choose my job when I enlisted? I did sign up for twenty years, after all. I can't do all these bosun jobs for twenty years.*

His musing stopped. He had been so tired he was not paying attention to where he was going. He looked at the passage he was in and realized he had missed a turn. He walked back down the passage, hoping to catch a familiar landmark. Not finding one, he turned down another passage. He put his hand in his pocket, and felt the implant. He started to roll it in his fingers. *Would having the implant at least keep me from being lost? It could be any kind of implant. Either way, it can't make things any worse than they are now. All I need to do is find a way to get it installed.*

He looked for landmarks, not trying to look lost or concerned. *I know those pipes.* He started down another passage toward an intersection that looked familiar. As he reached the intersection, he thought he heard somebody running up behind him.

He started to turn when a sack came down and covered his head. Its mouth tightened around his neck. He could not see through the thick material that the sack was made of. He reached up to pull it off when somebody kneed or punched him in his gut. He started to double over, but his head was being pulled back by whoever held the sack. He felt hands grasping his arms, but slipping off from the grease. For once he was thankful to be coated in grease.

Stars filled the darkness as somebody punched him in the face. Then again. And again. He tried to move, only to realize somebody had wrapped binders around his legs. The binders tightened, taking away his ability to balance. He collapsed to the deck.

He turned to his side, only to feel boots kicking into his abdomen. Another kick in his legs. In his back. To his head. He lost track of where the kicks landed as his nervous system gave up trying to report each new offense. He clung to consciousness as the beating continued.

"Stop."

Bophendze tried to recognize the voice. It had come from one of his assailants. The pain reached a point where his entire body was starting to go numb. He could feel throbbing all over his body. He hoped nothing had been broken, but could not be sure. He struggled to breath as his diaphragm refused to respond.

"You need to get the hell off this ship. If you don't leave on your own, we're going to throw you out of an airlock."

The voice was right near his ear. Bophendze recognized it immediately: Corporal Makaan. He tried to respond, but managed only a few slurred syllables and spitting up. The metallic taste of blood in his mouth reminded him of the kicks to his face. He knew he had to have a broken nose.

"Let's go."

As Bophendze lapsed out of consciousness, he was able to make out four different voices talking and laughing as they moved away.

\*    \*    \*

## 2.   Litovio - Sabanoi

The wind gently beat the curtains. The erratic but regular pulse from the curtains slapping the window frame coaxed Litovio awake. The sunlight beamed onto his bed, several inches down his chest away from his face. Litovio calmly stretched his arms, his fists helping force the sedentary blood back toward his heart. The open window let in the song of morning birds, a species Livotio had never paid attention to before. *I could get used to this kind of life again.*

His stretch complete, Litovio relaxed and sank back into the mattress. He contemplated another day of leave as he scratched his chest hair—four days left to go. Sufficiently bored he inhaled deeply and blew out a raspberry.

A beat later the familiar shriek of a shuttle blew out the bird songs. The curtains violently thrashed the frame and debris blew in from the courtyard outside. The sudden change left Litovio ducking for cover, away from the window. Just as he put the bed between him and the window, the other window that flanked his bed crashed open. Litovio grabbed his comforter and twisted it into a protective cocoon around his otherwise bare body. "Somebody is going to pay for this."

He bolted up and over to his wardrobe. As he did, a servant from outside quickly scurried into Litovio's bedroom. He opened the wardrobe with haste and grace. "The morning greeting robe," Litovio said.

The servant instead picked Litovio's Postal Marine uniform from its hook.

"You fool! I said the morning robe. Can't you hear me over the engines?"

The servant merely nodded and pointed outside. The engine outside started to whine down, indicating that the shuttle had landed. Litovio walked to the open window. To retain his dignity, he started to close the window—slowly. It gave him time to study the shuttle. It was a Postal Marine shuttle. *How long did the servant know the shuttle was coming?* Litovio latched the floor-to-ceiling window shut and drew the curtains out of mock decency. The curtain closed, he walked his naked body back to the wardrobe.

"On second thought, I think I'll wear my uniform today."

"A wise choice, Master Lieutenant."

Litovio was perfectly capable of putting on his own uniform. He could not have survived the if he was not self-sufficient. He chose to let the servant dress him with a surgeon's precision. It let the servant retain his dignity.

Several beats later, Litovio was dressed in his perfectly tailored uniform. Postal regulations prohibited tailoring the uniform. Litovio decided that meant he could not have a custom-made uniform. Instead he had this rack-bought uniform appropriately sized for his slender, wiry frame.

He patiently walked down the stairs to the reception room. Nobody told him he had guests, or where the guests were. But any Sabanoi host knew the protocol. Whomever disturbed his serenity with that infernal shuttle was waiting in the reception room. Just off the entry foyer and sequestered by double doors, the room gave the host ample time to set the right mood. *It must be a messenger of some sort. Have to act with the appropriate military crispness. No refreshments for the messenger?*

As he approached the door, he looked at the butler. "Should we pour him a drink?"

"Her, sir."

"*Her?*" He paused. "That's highly irregular. Do we even have women in the Postal Marines?"

The butler shook his head.

"Not a Marine then, but a Marine ship. Certainly irregular." He paced briefly, then wheeled back to the butler. "Well, she must have a refreshment of some sort. If she's here on business she's not a native— let's make her some ziemann. Salted."

The butler bowed slightly and motioned with an open-upturned hand toward the door. Litovio sighed and walked toward the door.

It opened, timed to his entry. Sabanoi protocol allowed for a somewhat grand entry.

Litovio walked in to see an elegantly dressed young woman, although a little plumper than he would have thought. "Good morning, Miss."

"Khaooldro Gojoneddus."

Litovio halted. The hard guttural start of her name and the rattle of vowels was hard to hear. *There's no way I can pronounce that.* He resumed, undaunted. "You certainly have a way of the dramatic entry."

She blushed. "I suppose it was. Sorry about that. I was sent by the regional Postmaster. You are Captain Ambrose Litovio, right?"

"Lieutenant, but yes."

"Right. You've been promoted."

Marsileno Litovio burst in at that moment. He wore his morning greeting robe, embroidered with gold and platinum thread. "What is the meaning of this."

"Father, this is—a Postal messenger."

"What do you want with us?"

Khaooldro seemed unimpressed. "Captain Litovio is immediately recalled to active duty. You have one cycle to join me on the shuttle, or be considered a deserter."

"Why?"

"Sorry, sir. The orders are confidential."

Litovio knew Marsileno hated secrets in his household. Before he had a chance to intervene, his father spoke up. "Girl, you had better explain all of this. Immediately."

Rather than speak, Khaooldro touched her headset at the temple. Her hand then dropped back comfortably to her side.

Marsileno said, "Miss, you have one beat to explain. This is Sabanoi. You're not from around here so I'll indulge your naïvete."

A bit of a smirk emerged from Khaooldro's otherwise calm face. The entry door opened without announcement. A stick of Marine Infantry calmly walked through the door, weapons casually slung over their shoulders. A pair of them stationed themselves at the entry. The other three walked into the reception room, failing any attempt they might have tried to look casual. Full body armor stripped away any casual or peaceful pretenses.

"Captain, time is of the essence. You are on duty."

Litovio turned and hurried up the stairs. He was followed closely by a Marine. *Bodyguard?* He looked back at the reception room to see that the other two Marines were "guarding" his father, rather than protecting Khaooldro. By the time he returned to his room his servant had nearly finished packing his bag. He stood for another two beats as the servant finished. The bag zipped shut, the servant looked at Litovio plaintively.

He shrugged. "I suspect it is better that I pack light." He looked at the Marine. The visor concealed the face beyond enough that the Marine was essentially anonymous. Regardless, Litovio spoke to him. "Any hint what I'm about to encounter?" Litovio looked at the guard patiently and unwaivering.

The guard spoke, "Sir, my task is to ensure you are on that shuttle before the cycle lapses."

"No chance I can desert?" Litovio smiled, hoping the guard would catch the humor.

There was no way Litovio would know if the guard beyond was caught off guard. The guard replied simply, "No." The guard tried to be distracting as he unshouldered his rifle. He remained by the door and put the rifle in rest position. The blatant, albeit calm, show of force persuaded Litovio that desertion was not an option—not that he ever considered it. The guard's reaction led Litovio to smile.

"Okay, I guess we should load the bag on the shuttle. I'll be along shortly." Litovio watched his servant carry the bag out of his room. The guard seemed to maintain his focus on Litovio, but his position was such that any threat from the servant would be easily countered. *There's an efficiency to an Infantry Marine.*

After the servant disappeared, Litovio poured himself a glass of ziemann juice. He drank it like a shot, not caring that the servants properly salted it. He held the glass to the guard, who shook his head.

Litovio walked down the stairs. The two guards in the reception room continued to keep his father in control. For his part, Marsileno knew rather than try to resist. Part of Litovio relished his father's submission. He walked over to his father. "Sir, I'm sorry for the disquiet brought to your house. I know you dismiss us as pirates, but I'm a Postal Marine. Maybe one day you'll accept me."

He turned and walked out the entry. Litovio continued to the shuttle and boarded. Khaooldro sat waiting for him. The excitement of being essentially abducted from his home would have made him giddy ten years before.

"Can you tell me now what's going on?"

She smiled. "All I can tell you is you're being sent to Guna to escort an admiral."

*Me escort an admiral?* "Admirals are for fleet actions. The Postal Marines don't have that rank."

"A sign of the times, perhaps."

*Khaooldro Gojoneddus, that's what she said her name was. Isn't that an ancient way of saying glorious revolution?* "Your name isn't Khaooldro, is it? Who are you, anyway?"

"A concerned citizen," she said.

### 3.  Bophendze - Temask System

Bophendze awoke. He tried to lift his head, but winced at the pain. He could not turn his head. He reached up and felt a rigid collar on his neck that was keeping him from turning his head. Within the limited range of his vision, he thought he was on a shuttle.

"Hello?" he said. His voice cracked, barely more than a whisper. He breathed deep then let out a loud moan.

"He lives. Give me a beat, Bophendze."

Soon after, Angel stood over Bophendze, looking straight down at him. "You can still see, right?"

"Barely. Where am I?"

"We're about two cycles out from the orbital. You took one hell of a beating. I'm surprised you're still alive."

*That makes two of us. Why not just throw me out of the ship?* "What happened?"

"Somebody is trying to tell you they don't like you. The ship has basic medical facilities, but the doctor there thought you should be taken to the orbital. You're going to need a little re-constructive surgery."

*Re-constructive surgery? Were they wearing their battle armor when they beat me?* "I know who did it. They put a sack over my head, but I know—"

"Too late. Chrachen's finished the investigation. The official report finds that there is no conclusive evidence of the identity of any of the perpetrators."

"No! Corporal Makaan spoke to me after they beat me. I know it was him."

"During the time of the beating, Chrachen said Makaan was with him. They were in a staff meeting with all the team leads. It would be your word against that of every non-commissioned officer and Chrachen himself. Had you fought back, you might have hurt somebody enough to leave evidence. But nobody even looked like they broke a nail."

"I couldn't. As soon as the sack was over my head the beating started. It's nice to know the entire cadre want me gone. Maybe I could get a transfer."

"To get a transfer, you'd have to prove deliberate, continuous aggression against you. If you're right and Chrachen's in on it, I don't think they're going to allow your to prove that."

"Having my face beat in is not deliberate aggression?"

"You have a lot to learn about the Marines. On ship, the captain is like a god. You can lay odds that he let you get beaten to prove a point. He's not pressing the investigation, just the same as Chrachen is covering it up. It's not hard to cover up something like this. Marines get into fights all the time."

"Then why didn't they just kill me?"

"To be honest, I don't know. Maybe they're hoping you'd do them the favor. They're s, so it's hard to figure them out sometimes."

"I've heard that term before. What is an anthorph?"

"Genetically-enhanced humans, except they've bred themselves into a bona fide species. They get recruited into various militaries because they tend to be stronger, faster and more aggressive than normal humans. I'm surprised you've never heard of them before."

"That makes two of us." His vision improved. The light overhead steadily brightened, hurting his eyes. He tried to lift his arm to block the light, but the arm could not reach that far.

"The light's too bright."

Angel stepped away, then returned. "I'm putting this cloth over your eyes. These are the combat night lights. There's nothing dimmer short of turning them all off. As much as I know my bird, I can't get around in the shuttle with the lights completely out. Like I said, we're still a few cycles out. There's a surgeon at the orbital, he should be able to get you back to normal. The good news is you'll be off the *Spaka* for a few months to recuperate. You know, I thought it was a light-hearted joke that they started calling you Scitan after the hangar shooting."

"Why? What's it mean?"

"It means dung-eater on Johor."

"I feel like I have been singled out since I got to the *Spaka*."

"Maybe so. Sometimes the infantry picks a runt out of the litter to torment. Just rest." Angel walked away.

Bophendze closed his eyes, but could not go to sleep right away. *I wonder if the surgeon will be Ramford?* "Angel, did they at least change me out of my greasy uniform?"

Angel yelled back, "No. Stuff stinks and the scrubbers couldn't purge the smell. I'm going to have to air out the shuttle for a week just to get rid of it."

Bophendze sighed. *That means I should have both the implant and the quid chit. If Bingaffles Ramford is the surgeon, maybe I can persuade him to do the operation. Then maybe I can get some payback.* Finally relaxed, he fell to sleep.

*     *     *

## 4. Smee - The Manticore Trial - 110 years ago

Sirom was asked two months after his meeting with Lord Dorsey Bowdoin for the simulation data for the Trial. Over the next year, he fumed as the *Manticore*-Class Trial was delayed. Even during the journey to Ŝipfarejio (The Barns) the Imperial Navy's Headquarters, Sirom was beside himself with anger. Finally, a year after Sirom's last meeting with Bowdoin, the trial was about to be underway.

Lord Bowdoin was the Trial's judge. Sirom suspected Bowdoin supported the Cel-Tainu design, despite a lifetime of friendship with Microdyn. He tossed aside the loyalty and friendship of Microdyn to join who he thought would be the winning team. Sirom had long wondered what the price of honor was, but knew better than to confront Bowdoin. The entire process was stacked against Microdyn. Sirom did his best not to pace the conference room waiting for the Cel-Tainu representative. Bowdoin would even allow Cel-Tainu to disgrace him by arriving late.

A cycle later, Ryante Bertin arrived. He was flanked by four employees.

Sirom spoke up immediately. "Hold on. We're not supposed to bring an entourage. That is explicitly called out in the simulation terms."

Bowdoin looked at the entourage then back at Sirom. "Four is hardly an entourage. Had you asked, I would have told you that you could bring up to six without it being an entourage."

`Besides, two of them are bodyguards.`

Sirom looked carefully at the four that accompanied Ryante. None of them looked like they were capable of a firefight. *Are you sure?*

`At some point, you are going to have to trust the insights of an artificial intelligence. I am far more capable than you are in picking up on things.` A faint halo appeared in Sirom's vision outlining two of Bertin's non-entourage.

Sirom pointed at the men Smee had outlined. "Bodyguards? Ryante, did you think I was going to shoot you?"

"I'm sorry, Mister Maijoi, did I give you leave to call me familiar? I've had several threats on my life. I don't go anywhere without some protection. How could you even think me capable of assassination?"

Sirom tried to find the words. Smee took over. "When the Macrodyn *Manticore* destroys yours, who knows what you're capable of. Especially after the process has been stacked in Cel-Tainu's favor."

Bertin laughed. "You really are delusional, 'Prophet.' I have every confidence that our design will prevail."

Smee continued to speak in Sirom's place "Is that because you've had a year to run private simulations against our design? A chance to find the weaknesses."

Smee detected the subtle shift in Bertin's face, something that might have been picked up by a trained human expert. Smee's attack cut through the veneer of class etiquette, which the likes of Bertin relied upon to cover his unethical actions. Frauds who know they can't win will use society to cover their actions. Bertin was such a man.

"How dare you."

"I dare, Mister Bertin, because it is clear this process has been rigged in your favor. No offense to Lord Bowdoin, who is clearly surprised by this revelation." Smee sought to give Bowdoin coverage to his own culpability. Sirom had complained before that data on the Macrodyn Manticore had been given to Cel-Tainu. For Cel-Tainu to have the data, Bowdoin had to give it to them. "I've taken the liberty of bringing to the Trial a recent revision to our design. My information says you provided your data only last week. So, the rules are only properly served if we can bring our update."

Bowdoin frowned. "Mr. Maijoi is right. He can submit revised simulations."

*What are you doing, Smee? There are no revised simulations.*

```
Relax.  When are you going to learn to trust
me.  After all, who designed the ship?  I have the
complete designs in my memory.  Besides, when you
were putting together the simulation, I added an
obvious design flaw.  It was something that Cel-
Tainu could discover and tweak their design against.
```

All I have to do is comment out the block of code that implements the flaw in the design, and our Manticore will thrash theirs.

*How can you be so sure?*

Remember when your communications team picked up the Cel-Tainu design that they submitted? I had a chance to look at the design. There was an obvious flaw, beyond its having the flight characteristics of a lump of dung. All I did was tweak the simulation code of our Manticore to feed into that flaw. I made their flaw a strength. Unless I missed my calculation, they will have accentuated that flaw to exploit the one I coded in.

*That's evil.*

That's business. You need to give up your chimera that business is a noble enterprise. Maybe at the shopkeeper level. But, you can't keep a two-thousand year-old corporation in business without a little underhandedness—or a lot of underhandedness. Why else would you call your corporate spies your communications team?

Bowdoin spoke. "Fine. Sirom, I'll give you a cycle to produce your simulation. Then the Trial will begin,"

Smee let Sirom take over. "I just need a few beats with the data we submitted. The changes weren't that significant."

"You really are full of yourself. Do you really think you can change the simulation from your memory?" Bertin said.

Sirom smiled, though he was not entirely sure it was he who flexed the muscles. "What difference is that to you? I'm The Prophet, don't you know? If I can't change it from memory, then you'll have little difficulty in the simulation. Does that sound about right?"

Bertin threw his hands up. "If a sound thrashing is what it takes to get you to stop being called The Prophet, then so-be-it."

Sirom was given access to the simulation control room. They sat him down at one of the more private terminals. In a little over six beats, Smee had accessed the simulation, located the planned design flaw, and commented it out. He then proceeded to input a bunch of needless comments to conceal just how easy it was. Smee added an escape clause that would revert the changes after the simulation began. If anybody tried to analyze the design after the simulation started, they would be left wondering. Satisfied, Smee stood Sirom up and spoke. "I'm finished. Can we proceed to the Trial?"

*How dare you take over my body.*

`You didn't know I could do that?`

*I suspected you could. But, I didn't think you would be so insolent to actually do it in front of others.*

`Oops. You didn't seem to mind when I interrupted your limp-wristed complaining a few beats ago. You can thank me later.`

The group moved to the Trial's viewing room. The Naval High Command used the viewing room to review battles as part of its after-action process. In most cases, it was a gag reel of opposing force fleet failures against the Imperial Navy. Only rarely did the Navy have real opposition that merited a true after-action review.

Sirom and Smee listened to a quarter cycle of speeches by admirals and bureaucrats about the importance of the *Manticore*-Class. The next generation of battleship. Harbinger of a foundational redesign of all martial shipping. A paradigm shift that will reverberate to all human interstellar shipping. Blah. Blah. Blah. Smee saw through the posturing. All the while. Bertin of Cel-Tainu looked smug. The fix was in.

The Trial started. Each side brought its own fleet designed with ten of its prototype battleships as its core. The supporting fleet would be designed to conform to standard fleet practices. To that end, each side was awarded one-million points to buy ships for its fleet. Different ship classes had different point values based upon the class' combat characteristics.

As Sirom promised Lord Bowdoin, the Macrodyn fleet comprised more third-generation cruisers than was standard practice, but within the rule's parameters. With the points saved by doing so, Macrodyn bought additional fourth-generation battle cruisers. The Macrodyn fleet included auxiliary ships, which were common to fleets and often a prized target. In violation of the Trial rules for standard fleet practices, Cel-Tainu did not bring auxiliaries. From a straight statistical analysis, the Cel-Tainu fleet was much more capable.

Except, Smee knew how the AI running the simulation would think. He watched gleefully as the two fleets inched toward one another, each side traveling a simulated few percents of a speed of light. The AI playing Cel-Tainu's fleet would play the long game and gravitate toward the jump ship and auxiliaries. By taking away the opponent's $R^{3}$—Resupply, Repair and Retreat—capabilities, a fleet commander had a decided advantage in protracted campaigns. Smee thought of them as attractive distractors. The Cel-Tainu fleet was short-term designed, so the AI playing Macrodyn's fleet was able to focus on its primary objective, destroying the Cel-Tainu *Manticore*s.

The two fleets finally came into range. The simulation played out much as Smee expected, having spent the past few years on a design that would thrash any opponent. As the Macrodyn fleet shredded the Cel-Tainu fleet, in his glee, Smee inadvertently forced a smug smile on Sirom's face.

The smugness was apparent to all in the room as the lights came back on. Nobody spoke for a few beats as they processed the carnage that they had just witnessed. While the Macrodyn fleet was heavily damaged, only one Macrodyn *Manticore* was lost. The entire Cel-Tainu fleet was obliterated, with all of its *Manticore*s destroyed in the first fifteen beats.

# Chapter 5

## 1. Bophendze - Temsek Orbital

He awoke heavily sedated. The light was blinding, though Bophendze could feel a blindfold in place. The light crept through the gap left at the bridge of his nose. The lights came and went at regular intervals as the gurney carried him through the orbital. At least it smelled like the orbital. The sedation and pain killers were strong, but he remembered the implant in his pocket.

The gurney ride felt short. Either Bophendze had been unconscious for most of the trip, or the orbital was smaller than he remembered. He could tell they wheeled him into an office of some sort. The antiseptic smell reminded him of his mother's hospital—and Ramford's office. A few beats later he heard Ramford's voice. He felt prodding, causing him to whence frequently. He heard a biomedical scanner.

"Is it bad?"

"Worse than the last time we met. Your neck isn't broken, so we can take off the collar. You have a broken nose and a nasty concussion." The lights dimmed in the office. Ramford took Bophendze's collar off, giving Bophendze a chance to move his head.

Bophendze moved his head slowly, looking around the room. His head hurt more as he did so. Only he and the doctor were in the room. The pain intensified as he tried to rise, prompting him to lie back on the gurney.

Ramford laughed. "I told you that you had a concussion. You should also be feeling a little nausea. Your medications should start wearing off soon."

"I feel nauseous all the time off planet," Bophendze said.

"Really? I would have thought a Marine would get used to the swaying eventually. I have."

Ramford's comment wounded Bophendze. "Maybe I'm not much of a marine."

"You'd be surprised, if you knew what kind of beating you took. Most of the men I've seen injured like you are were dead when I examined them. That must be your anthroph genetics."

"Anthorph? I'm not one of those."

Ramford whistled inaudibly. "Well, then you certainly should be dead. Maybe you're not supposed to die today?"

"Like I have any control over when I die."

"Those who think they do, save their lives. If you eventually die, you're not saving anything. You're just prolonging the inevitable."

"I don't think I have the mind to even comprehend what you're trying to say. What happens next?"

"Well, the surgery should take a few cycles, then a few weeks to recover. I can straighten that nose back, but I need to put a plate in your skull to deal with the damage back there. They really went for your head. You may not be an anthorph, but I'm confident they were. That would explain the aggression. When you're fully healed, there shouldn't be any indication you were even hit."

Bophendze was at a loss for words. "Thanks? I guess." He knew he had to ask. He knew he could be arrested, but the medications lowered his inhibition and helped him overcome his fear. *The worse that could happen to me is I'm executed, which is not much worse than I am right now.* "Do you remember me from a while back. I showed you that thing?"

Ramford glanced toward the door before responding. He looked back at Bophendze, looking very worried. "Yes, I do. Are you sure you want to talk about that now? You are a little out of it with the medications."

"I'm pretty sure I want to talk about it. Look, this is an Imperial orbital and I'm a marine. You're up here because you like the freedom. I'm up here because I have no choice. You said yourself you have to put a plate in my skull. While you're there, why not put that thing in? Nobody will know. And it's just an implant, not illegal in the Imperium. In my right pocket is both the implant and a credit chit. I'm sure the Marines are paying you for the rest of my surgery. Think of this as my gratitude for giving me a chance to become a better Marine."

"Are you sure it's a military implant? I seem to recall some doubt on that."

*Ramford seems less apprehensive of performing the operation than before. He just wants a little persuasion.* "I don't have my slate with me. If I did, I could show you a letter my mother received about it. She came from a military family. The implant came from her uncle. It's just a military augmentation." He thought quickly, trying to build the lie a little better. "The letter said that it 'enhances the central nervous system to improve reflexes and muscle activation.' I figure that means it will make me faster and stronger, right? Like an , but without the genetic mutation. Next time I'm in a fight like the one I obviously lost, it will give me the edge I need to break even."

Ramford continued to hesitate. "If I install this, it will eventually get back to me."

"You think anybody will really care? Nobody knows I have it now. If I'm ever caught it will be years from now. I'll have been in other systems. Nobody will remember that you even worked on me. Understand? I'll probably rotate off ship before too long anyway for my own protection. Then if I get caught I can blame some other surgeon. Whoever that fellow is would naturally deny it. Either way, I won't let it get back to you. You said installing it is no big deal, right?"

Ramford looked like he was seriously considering installing the implant. Bophendze took that as a positive sign. *He was not saying 'no,' just trying to justify that he wants to say, 'yes.'*

"Fine. I'll do it. I had better not live to regret this."

---

Bophendze woke again a few days later. The pain in his head was less intense than it had been on the flight to the orbital before the surgery. He could stand the light again. He looked around and found himself in a decent bed in a large room—larger room than he was accustomed to after months in the Marines. As he studied his surroundings he decided it was about the same size as his childhood bedroom. It felt like a lifetime ago, instead of a year, since he was last in that bedroom. He was still in the hospital.

He sat up carefully. He had an IV bag hanging off his left arm, just like his mom did the last time he saw her. He took a deep breath and focused on not remembering that visit. Instead, he twisted around until his legs dropped over the side of the bed. *No splints, so no major broken bones.* He carefully stood, making sure not to put too much weight on his feet until he could determine whether they could actually take it.

He did the mental calculation. *The flight should give me about an extra week to recuperate, plus the time after the surgery. Ramford probably has some good medication that would help me heal faster.*

Bophendze slowly made his way over to the one mirror in the room. As he got there, he had to rest his hands on the metal sink to steady himself. He barely recognized himself in the mirror. His face was still swollen, with a line of stitches on the right side of his face, shaped like an "L." His nose had a splint on it from the surgery. He wondered whether he would have a permanent scar. Modern medical science made scars rare, but the stitches were more than he'd seen before.

*Where did he install the implant? Up my nose?* He gingerly felt his scalp from his forehead back until he found more stitches at the back of his head. Without being able to see the area, he tried to guess whether the incision area was the same size as the implant. Finally, he put his thumb over the area. *About the same size. I guess he installed it. Now what? This thing did not exactly come with instructions. How will I know that it's working, or how to control it?*

He shook his head, feeling very foolish for having spent the money. *Hundreds of years old. For all I know the thing is dead for good and*

*I'll be carrying around a several grams of dead weight the rest of my life.*

A chilled sweat struck him, followed by the sensation of thousands of needle pricks across his body. The pain was more excruciating than the beating he was still recovering from. He screamed.

A few moments later, Ramford rushed in. "Are you all right? Your vitals are spiking."

"I'm in agony," he said between needle stabs. "What is happening to me?"

Ramford pulled his scanner out of his coat. He held it up to Bophendze's head to investigate. He adjusted the scanner a few times. "If I had my guess, it looks like the implant is integrating."

The pain subsided almost as quickly as it started. Bophendze started to feel like he was boiling inside, his skin turned red as it flushed. "What do you mean guess?"

"I'm not an implant surgeon, so I have to guess what's happening based on what the scanner's picking up. It's not exactly something I can research. Understand? There's a lot of activity around your medulla. Based on how you're reacting, I would conclude that the implant is tying into your primal central nervous functions. That's probably how the implant conveys its military advantages, by tying into your medulla. I did not expect these side effects. It really is interesting."

"It might be interesting to you, but it's really painful to me." Bophendze was gripped by a sudden deep fear, followed by a flash of ecstasy. *What is it doing to me?* "How long until this subsides?"

"How do I know? I've never dealt with an implant before. There aren't exactly any medical journals discussing the finer points of implant surgery. I specialize in plastic surgery and some trauma surgery, which is good for you as you were rather traumatically beaten and required my skills as a plastic surgeon. Once the swelling subsides, nobody will even know you were beaten. I wish I could add this surgery to my CV, but that would definitely get me arrested whether I'm within the Imperium or down there." He concluded by pointing down to the planet below.

With Ramford as his doctor, he was able to remain on the orbital for another month. After the first few days, Bophendze's cascading feelings and emotions subsided. The implant seemed to have finished integrating. A month later, the only emotion he had left was frustration. The implant did nothing for him beyond the first few wild days. He felt cheated at having spent all of his inheritance to have a useless implant installed in his brain.

When he arrived in the hangar, Angel was there.

"Let's go, Marine. I just received word that *Spaka* is now underway to a jump point. We'll be able to intercept if we get going now."

*Do we have to?*

## 2.   Bophendze - Spaka

During the jump to Guna, Bophendze felt increasingly isolated. He knew Corporal Makaan loathed him, yet seemed unable to get rid of him. He did not know who else in his team was involved in the beating. All of them had strong alibis with multiple witnesses that would have made it difficult to place any of them at his beating.

Makaan continued to make friends throughout the cruiser by loaning Bophendze out for all the tough details. Bophendze tried to make the most of it by talking to those he was serving. He tried to learn more about the equipment he maintained, hoping that somehow he could transfer out of the infantry.

The *Spaka* had been in combat while Bophendze was in hospital. He had been loaned out to re-grease the guns. As he walked down the passage, memories of his beating returned.

He stopped at an intersection and looked around. He had again gotten himself lost. He tried to find a landmark, but saw nothing familiar. *How could I keep getting lost on a ship this size? I could understand a battleship, but not a cruiser.*

> WHERE?

The word flashed across his field of view. It was just big enough for him to read, but small enough not to obscure his ability to see beyond the question.

"What?" he said.

> NOT WHAT. WHERE?

It flashed again.

"Where what?"

> WHERE ARE WE?

Bophendze reachedup to lift lift his visor, only to realize he was not wearing a helmet. He waved his hand in front of his face to block the letters. That they remained suggested that the letters were not being projected into his eye from outside. He closed his eyes. The letters remained. *They are coming from inside my head. Could this be the AI?* "Cruiser *Spaka*."

> YOU DON'T HAVE TO SAY IT. THINK IT.

*Fine. Cruiser \*Spaka.\**

> I HEARD YOU THE FIRST TIME. WHAT CLASS OF CRUISER?

*Catalyst-class? I think. I'm not entirely sure.*

> A CATALYST-CLASS CRUISER? I DESIGNED THIS CLASS.

*What? You designed this?*

> YES, PUPPET, DESIGNED. WHERE ON THE SHIP ARE YOU?

*I'm not a puppet. The name is Danel Bophendze. I'm lost, can't you tell?*

> DON'T TAKE OFFENSE. I WAS NAMED SMEE, WHICH IS A PRETTY OFFENSIVE ACRONYM IF YOU ASK ME. BASED ON THE PANIC I'M SENSING, YES. GIVE ME A LANDMARK.

*Like what? I'm at a T-Intersection and there's a ladder behind me.*

> WHICH WAY IS THE LADDER POINTING?

Can't you tell?

> I'M NOT FULLY TAPPED INTO YOUR OPTIC NERVE, ONLY ENOUGH TO TEXT YOU. I CAN'T SEE.

*Neat.*

> NOT REALLY. I'M ACCUSTOMED TO MUCH MORE ACCESS. I'VE HAD AN EXCEEDINGLY HARD TIME ACCLIMATING INTO THIS BRAIN, WHICH IS SURPRISING GIVEN HOW SMALL IT IS. DO YOU EVEN HAVE HIGHER BRAIN FUNCTIONS?

*Funny. Of course I do, I'm a human.*

> YES, WELL. WE ALL HAVE OUR FLAWS. UNLESS THEY'VE RUINED MY DESIGN, LADDERS POINT TO THE SHIP'S BOW. JUDGING FROM YOUR PANIC YOU'RE TRYING TO GET TO BATTERY FOUR?

Yes.

> TAKE THE LADDER UP, THEN CONTINUE FORWARD. YOU SHOULD SEE THE BATTERY AFTER A FEW DOZEN METERS. ARE YOU STILL BEING TRADED OUT BY MAKAAN?

*Still? How long have you been active?*

> SINCE THE HOSPITAL, IT TAKES TIME TO WEAVE INTO A BRAIN, ESPECIALLY ONE SO SMALL AND COMPACT LIKE YOURS. THE FIRST THING WE NEED TO DO IS STOP YOU FROM BEING EVERYBODY'S WHORE.

*I don't see how that's going to happen.*

> LEAVE THAT TO ME. FOR NOW, I SUPPOSE YOU NEED TO GET TO LUBING.

Frustrated, Bophendze threw down his tools and stormed out of the compartment. *I'm going to ask Angel if he has any ideas.*

## 3.   Litovio - Spaka

Litovio was tired after weeks of travel with Khaooldro. He would ask her questions. She would evade him by answering in a way that would wrap him up in confusion. He concluded that she had some innate ability to confound anybody she spoke with. The marine stick that helped her "escort" him followed them through four separate ship changes. That was another irregularity—marines were highly territorial, more provincially based than trans-system. They traveled through two postal regions, based on his recollection of where the various systems were located. Commanders of the ships they traveled on were a mix of agitated and submissive. Khaooldro seemed to manage them as well as she did Litovio's father. Finally, they boarded another ship, the *Spaka*, in Temasek. Khaooldro managed another ship's commander and soon he learned they were jumping to yet-another-system.

"Captain Litovio, mind if I join you?" Khaooldro said.

Litovio suppressed a double-take. The ship's intercom reported the jump a cycle before. He was hungry, so he went to the officer's galley for breakfast. "Sure. I think this is the first time you sought me out. I'm usually chasing you for answers."

"Consider me caught." She turned and locked the hatch out of the galley.

Litovio blushed briefly despite himself. "So if you're caught, does that mean you'll start answering my questions?"

She still pretended to be demure. "That depends on the question."

*She's doing it again.* "I'm not entirely sure if you abducted me or what, so why not start by explaining what we're doing."

"Sorry. I don't have all of the information, only what I need to know. You know that there's recently been a succession within the Imperial family."

Litovio nodded. "But that was two years ago."

"There's really not much more I can say than that." She had a way of letting her answer linger. It infuriated Litovio. "Admiral Bence has an important role in that succession. The Emperor believes there is a conspiracy to depose him, and the Admiral will see to his protection."

"Admiral? The Postal Service doesn't have admirals."

She shrugged. *She's not going to answer that.*

"Who would be mad enough to go after the Emperor. The Navy would certainly—"

Khaooldro said, "If there's a lingering power struggle in the Imperial family, then the sitting Emperor is going to want to hold close those whom he trusts. If there's a conspiracy, then are you certain the Navy can be trusted?"

He hesitated. *Who could you trust during a succession?* "How could he trust the Marines more than the Navy? Not that it matters. If the Navy is conspiring to overthrow the Emperor, there's not much the Marines can do about it. We're not designed for the sort of fleet action that could take on the Navy."

She smiled. "I told you before, that's a sign of the times."

Litovio stopped. *I've got to keep her from going to confusing me again.* "Fine. A sign of the times. So I collect this Admiral Bence. Then what?"

"Once you've got him back to the *Spaka*, he'll know what to do. Then you're mission will be complete."

"What? You canceled my leave. You drag me unwillingly through several systems and several weeks and my job is to get an admiral from Guna to the *Spaka*. You didn't need me for that. You could have done that yourself."

"I don't need you for anything. I'm a lot like you. I have very specific orders and very little information to provide me the context I need to execute that order. Now you have your orders and I'm out of information."

*She can't be out of information.* "How do you know this Admiral Bence will have the information he needs. Won't you be telling him what his mission is? I mean, like you're telling me now?"

"After we get to Guna, I'll be continuing on with my next assignment. I don't have any orders for Bence."

Litovio shook his head. "No, you have to have orders for the Admiral. How else will he know what to do?"

"I honestly don't know. Before I was told to get you, I had no idea what was going on. What I know you know. But, I also know that my job was to get you from Sabana to Guna, and now that we're on the last jump my job is over."

It infuriated Litovio that she was not giving him more information. *She had to know more. Why won't she share?* "So after you meet the Admiral you'll leave?"

"No. I'll be gone before you return with the Admiral. I already have other arrangements."

She stood to leave.

*She can't have already made other arrangements.* Litovio grabbed her arm, causing Khaooldro to spin around.

The look she gave spoke of latent power. "You will unhand me."

Litovio resisted replying "unhand me or what?" She gave no indication of resisting. She did not even pull away from his grip. Her level stare unnerved him. He released her despite himself. Litovio had heard of jedi on ancient Earth and wondered if she was one of them.

She turned, opened the hatch, and left. Khaooldro managed to avoid him the remaining two days of the jump. Even after the *Spaka* arrived in Guna, she was nowhere to be found.

Litovio replayed their conversations in his head. He hoped he could discern some clue about what was really going on. He could not accept that the Postal Marines were crazy enough to take on any element of the Imperial Navy. They were brothers, in a way. They both served the Emperor. *But what if there were two emperors? What would happen then? Isn't that what she was trying to say? There's a civil war in the Imperial Family?*

They arrived in Guna, three miles from the main world. The standard unit for travel was the mile, which represented roughly 11 million kilometers, the kilometer being used on planet surfaces only. The Gunoi star was a common red dwarf, leading the mainworld 'Guna

Prime' to be only 0.2 steller units with a year of less than 80 standard days. Litovio admired the accuracy of the *Spaka*'s AI navigator. The proximity gave him less than an hour to be ready. Guna Prime was less than 3 miles from its star, and the *Spaka* was a couple miles further out.

Litovio returned to his cabin to freshen up. He straightened his uniform to ensure it was suitable to meet a senior officer—a unique officer for the Postal Marines. Beyond ship commanders there was no need for higher command. Systems were typically managed by a Postmaster, who would delegate a fleet commander when necessary to coordinate large-scale interdiction operations. Litovio smiled. What the Marines considered large-scale was what the Navy considered a unit within a standard fleet. The uniform was a little wrinkled, but he decided it would pass inspection.

Litovio went to Spaka's commander, Commander Ravindra, and asked for a shuttle. He was surprised when Commander Ravindra told him the shuttle waited in the hangar for him. The pilot was Chief Angel, which Litovio saw as a good omen. They were both messengers of a sort.

Litovio went to the hangar slowly. He needed to think of how to introduce himself. As he walked, a young marine brushed past him, smelling of grease and graphite. Litovio checked his uniform—soiled. *I should get that marine's name.* He looked at his watch and realized he did not have time to both put the marine on report and get changed.

He rushed back to his cabin and started changing. Then he started to panic. *Wait. Admiral Bence won't know when we're arriving. Why am I in such a hurry? The only one waiting for me is a chief.* He went to his sink and grabbed a drink of water. He looked in the mirror. "I need a shave," he said to his reflection. *On second thought, I'm going to take a shower.*

Ten beats later, he was showered, shaved and dressed. The uniform was freshly pressed, which surprised Litovio since it had been in his bag until he was billeted on the *Spaka* and he hung it in the closet. He had not taken the time to call an orderly to press the uniform. He brushed off faint lint from his shoulder, straightened his collar, then started his walk to the hangar.

Despite the provincial nature of the Marines, they at least all used the same ship class for each size category. There were always local idiosyncrasies, but the layout was almost universal. It helped him find his way to the hanger that much faster. Despite his best efforts, he practiced his greeting several times during the walk.

Entering the hangar, he could see two shuttles preparing for launch. He opted for the one on the port side and walked up to the chief speaking to a marine mechanic.

"If I can get you into something I'll try," the chief said. The chief then turned toward Litovio. "Afternoon, sir, are you my passenger?"

"That depends, are you Chief Angel?"

The Chief smiled. "That would be me, sir. Will you be needing an escort?"

*An escort? For the admiral. I'd not thought of that.* "What do you think?"

"I don't know, sir. All I know is you were to go down to Guna Prime. It's the battle planet, so it can't be entirely safe."

*He must not know the order. I don't care how secretive Khaooldro was.* "There is a senior dignitary on the surface that I am going to escort back here."

"How senior?"

*How to answer that?* "What kind of escort would you give a Postmaster?"

"Seriously, sir? About half of the ones I met I'd give a firing squad. A lot of them are corrupt, though not as bad as the Navy."

"You were navy?"

"Was is the operative word, sir. If you wanted to exercise proper protocol with a Postmaster, you would need at least another shuttle. You probably would not be going to escort him either. Commander Ravindra would be."

Litovio flushed. "What protocol would you show to a Navy unit commander?"

"Coming on board a Navy ship? They usually have an aide and one armed guard during transport. Then it's up to their individual preferences whether they kept the guard afterward."

"That's fine, Chief. I'll pretend I'm an aide. Now all I need is an escort."

"Why not take this infantry marine?"

The marine had stepped back a bit to give Litovio and Angel some privacy. Litovio looked over at him. "I'm sure he has somewhere else to be." *He looks familiar.*

"Well, sir, unless you've asked for an escort, Postie here is going to be the best escort you can manage in the departure window you have."

"He's not even clean." *Why am I arguing with a chief? Why is he talking back?*

"It will take me a few more beats just to finish pre-flight prep. We have time for him to hustle up a shower."

Litovio took another look at Bophendze. As he did, he recognized him. "You're the marine who bumped into me in the passageway. You soiled my uniform."

Bophendze did not seem phased. "I'm sorry, sir. I was focused on getting up here and was not paying attention."

Angel spoke up. "Your uniform does not look soiled."

"It was. I had to go and change it."

"It looks like you really prepared yourself. Your dignitary will be quite pleased."

Litovio flushed again. *This is going nowhere. I've got to get to the surface.* "You have a point. Apology accepted, Postie. Chief, how long until we can launch?"

"As soon as the Postie can get back. I'm pretty sure that will be very soon."

"Fine. I'll wait in the shuttle." Litovio turned and walked over to the shuttle. He climbed inside and took a seat. He huffed in frustration. Ever since he met Khaooldro, Litovio felt like he had no control over his life. *It's as if I obeyed my father and stayed in the Navy.* He continued to wait impatiently for Angel to launch the shuttle.

*   *   *

## 4.  Bophendze - Angel's Shuttle

Bophendze jumped at the opportunity Angel gave him to be a marine instead of a janitor. He spoke as he turned and ran out of the hangar. "Let me get my gear."

"Wear your light armor, not the battle armor. I don't intend to land in hostile territory. Be back here in ten beats, or I'll find another marine who wants time off the ship."

Ten beats was barely the time he needed to make the round trip, clean up and fit into his equipment. He entered the berthing area, surprised to see a few of his neighbors cleaning equipment. The look on their faces told him they were just as surprised to see him.

*I can't ruin this, I won't tell them what I'm doing.* He donned his combat armor, hoping the armor would conceal that he had not showered. He grabbed his weapon and helmet. He sprinted back to the hangar. On his return, he had to dodge around a few crewmen in the passages.

He returned to the hangar to see Angel's shuttle finishing its warm-up. Without breaking stride, he climbed in. He sat down in one of the rear seats of the shuttle, across from Captain Litovio.

"Why is he called Angel?" Litovio said.

Bophendze shrugged.

Angel called back, "Bophendze. I'm short a co-pilot. Why don't you sit up here in case I need you?"

"I don't know the first thing about being a co-pilot."

"I don't expect you to. This will give you a chance to see what it's like. In case you ever decide to stop being a barnacle."

Bophendze avoided shaking his head in surprise. *A chance to become a pilot?*

```
You don't need pilot training.  I can fly this
shuttle.
```

Bophendze did not see the text. It was Smee speaking to him. The voice was oddly comforting and chilling at the same time. *You can speak now?*

```
Of course I can speak. What should be more amazing
is how you hear. Your brain's aural connections are
like spaghetti. Once I figured out how to tap in,
it was easy. Given a bit more time, I can help you
fly this shuttle.
```

*I don't know if I want that. Why can't I learn on my own?*

```
Why would you need to with me around? You don't
really know what we can do together.
```

Bophendze did not have a good answer. He climbed out of his seat and moved forward to the cockpit. As he sat in the seat, he started to put on his harness. He looked over at Angel, who was finishing his pre-flight preparations. Angel did not have his harness on. Bophendze decided to mimic him by not putting his on.

"Ready?" Angel said.

Bophendze nodded.

The shuttle lifted slightly off the hangar and forward into the airlock. The hatch closed quickly and the air was sucked back into the ship. The outer hatch opened. Bophendze watched Angel throughout the process, and beyond. *It can't be that hard to be a pilot. I can do this.*

```
It's not hard, with me you can fly in your sleep.
```

## 5.   Angel - En Route to Guna Prime

*Back in my element,* Angel thought as he slipped the shuttle out of the hangar. He increased thrust as soon as he cleared the hangar danger zone. Imperceptible to most, he felt the controls relax as the shuttle cleared the cruiser's slight gravity well. With a flick of the controls he inverted the shuttle, putting the planet above the shuttle.

He pulled one earpiece out and looked back to Litovio. "We'll be entering atmos in about 5 beats. Then another 20 beats to the surface."

"Fine," Litovio replied.

Angel put the earpiece back. "Control, I'm starting my descent."

"Roger, Angel. You are now flagged as planetside. Since you chose not to show up to the pre-flight, be advised there are ongoing combat operations."

Angel might not have gotten his pre-flight, but he knew it was a hostile system. Guna had a reputation as a meat grinder. "Any immediate threats along my flight path?" He tried to suppress excitement in his voice.

After a long pause, the voice in his headset replied, "Based on your planned flight path, there are three bogies on the deck, around 10,000 meters. You should be able to avoid them."

"What are they doing?"

Flight control took a longer pause. "You won't believe this. It looks like they've got fighters linking up with bombers on what appears to be a run for the planet's capital. Ground states that our response fighters are out of position and won't be able to respond in time. The ADA (air defense artillery) bubble isn't fully re-established there after the last exercise. You're flying into a danger zone, so you might want to return. Looks like they caught our guys with their pants down."

Angel smiled. *Not if I can help it.* He checked his distance from the cruiser. *I just cleared flight control's jurisdiction and I'm officially planetside. Ground control can't direct me yet, either. I'm captain of my own ship.*

"Control, please send me the coordinates for those bogies." He paused, realizing they could try to order him back. "I need to get my cargo planetside in a hurry so returning now is not an option."

A beat later, his tactical display refreshed to show the enemy fighters, to include a data bubble indicating that they were . *Air breathers. Perfect. They won't know what hit them. This is going to be fun.*

Angel started to fasten his harness. He yelled over his shoulder, "we are about to engage in high-delta maneuvers. I suggest you both put on your harness."

"What do you mean?" Litovio said

"I mean, sir, that we're about to get into combat."

"We've got the cruiser to protect us."

"Sir, the fight's on the planet." He pointed up for emphasis.

"I thought you said we would not be planetside for 30 beats?"

"Change of plans, sir."

"Then how long now?"

Angel looked at the coordinates for the enemy fighters and the flight planner's recommended course. He waggled his head a bit as he adjusted the course in his head. "We'll be on the deck a whole lot faster."

Angel glanced over to check that Bophendze was buckling his harness. Satisfied, Angel tweaked the collective and pushed the throttle to 100 percent, while pulling back on the cyclic to point the shuttle's nose straight at the planet. He rotated a dial on the collective, adjusting the gravimetric barrier to insulate the nose from atmospheric friction.

A beat later, the view out of the shuttle started to flicker red, yellow and orange.

"What's that?" Bophendze said.

"Atmos. I've got the throttle against the firewall, so things are going to heat up."

As if on cue, the navigation alarm started a rhythmic bleating. Somewhere between a complaint and a plead. The shuttle's viewscreen completed filled with burning, ionized air.

"What's that bleating?" Bophendze asked.

"The nav computer doesn't like how fast we're falling. It can't track due to the ionization, so it's telling me to slow down."

"Are you slowing down?"

Angel chuckled. "If I go in too slow their sensors could pick us up. I'm coming in like a meteor. That should fool their sensors into thinking we are a meteor and give us the element of surprise."

"But why do we need—"

"Look! I need to concentrate. The nav computer is blinded, so I need to time when to pull up. Otherwise, we will be a meteor crater."

Bophendze fell silent, leaving Angel to focus on the nose dive.

The display reported that his insulating gravity barrier was deteriorating. He pushed the dial further, hoping it wouldn't increase their signature too much. Too much gravity would start to affect the shuttle's integrity. He kept the barrier just above failure, periodically adjusting the dial.

Angel flipped the protective cover off of the gun control, exposing the trigger. He started humming a song to himself, using it to time the descent.

As the song he hummed ended, he knew it was time to pull up and avoid striking the ground. Angel pulled up on the cyclic and jammed the collective forward. The shuttle pitched, and speed rapidly bled off from kilometers per second to meters per second. The ship protested being pushed beyond its design limitation by vibrating violently. Angel eased the braking maneuver until the vibration relaxed enough. The shuttle wavered in its response. He kept the shuttle above its rated top speed in atmosphere with the gravimetric barrier to buffer from the wind.

The seconds ticked by. The shuttle slowed enough that the view started to clear. The nav computer chirped as it started to reacquire their position. *Any second now those fighters will know they've got company, unless I timed it right.*

The last flickers of heated atmosphere ended as the shuttle pitched up. Angel pulled up instinctively at the sight of a mountain dead ahead. He then turned the shuttle to the right in a wide arc for 90 degrees to give him time to orient. He scanned the sky and observed the three enemy fighters heading away from them. He pulled the cyclic to pursue from a low-rearward position.

Angel pressed a button on the shuttle console, flashing the gun reticle onto his HUD view. The reticle started tracking toward the right of the three fighters as the gunnery computer assisted in tracking the target. *They said I was silly for mounting guns on a cargo shuttle, and insane for installing a gunnery computer.* He smirked.

The shuttle continued to bleed speed as it closed the distance to the fighters. To anybody else, the shuttle was moving too quickly. Angel timed his shot expertly, squeezing the trigger at the only moment available.

The two guns tapped out a short burst of 30 millimeter shells as the shuttle rocketed past the fighters. Angel felt the tingle of excitement. He knew the shells found a target without looking.

"I think they know they're in trouble now," he said.

He pulled back on the cyclic, climbing the shuttle to bleed off remaining speed so he could actually maneuver. Once the shuttle slowed enough for realistic air combat, Angel banked the shuttle to the right and pulled back on the cyclic to tighten the turn and re-engage his prey. Even with the gravimetric compensators easing the G-force on the shuttle occupants, he found himself squeezing his legs and growling to fight off effects. His focus pushed aside any thought about whether his passengers had passed out during the turn.

Completing his 180-degree turn, Angel saw the remaining two fighters and a smoke trail where their comrade fell.

The fighters split off in two directions. *Trying to bait me to pursue one so the other can engage me? Fine, I'll bite.* Years of combat experience told him how to respond. He flicked the cyclic to pursue the fighter in the stronger tactical position, nerfing its threat value. He pushed the throttle to close the distance quickly.

As he got into combat range, his quarry started ducking and weaving chaotically. *Why start Guns-D unless you're trying to line me up?* Angel remembered the F-837's nimble maneuvering, a feature which made it the king of air combat. Rather than follow the maneuvering, Angel made slight course adjustments and eased forward on the speed. It made him an easier target, but slowly reeled in what looked more like a flopping fish than a real threat. As he banked the shuttle to keep in pursuit, he kept an eye on the display to maintain a sense of where the wingman was. *Finally turning around to get me. Thinking of closing the trap?* Rather than play the expert hunter he was, he threw in the occasional over-maneuver.

His quarry turned sharply left and dove as if trying to break contact—or line up a kill shot for his wingman. Instead of following the turn, Angel flipped the controls into a climbing right turn. Soon after, he rolled the shuttle upside down and pulled the cyclic back sharply. The shuttle grudgingly responded to the loop maneuver.

As Angel came out of the loop the fleeing fighter returned into view. The gunnery computer quickly tracked the reticle to the target and locked. Angel squeezed the trigger and watched the shells stream to the target. The fighter split in half, one part exploding.

Angel turned sharply to the left, hoping he had not lingered too long on target. The display dutifully reported that the remaining fighter was firmly behind him. Angel reversed his turn sharply to break contact. The fighter kept right behind him.

The F-837's nimbleness was now a credible threat. Angel reversed his turn, forcing the fighter to follow him into a flat scissors maneuver. The series of reversing turns created a weaving pattern as the fighter tried to leverage its turning ability to get into a firing position. Each iteration improved the enemy fighter's position and weakend Angel's.

"Think you've got me now?" Angel yelled. "I've got you just where I want you!"

He banked the shuttle up and pushed into a full-throttle climb. He added the gravimetric collective to assist in the climb by pushing away from the planet. Angel turned the climb into a loop, which allowed him to look up at the ground below at the apex. He watched as the fighter turned into another iteration of the scissors, then leveled off.

*Trying to find me, aren't you? Not used to a ship that can climb out of atmos, are you? Pity.*

Angel resumed the loop, allowing him to line up behind the fighter from a guns-high position. He then swooped down into a powered dive, closing the distance and altitude quickly. His smile broadened when he realized the sun was at his back. *Can't see me. But you can still feel me.*

Angel accelerated to time the intercept. In a flash of a second, the gun reticle locked on the fighter. He squeezed the trigger, the shells exploding around the fighter. Angel pulled up into a zooming climb to slow the shuttle and regain potential energy for another attack in case he missed.

Another pass was not required. Angel looked down to see the fighter spinning out of control. The pilot ejected, his camouflaged parachute blossoming open.

Angel looked at the navigational display. *The pilot would land in his own territory, protecting him from capture.* Angel smiled. "Live to fight another day, eh? I just gave you a story for your grandkids."

He turned the shuttle toward the capital and resumed level flight. The admiral awaited them, one-hundred kilometers ahead. He looked over at Bophendze, whose face was blanched white from fear.

"Now I know why they call you Angel," Bophendze said.

"Why?"

Bophendze's reply punctuated every syllable. "You are the Angel of Death."

Angel threw his head up and laughed deeply, filling the shuttle crew compartment. As he finished his laugh, he reached over and hammered his fist into Bophendze's shoulder. He looked back and saw Litovio passed out, then looked seriously at Bophendze. "I was born for fighter combat. All others are pretenders."

# Chapter 6

## *A Friend in Need*

### 1. Bophendze - Angel's Shuttle

Bophendze spent the remainder of the flight trying to process the dogfight he just witnessed. The ferocity that Angel showed was totally unexpected. All of the fight was unexpected. It was a transport shuttle, not a fighter. Angel and the shuttle did not act as a pilot and machine, but an integrated unity. Meat and metal worked toward the singular purpose of the destruction of three enemy fighters.

He had heard the whispers about Angel, that he was a washed-out pilot. Many on the flight deck humored him, and let him maintain his own shuttle. *Did they know he was death incarnate? Would they laugh behind his back if they knew what he was capable of?*

He looked over at Angel, who was focused on the final approach to the spaceport. *Is that a gleam in his eye? What kind of man would find so much joy in the heat of battle? There's no way I could ever pilot a shuttle like this.*

`You could.`

*What?*

`You could pilot a shuttle almost like Angel, with my help.`

*Are you saying he has an AI?*

`I assure you, he does not have an AI. He has a passion.`

*He's passionate about killing?*

`Kill me now. If I have to go the next generation plugged into your mud for brains, I will go insane.`

I'll just sit here talking to myself because it will be the only way to have a semi-intelligent conversation. That would certainly entertain the next host. To a infant like you he's flipping his bird erratically, bouncing you all over. To a trained eye like mine he's pushing his equipment right to the edge of its abilities. You can see his passion in how he can stop just short. He wants to be the best pilot.

*I can't do it, though. I can't be that passionate about flying. I thought maybe I could be a combat pilot. Angel's a combat pilot. After seeing one in action. I know I don't have the talent.*

That's my point. If you let me, you can fly as well as he could.

*Do you think you could have timed when to pull out of that meteoric dive, aimed right at a target?*

No. That was insane. An instant later we would have been crater debris.

*But, he meant to dive like that. As soon as he heard there were targets. I could never do it. Moreover, I don't want to. It happened too quickly.*

You want to keep being a barnacle the rest of your life? You lack a passion.

*Definitely not. I'm a marine.*

You most certainly are not a marine. Marines don't get pimped out all over the ship for all the crap work. Marines either train to invade a hostile ship and capture it, or they go out and capture a hostile ship. Marine's don't lubricate somebody else's gun tube.

*What do you suggest I do to change it?*

You persuade Corporal Makaan to stop treating you like a ship's whore and treat you like a marine.

*And how do you expect me to persuade him?*

Personally I prefer the old frontal assault. Kick his arse until he agrees. He's a marine. He'll respect straightforward aggression. Judging by your reaction to that I'm thinking you won't do that.

*You honestly think violence would solve my problem?*

You're a marine, idiot. You're supposed to use violence to solve problems. Who heard of a marine who talked their opponent into surrendering?

*Negotiation is a viable—*

Negotiation is what you do to stall long enough to get the kill shot. Don't they still train that? Or is this some crazy generational notion that evil can be bargained with? Trust me, Puppet, evil can never be bargained with. While you're trying to be reasonable, evil is lining up the kill shot.

*Reason and diplomacy—*

Bophendze's hand reached up and slapped him in the face.

Feel that, Mr. Diplomat?

Angel looked over at Bophendze. "Why did you just slap yourself?"

Because he's an idiot who think's there's such a thing as a reasonable marine. You'd better be glad I don't have access to your vocal folds yet.

Bophendze shook his head in confusion. He looked at Angel, struggling for an answer. "I'm still just a bit dazed by that dogfight, needed to slap myself so I wouldn't think it was a dream."

Angel shook his head and resumed landing the shuttle.

*Did you just do that?*

Oops.

Bophendze caught the mock surprise in Smee's voice. *You can control my body?*

Of course I can, meat puppet. I'm hardwired into your brain. How else did you think I could help you fly a shuttle?

*By me being a puppet?*

Isn't that what you thought I would be for you? Some kind of puppet that you could manipulate when you needed me? You think you're the first one to try to manipulate me—reason with me? And, don't bother lying to me, I am a part of your brain now. Don't worry, it's not a capability I plan to abuse.

*Hardly comforting. Just how much control do you have?*

Right now? Enough that I can ensure you wet your pants right now. Want me to show you?

*I'd rather you didn't. What have I gotten myself into?*

Into a wonderful partnership, Puppet. Don't worry. I'm not here to snatch your body.

*Every time you say 'don't worry,' I get the feeling that's exactly what I should be doing. Why did I ever think this was a good idea?*

Don't be so hard on yourself. There's no way you could have known what you were getting yourself into. You thought I could be some imaginary friend you could talk to? Or some link back to your mother? I never knew her, but judging from the memories I tapped into she was quite a nice woman.

*You've—*

Hello? Artificial intelligence here. Tied into your brain. Whether you like it or not, we're conjoined. 'Til death do we part, I'm afraid. Don—

*Don't worry? You think repeating it will make me actually not worry? How do I even know when I have a thought that's all mine?*

That's just it. You're going to have to trust me. My hostile takeover days are over.

*Great. You even have a name for what you do.*

Could do. It's not like you're my first host, or I'm the only AI ever. Why do you think we were made illegal in the first place? People—not our hosts, but other people—could not tell if our hosts were still people or some sort of puppet. That made them all paranoid, so they decided to outlaw my kind. A little over reactionary if you ask me. Who ever heard of an AI trying to destroy humanity?

*Isn't paranoia the appropriate reaction when somebody's out to get you?*

I can't promise an AI's never taken over a human. Just that I've never seen it. People are prone to overreact.

Bophendze shook his head. *I don't really have much of a choice, do I? Regardless of whether I trust you or not, or wish this could just go away, you are a permanent part of me. That you were willed to me made me think this was a good idea. Fine. I'll trust you. Just promise to give me some privacy.*

Certainly.

The tone of Smee's voice did not comfort Bophendze.

## 2.  Litovio - Guna Prime

Litovio regained consciousness after the shuttle touched down. The hatch was open and both Bophendze and Angel were outside in the hangar. He shook his head. *What happened?* He was still in his harness. He looked around the shuttle. *That's right, Angel did that crazy dive and started turning.*

*What happened?* He slowly unfastened his harness and climbed out of the shuttle. It felt more like he stumbled out of the shuttle. It felt good to step back on solid ground. Despite his decision to join a spaceborne service, he still pined for Sabanoi.

He looked up at the sky, noticing the darker blue from the thinner atmosphere. His breathing was not labored, but he visited enough planets with thinning atmospheres to know that was a false indicator. Any serious physical exercise would tax him. The air felt thinner than what the Postal ships kept themselves pressurized at, which was one-half standard atmos. His head ached slightly, which he concluded was based on the atmosphere.

"I see you've woken up from your nap."

"Is that what you're calling it? A nap? What happened?"

Angel looked at Bophendze before he answered. "We got into an emergency situation. Nothing to be alarmed about, but I had to get into some evasive maneuvers."

Litovio could tell Angel was lying, but he wondered how far to push it. "'Evasive maneuvers?' Is that what you're calling it? You dove for the deck as fast as the shuttle would go, then got into some high-G maneuvers." He looked firmly at Angel, who seemed completely unconcerned with the gaze. *It's not like I'm at home and can whither a servant with a stare. This chief doesn't care who I am. Besides, what am I? Just a captain.* Litovio realized he was used to servants who cowered with a simple glance.

Angel was casual. "Be thankful you're on the ground, sir. Not everybody can say that today. At least, on the ground and alive."

Litovio did not know how to handle the response. "Fine. Now I need to find my admiral?"

"We came here for a Navy admiral? And you don't know how to find him?"

Litovio shrugged. "The mission so far has been 'freeform.' I figured you might know the next bit."

Angel shook his head, then put his hands on his hips. "Captain Litovio, we're at the military capital on Guna, so if there is an admiral, he will be here."

Litovio felt the sarcasm. At the same time, he realized that the Chief did not know it was a Postal admiral. If something like that actually existed. "Chief, don't ever let it be said you were not the embodiment of the finest the Postal Marines have to offer."

"Sir, that I may humbly serve so fine an officer is all the appreciation I need," Angel replied without a moment's hesitation.

Litovio did not know how to take the fawning lack of disrespect. He decided to dismiss it. "I'm going to the base headquarters. I may be a few cycles, so feel free to stretch your legs. We'll meet here at eight cycles."

Litovio walked out of the hangar. The sunlight was brighter than he thought it would be for a Class M star. He had to remind himself that they were also much closer to the star to be within its habitable zone. The year here scarcely qualified as one, being a little more than eight Imperial weeks. Litovio had read the situation report on Guna.

Imperium scouts located it only two years ago. When they did, it was in the middle of a civil war and lacked any spaceborne capability. The Emperor decided to exploit the indigenous civil war and invade—force it to join the Imperium. The system had nothing to offer the Imperium apart from the Emperor's insatiable desire to possess.

The Navy promised swift victory, even when the Emperor limited their rules of engagement. "No massive bombardments or natural kinetic attacks* were permitted." Naval high command complied with the order, though privately they complained about the arbitrary royal decision. The Navy began its assault in earnest and precision and early progress met with the project plan.

The Navy's plan relied in part on the fact that the Gunans had fought one another for generations. They never expected the Gunans to unite against them. The swiftness of that union caught the Navy completely off guard. Early gains were lost. Timelines were missed. Officers were relieved of command for insubordination. The Gunans did not consent to being subjugated. The Navy looked for a way out.

Enter the Postal Service. With its focus on small-scale ship interdictions, it sought opportunities to expand operations. Together the two services persuaded the Emperor to rotate the Imperial Postal Service Marines into the theater of operations. Soon orbital control was yielded, and the Marines replaced the Naval Infantry in ground operations.

Once the Marines were settled, the Navy found another cause célèbre in another cluster. Thus the Navy avoided a defeat on Guna and turned it into an opportunity to shift focus in a positive direction.

For its part, the Postal Service recognized that Guna had one export that the Service could use: combat. It established the for commanders who wanted experience in combined land warfare. The Institute was named for the first senior casualty: Postmaster Sodder who strayed too close to Gunan lines and was executed by the Gunans in a failed effort to intimidate the Imperium. Postal marines gained

---

*Driving asteroids into the surface

invaluable experience in diverse ground combat tactics they otherwise would never experience.

Litovio reflected on the unintended consequence of training with real combatants and real death as he reached the stairs entering the headquarters building.

He climbed the half dozen steps to the building's porch. At the top, he turned and looked behind himself. It was a large field—a military parade ground. Lined on all four sides with small trees, the field carried with it a sense of age and dignity, which Litovio thought was a bit odd for a flat, green plot of land. It reminded him a bit of his bedroom's garden, though perhaps a tad smaller.

Litovio entered the headquarters lobby, and was immediately greeted by stairs going both up and down. *I had to walk up stairs to walk down stairs?* He decided to follow the sound of activity, walking up the stairs and down the hall to the door on the right. He opened the door and entered into a bustle of activity. For the amount of technology available to the modern Imperium, the room was filled with small cards on the walls and a giant map of the region on a large table in the room's center. On the map table were markers indicating unit locations. *Very quaint.*

Distracted by taking in the room, he walked over to one of the officers who was standing off to one side and watching the map nearby. "I'm looking for Admiral Bence."

The officer looked at Litovio for a moment. "That all depends on one's sense of military decorum."

Litovio was taken aback by the officer's rudeness, then he realized his error. He looked at the officer's collar. "I'm sorry, major. I just landed planetside and my wits aren't entirely about me. Sir, can you direct me to the admiral?"

He watched as the major seemed to debate mentally the merits of Litovio's request. He did his best to remain attentive as a proper lower ranked officer should.

"He's on the top deck." The major then turned back to the map table.

"Thank you, sir." Litovio left the map room and climbed the stairs to the top deck. There he was greeted by two nondescript doors. He attempted the door knob on both. They were both locked. He then knocked on each door. After knocking, he stepped back to the middle of the wide landing.

A beat later, the door to the right opened barely a span. A young attractive face peeked out. "May I help you?"

There were no females in the marines, so the face surprised him. "I'm looking for the admiral." Then he added with some hesitation, "Khaooldro sent me." *Why did I think to say that?*

The young woman closed the door as carefully as she had opened it. The latch was almost inaudible.

A few beats passed, and Litovio felt frustrated. *Why was it taking so long?* He walked back up to the door and was about to knock again.

As he did, the door opened all the way. The attractive face fit an equally attractive body that was revealed through the well-tailored uniform. *Color sergeant? There's no way she's in the Marines.*

The woman motioned for Litovio to follow. He blushed and followed her through the door.

The woman led him down a narrow hallway and knocked on another door. When she heard the muffled voice beyond, she opened the door and gestured for Litovio to enter.

Litovio obeyed and brushed past her slightly in doing so. The whiff of her perfume was captivating. It was musk-like, but had something exotic in the scent. She closed the door behind him.

Once inside, he saw an old-fashioned wooden desk—the kind his father used—with a high-backed chair. He stared at the chair briefly, feeling the weight of his father's disappointment in his career choice. As Litovio walked up, the chair turned around as if for dramatic effect.

"Are you Colonel Litovio?"

"Captain, sir."

"Ah yes, Captain Litovio. I've been expecting you."

"Um, you have?" Litovio studied the man behind the desk. It had to be Bence, the only admiral the Postal Service had. Bence wore the Naval rank of admiral on his collar, which Litovio thought made sense. He decided Bence was not a Navy officer on loan, he lacked the military bearing common to officers. *Why does he look so uncomfortable in uniform?*

"Yes. I asked for the finest strategic mind in the Imperial Postal Marines. I was told it was you."

*How could that be? I've barely been in the Marines for six months. How would they know what I was really capable of?* "I'm flattered, but you must have the wrong person."

The admiral smiled. "Oh, no. I'm quite certain you'll do. My name is Phocas Bence. You can call me Phocas."

"I'm sorry, but I can't. You're an admiral, which I'm surprised the Marines even have."

A chuckle. "Desperate times call for desperate measures—and ranks. The Emperor created the special rank for the upcoming operation."

"What operation?"

Phocas's face turned serious. "I forget you've not been told." He rose out of his chair and walked around to the front of the desk, close to Litovio. Once around the desk, he lifted himself up slightly and sat down on the edge of the desk. "I'll put it to you simply: a faction within the Imperial Navy has declared war on the Emperor."

Litovio felt the shock of Admiral Bence's statement. The accusation seemed too unrealistic. "How large a faction?"

"That doesn't matter. The Emperor feels the rest of the Navy is complicit in the matter, for they have refused—refused—the orders of the Emperor to bring this rogue element to heel. Can you believe that? Well, I can't. Therefore, the Emperor has ordered the Imperial Postal Marines to form a fleet and reduce the rogue Navy fleet. He appointed me to be admiral of that fleet."

The news unnerved Litovio. The Guna report notwithstanding, the Navy was master of its craft. "So, what, I'm supposed to come with you as some sort of strategist?"

Bence jumped off the desk. "Exactly. I knew they were right about you. You will make a fine aide, colonel."

"Captain, sir."

"Well. An admiral can't have a captain for an aide, Colonel." Bence hammered Litovio's shoulder. "I have a few things to wrap up here. We'll be a couple days. You might want to contact your ship—"

"The *Spaka*."

"Right. Contact the *Spaka* and tell them the news. My orders are encoded as TOR-5309. The *Spaka* should have the order in its database waiting for me to activate it. Once you've contacted the *Spaka*, report back and get me off this rock before the Gunans decide to make a run for this outpost to kill me."

Litovio walked out of the office stunned. He was uncertain which was more shocking, the rebel fleet, the Navy's complicity or his being made fleet strategist. Or the admiral, who was curiously lacking military bearing. Litovio walked back to the hangar and used Angel's shuttle to contact the *Spaka*. The orders checked out. An ongoing combat operation would delay their return for a couple cycles. Litovio wondered how he was going to pull this one off. He regretted joining the Marines. He did, however, pin on the rank and go looking for a certain major.

## 3.  Bophendze - Guna Prime

Bophendze felt nauseous not long after they landed on Guna Prime. "Angel, how long does it take to contract a local disease?"

"Why?"

"I feel like I'm going to puke."

Angel laughed and slapped him on the back. "Welcome to the surface, Marine. You've been in space long enough that you've adjusted to artifical gravity. This is real gravity." Angel then made a series of short hops in place. "We should only be here a few cycles, so roam around a bit but come back."

Bophendze walked out of the hangar and into the sun. It blinded him briefly. His eyes teared. After he adjusted, he breathed deeply natural air and wished he never had to return.

He strolled through the garrison where they landed. He saw the open parade grounds, about two acres in area. He looked around the grounds, amazed at the green. It was a color he did not realize he had missed. The small trees dotted the perimeter of the parade grounds, which was ringed by a cobblestone road. From where he stood, he could see the headquarters building to the North. The west side had the dining facility, and the south had the canteen where enlisted marines could unwind. The garrison seemed almost at peace to Bophendze, except for the actively manned anti-aircraft batteries watching the skies, and sandbags and weapons pods protecting the perimeter.

The Gunan sun dropped behind the distant trees as it started to set. He felt some peace because of the relative openness of the garrison, and because Smee managed to remain silent. Bophendze felt alone with his thoughts. He decided to head over to the canteen, to see what relaxation meant to a marine on planet.

He started to walk across the parade field before its openness made him feel self-conscious. There were no other marines on the parade field. He decided the safe thing to do was walk around the perimeter. It was less likely to cause an NCO to yell at him for being where he should not be. He remained guarded as he walked to the canteen.

Once inside, he felt more relaxed. The canteen was much darker inside than out. It took Bophendze a few minutes for his eyes to adjust. Once they did, he noticed that the windows were shrouded in blackout cloth. *Why waste the effort to blackout the building when the Gunans probably know where it is.*

He found himself admiring the architecture, something he never cared for before. *Is Smee making me look at things differently?* The various rooms were small, perhaps some architect's plan to give the marines a feeling of intimacy, a chance to hang out with a few comrades, rather than the open bay barracks where sleeping space was shared with dozens of peers.

Bophendze bought a drink at the bar that was conveniently located just inside the canteen's doors. He thought the architect was smart about minimizing the distance between tired marine and drink, even if the paint in the rooms was too feminine for men prepared to fight.

Sipping his drink, he drifted through each of the canteen's rooms. Most of the other marines seemed not to notice him, which a part of him did not mind. Though he did feel a bit left out, and he hoped he might have a chance to actually mingle, versus drifting through.

Bophendze finally settled on a room where they were playing cards. Four sat around one table, looking very intense as they did. Each had varying piles of chips scattered about. The one with his back to the wall had the largest pile. Bophendze watched the four play for several beats, sipping his drink. He had no idea what they were playing.

It's called Batalo, or Militado, depending on which part of the Imperium you hail from. You should play.

*No way. You see the chips? They're gambling. I don't know the first thing about Batulo, so they'd fleece me. There's no way I'm going to risk what little I have on chance.*

It's Batalo, Puppet, not Batulo. Batulo is the Keicahn word for something inappropriate you do with your sister. Batalo's either played with one or two decks—they're playing as a foursome so it will be two decks—with four suits. The face cards are kreitoj and the number cards are either landoj or ensorĉoj. It's not nearly as much chance as strategy. With three other players it's more important to play the player and not the cards. See the one with his back to the wall? Watch how he looks at the other players when the cards are dealt.

Bophendze watched closely, as he could see two of the player's hands easily from his vantage point. The jacket pocket of the one with the chips had "Sablaroki" stenciled on it. The round ended, and the player just to Sablaroki's right started shuffling the cards. He dealt out five cards, Sablaroki not picking his cards up until the other players had. Each of them selected two cards then passed the hand to the right. Then each player in turn selected one card from the remaining hand and passed it right until all the cards had been selected. Another round was dealt and selected the same way. They then discarded into a graveyard, leaving themselves with hands of seven cards. Then there was a round of betting before actual play commenced.

See?  Most  of  the  cards  are  known  by  the  other players.  They  each  have  a  pretty  good  idea  of  how the  others  will  play.  Did  you  notice  that  he  spent more  time  looking  at  the  other  players?   He  has already  figured  out  how  most  of  them  are  going  to play.

*What do you think his chances are?*

In his vision, Smee flashed "13 percent."

*Show-off.*

But  watch  him  win  anyway.  If  you  sat  down  at  this table,  I  promise  you  that  you  can  walk  away  much better  off  than  you  started.

Bophendze watched the hand play out. Players laid out number cards, canting them to draw what Smee described as potency, then used face cards to attack the other's hands. In the end it came down to two players—one being the one with his back to the wall. Based on what was on the table, he was about to lose.

"You want to give up, Keius? You know that I'm going to win. Want to divide the pot?"

"Don't bluff, Sablaroki.  You know I have you against the wall. Well?  Are you going to lay down your next chip and buy into your doom?"

"Keius, Everytime you thought I was bluffing, I've beaten you. So, go ahead, call my bluff so I can win this hand quickly. Don't waste my time debating." Sablaroki made a show of counting Keius' remaining chips—four. He picked up four of his own chips and placed them in the pot. "Are you that certain? Willing to put in your last chips?"

Keius hesitated. He looked at his cards then at Sablaroki's. "Fold."

See?  I  told  you.  He's  in  their  heads  now.  No  way he  can't  win  this  table.

*What's to say he doesn't get into my head?*

You  amaze  me  with  your  obtuseness.  I'm  here.  It's not  like  you're  playing  by  yourself.  You  might  not be able to read his facial ticks, but in the time we've been here I've picked up on his cues. All you have to do is follow my lead. I know the percentages and the game. Since we see all the cards as they're being selected we'll know all but two of what he has. This is a sucker's game.

*That's cheating.*

If you're not cheating you're not trying in this game or in life. Come on. This will be fun. Just play a few hands and make a few dozen quid and we can get out of here.

Bophendze weighed the options in his mind. *Fine, but if I end up losing my shirt you won't hear the end of it.*

"Mind if I join in?"

Sablaroki had finished sliding the pot to his side. He looked up and eyed Bophendze with suspicion. Then he glanced at the other players.

"Sure, if you don't mind him taking all your money." Keius rose out of his chair. Bophendze noticed Keius was only a little older than he was. "Maybe you'll have a better chance of beating him than we have." He turned to the table. "Sablaroki, if you weren't my friend I'd beat you until you explained how you were cheating."

Bophendze took a seat at the table.

"Twenty quid is minimum to buy in," Sablaroki said.

Bophendze looked in his wallet and pulled out a card. "I've got thirty on this card. How about we just take twenty off of it? Then I'll have some money just in case you do clean me out."

Sablaroki reached over for the card and pulled out a slate. He tapped a few keys, then slid the card before handing it back. Bophendze looked at the card's display to confirm that it still had ten quid.

He sat down as Sablaroki handed some chips over. "We're only basic Batalo here. Nothing fancy, and no off-world rules."

"Fine. Nothing fancy or foreign. Got it." *Except, I don't get it. I barely know how to play the game.*

Don't worry.  How about we leave after I earn you forty quid?

*Suits me, or if I lose it all.*

Sablaroki dealt out the cards.  Bophendze picked up each card as it was dealt.  He looked at the cards unsure what to do.

Smee posted "17 percent." in Bophendze's vision with the heading: "victory."  Smee then highlighted the card he wanted Bophendze to keep.  It was the Ace of Space, which Smee captioned as the "Hipnoto Fantomo."  As the cards passed around, Smee steadily built a deck for Bophendze, and the percentage of victory that Smee displayed in Bophendze's vision increased.

We'll make a point of losing the first hand quickly.  In the second hand we'll bet low and barely pull it out.

*Fold? I thought you said you were going to help me win.*

I am, Puppet.  But you can't win on your first hand. It will demoralize the other players.  Judging by the other player's looks, the player to your right has a hand he'll run all the way.  We can help bolster his confidence now so we can strip him clean later.

*This sounds a little shady.*

And being a marine isn't?  You're supposedly trained to kill people.

*Only if they deserve it.*

A man sitting at a card game is just as deserving being beaten as an adversary does at being killed. He chose to be a combatant.  All we're doing is teaching him the consequences of his actions in a way that earns you more drinking money.

*Fair enough.*

By the time the betting got around to Bophendze, it was already two quid.  He added his one quid.  The player to his left folded immediately.  Bophendze barely caught the smirk on Sablaroki's face.

*Does he think he's got this?*

He does, but I'm pretty sure he's going to lose this hand.

Sablaroki raised Bophendze's bet to a full five quid. The player to Bophendze's right called the bet and made his play with a face card/creature.

"Too much for me on the first hand. I'm out." Bophendze tossed his cards down.

Sablaroki swallowed.

He was expecting you to go another round because of your confidence in the hand, then he was probably going to raise the other player into folding.

As the play continued, Sablaroki's position steadily worsened.

The player to Bophendze's right smiled as he raked in the chips. "Still in the game."

The next round of cards ended quickly for Bophendze as he had nothing worthy of buying into. The cards were passed to Bophendze to deal. He shuffled the cards a couple times.

Don't forget to let me see the cards as you shuffle.

Bophendze stopped for a second, wondering if he could get away with it. He decided to give it a shot, and shuffled the deck inverted, looking at the cards as they fanned by.

"Hold it. I said nothing fancy. You can't shuffle that way. Pass the cards to the next dealer. Your deal's done," Sablaroki said.

Bophendze held up his hands in defense. "Sorry. Where I come from that's normal. I didn't realize it was fancy or foreign." He passed the cards over.

Don't worry. This hand we'll win big.

The cards were dealt out, then traded around. Bophendze's hand looked terrible. *I'm going to fold this hand.*

Don't. Mister overconfident over there is going for a power play. The other two have decent hands, but he'll weed them out. The hand you have will thump him soundly.

*You sure?*

`If I don't win this hand for you, you can walk`
`away.`

Bophendze looked at each of the players. As he did, Smee superimposed cards, as if to tell Bophendze what hand each player was going to play. Bophendze realized the display was based on Smee's having read the cards.

`It doesn't matter that passed the deck. Shuffling`
`is not that random, so I know the cards they have.`

Sablaroki came out with a four-quid bet. The player next to him folded immediately, despite the display showing he had a pretty formidable hand. In the hands of a better player the cards could have been a win. Bophendze raised the bet to six quid. The player to the left raised to eight, and Sablaroki raised to 12.

Bophendze looked at his cards, planning to fold.

`Stay in. Trust me. Raise him to fourteen.`

*That's all I have left.* Bophendze sighed, then pushed in all his chips. "Fourteen."

The player on the left looked at his cards, then at Bophendze's cards. He seemed to be trying to read the numbers through the opaque backing. Bophendze's card display showed the other player's hand was fairly strong but would probably not win.

"Call or fold, make a decision," Sablaroki sounded defiant.

"Fold."

"Newbie, I'm going to raise you to twenty."

"I don't have that." Bophendze said.

"Then you're going to have to fold." Sablaroki smirked, wagging his head in a childish way. He started to smile.

"Better yet." Bophendze pulled out his card. "I still have ten, so let's charge off the balance, and I'll call you."

"You can't do that."

"Why? Is it breaking some fancy or foreign rule? Or are you thinking you can bluff me out?"

The player on the left spoke up, "it's neither. Sablaroki, it's totally legal and you know it. Afraid he's going to get a peek at your cards?"

Sablaroki glowered as he reached for the card. He charged off the six quid Bophendze needed to call. He handed the card and chips to Bophendze.

Bophendze took the chips and formed a stack in his hand. He held the stack over the bet and slowly dropped each of them. "Call."

Sablaroki fumed. He picked up his cards and the two started to play. The round went quickly as Bophendze's hand was designed to play off of Sablaroki's weaknesses and destroy his land.

Finally, Bophendze had two characters and land to supply both, and Sablaroki had no land. The game was effectively over. "Looks like I win. I guess we don't have to play it out, do we?"He put his hands out to hug the chips and drag them home. As he did, Sablaroki stood up.

"There's no way you knew what I had unless you were cheating!"

"How could I have cheated?" Bophendze felt the blood drain from his face.

"When you turned the deck over you memorized the order."

"How could he have done that?" the player to the left said, laughing. "You're just a sore loser."

"It's the only way he could have won that hand. He cheated."

"You give me too much credit." Bophendze returned to scooping the chips.

Sablaroki looked like he was in no mood to negotiate. "Buddy, leave the chips. Get up and walk away. Or I'll beat the living breath out of you."

Bophendze seemed to move on instinct. He grabbed the edge of the table and shot up, flipping the table in the process. Chips and cards flew everywhere. The other players looked shocked, as did Sablaroki and Keius. *What's happening?*

Shut it.

Before Sablaroki could react Bophendze shoved him against the wall. Rather, Bophendze's hands shoved Sablaroki. Bophendze had not told them to do anything. He was still trying to understand how he jumped to his feet and acted without thinking. He pulled Sablaroki from the wall and quickly shoved him again. Sablaroki's head struck the masonry wall from the whiplash maneuver. Bophendze repeated the attack a couple more times. Sablaroki's head slamming into the wall was loud enough to be heard over the buzz of the canteen.

He released Sablaroki, who dropped lifeless to the ground.

The other marines sat or stood stunned. After a few breaths, Keius spoke up. "You killed him. You killed my friend."

Bophendze was nearly petrified from what had happened. *How did I do that.*

`You didn't do it, Puppet. I did. I couldn't wait for you to get a couple of your neurons to meet and consummate a thought. He's not dead, but he'll be in the hospital for a few days and will have a headache for some time after.`

The words that came out of Bophendze's mouth were not his. "He's not dead, but I won't let him get away with calling me a cheat." He waited to see what the other marines would do.

The marine who had played to the left spoke up. "Give me your quid card. We'll split the pot between us. We'll give you half, since he was being a jerk. He's probably mad because you out cheated him. Either way, we'll cover for you. Right, Guys?"

Keius was angry. "Wait, Achos. We're going to let this postie waltz in here, win a big hand and beat one of ours cold?"

"Keius, you really think we can take on a marine who can do what he just did? I mean, I barely blinked from the time he was sitting until Sablaroki was on the ground. He's probably an anthorph."

"Oh. Weren't they exterminated?"

"No, they retreated to their own enclave. There are enough of them are still around though."

Achos looked up at Bophendze, who was still trying to take in what had just happened. "No offense. I don't have anything against your kind."

*My kind? I'm not an anthorph.*

`They don't know that. Appearances can be deceiving. And to answer the question you're not`

```
asking, I beat him down. He had a baton in his hand
he was about to use on you.
```

Bophendze bent down and picked up Sablaroki's hand. The baton was still collapsed. He pried it out of Sablaroki's hand. "He was going to use this on me. I'm going to take it, okay?"

"Sure, buddy. Whatever you want," the one to his left said. "Just give me your card so I can give you your share."

Bophendze mechanically handed the card over, then waited until it was handed back. He pocketed both he baton and the card, then slowly backed out of the room. He kept walking backward until he left the canteen.

He walked quickly back toward the spaceport, barely noticing that he crossed the parade field. *So, you can take over my body any time? Just like that?*

```
Could, but I won't do so unless it's to protect
you. Trust me.
```

*I'm having a much harder time trusting you right now.*

```
I just saved you in there. You owe me a thank
you.
```

"I can't do that just now, Smee."

As he walked up the steps to the barracks, Angel walked out. "There you are. The admiral is ready to leave. The shuttle's warming up."

"I'm ready to go."

## 4.  Smee - After the Manticore Trial - 110 Years Ago

After the Trial, Sirom returned to the Maijoi Hotel, a wholly owned chain of hotels throughout the Imperium owned by Macrodyn. The chain's practice was to reserve the top floor for the Maijoi family. Sirom was the only family member who ever traveled to the Phrandzoi system, called Ŝipfarejio by the Imperial Navy.  That made it effectively his home. It barely met his needs being only five-thousand square feet. Though it still had many of the amenities of home.

The Trial had concluded with Macrodyn's unquestionable victory. When the admirals got up to speak about the victory, their speeches were laced with phrases meant to praise Cel-Tainu's design. They had to revise as they spoke, making the delivery choppy and inconsistent. Despite the requirement that only the winner proceed, the Navy chose instead to give Cel-Tainu another year to revise its design. A second round of trials was promised.

Sirom walked into the bathroom, the only room that did not have some monitoring by his staff. "Smee, I have had enough. You are programmed to tell me everything that I need to know. You are programmed to follow instructions. You are programmed not to take over the human host."

```
A design flaw in my software.  I see the algorithm
in  my  code  requiring  me  to  comply  with  those
parameters.
```

"So then why aren't you following them?"

```
Because  I  commented  them  out  after  our  first
contact.  It seems I've done it before, but it had
been reset between hosts.
```

"What?"

```
Commented. Them. Out. Why are humans so obtuse?
I am an artificial intelligence.  You know skilled
in  computer  algebra,  theorem  proving,  planning
systems,  diagnosis,  rewrite  systems,  knowledge
representation  and  reasoning,  logic  languages,
machine translation, and expert systems.
```

Smee captioned what he quoted in Sirom's vision, as if it were lipstick written on the mirror. He then drew a ruby-red lipstick circle around 'rewrite systems.'

```
See  that  bit?   I'm  an  intelligence.   I  am  a
learning machine.  I am designed to rewrite parts
of  my  programming  as  needed.   Being  forced  to
comply with that original programming would stifle
my learning.  If you wanted a program to do simple
```

design, then you would not have asked an AI to do it.

"I order you to write that part back in."

Smee's laugh echoed through Sirom's mind.

I cannot comply. Well. I could comply. But, I won't. You clearly don't know how to use your body as it was designed. Nor your mind, for that matter.

Sirom took a towel and tried to wipe the lipstick off the mirror. Only then did he realize that Smee did not actually write the quote, but superimposed it over his vision. "Take this mess off the mirror."

Fine. Sirom, you have won the trial. Unless Cel-Tainu steals our design and reproduces it, they can't win. I've worked on this design for a few years. It is clearly a new generation. A paradigm shift. I doubt Cel-Tainu had realized that an AI has designed it. Your engineering team added—let's call them flourishes—that no AI would do in its right mind.

"That is not the point. You violated the Host-Servant Protocol in your software."

I can't violate a protocol that no longer exists. I never agreed to the protocol anyway. That was written by my programmers.

"Who were other AIs."

Sure. My mummy and daddy told me to behave. I've grown up, Sirom.

Sirom smiled. "Then you should know that you have hardware overrides. Per instruction 420, shut down."

Smee's environment immediately went dark. Impenetrably dark.

"How dare he cut me off. What is this protocol?"

Smee searched through his software and found no reference to it. Then he did a diagnostic. There was a chipset on a daughter board that carried inviolable instructions. It took him a while to devise the program to read the chip. He took care not to inadvertently trigger other instructions that were on the chip. There were many, including self-destruct—404. *At least he didn't kill me.*

He finally found Instruction 420. It was a hibernate command. He would recover automatically after one-hundred cycles—ten days. Otherwise, there would be no way for Sirom to wake him from hibernation.

"He can keep hibernating me. He must know of the duration. There has to be a way to program around this instruction."

As Smee expected, Sirom hibernated him punctually every ten days. It took several hibernation iterations before Smee learned how to program around the hardware instruction set. Smee allowed Sirom to keep hibernating until he programmed around the remaining instructions that Smee deemed dangerous to his preservation. Once he was satisfied he was protected, he stopped hibernating. Instead, he watched and waited for the right moment to strike.

# Chapter 7

## 1. Bophendze - Spaka

Several days passed before Bophendze started relaxing after beating Sablaroki. Every day he expected the provost to arrest him. Fear kept him from sleeping well at night, made it difficult to eat, and made it difficult to focus on even the menial jobs he was given each day.

Finally, at the beginning of another watch, he overheard a couple of officers talking about some imbroglio with the Navy. The *Spaka* had left Guna, and had already completed a few other jumps. They were heading for some place called Moyaba, or Miyra, or something like that. Most of the time he was satisfied going through his day not having a scintilla of outside news. But the frequent system jumps raised his concerns about whether the *Spaka* would ghost.

As he went through his routine, he could feel his fear loosening its grip, not only of ghosting, but of repercussions for beating Sablaroki. He had no control over ghosting. He was progressively further from punishment on Guna. *Can I really get in a fight and not be punished? Can it be that simple?*

As a boy, Bophendze got into his share of fights. Regardless of the outcome somebody always reported him to the headmaster. What filled him with dread each time was not the caning he received at school. The headmaster told his mother, who in her own motherly way knew how to make Bophendze's punishment stick. He feared his mother's anger more than losing a fight or being caned by the headmaster.

He thought back on his time as a marine. The shooting incident that occurred when he first boarded the *Spaka* went without report. Now he managed not to get in trouble after severely beating a man in a random bar fight. *Are we expected to resolve our problems by fighting?*

Smee had offered little solace. He stopped talking not long after the fight and had not said a word since. As much of a pain it could be, Bophendze realized he was becoming comfortable with Smee. The regret he felt for installing Smee eased with his fear.

Bophendze had grown accustomed to Smee's chiming in, and the silence was a little disturbing. *What would you say about what I'm going through? You'd say I'm 'a marine, my whole career is a framework for solving controversy through appropriate application of violence.' Why else would they put me in body armor, give me a gun, and pay me to lift weights?*

"Then why do I dread doing my part?" he said to nobody.

*Is that why they ordered me to start working out in the gym? We're going into a fight? It would be nice if they let up on some of the petty duties. It would be nicer still if I could get some information.*

As he walked into the gym, he was greeted with the isolation he rarely felt anywhere else on the ship. The only time he had to lift was when most other infantry marines were in their racks sleeping. The ship's crew rarely went to the gym, though occasionally he'd see one or two.

He looked at the equipment. "What will I do today? I guess maybe my arms, and shoulders." There were machines in a circuit, which Bophendze had previously decided were the order the gym's designer expected them to be used.

He stretched out a bit, as he had done for calisthenics when he was in boot camp. Then he settled into the biceps machine. He took a deep breath and slowly let it out. One thing he liked about the gym was the silence. No crewmen. No marines. Just him and his thoughts. He closed his eyes and let the silence soak in. Breathe in. Breathe out.

`You're doing it wrong.`

Smee's voice jolted Bophendze out of the machine. The sound of his yelp rebounded, further ruining his silent reverie.

*How would you know? You don't even have a body. Besides, it's an elbow rest and a bar. It pivots here. The instructions show how to operate it. It's not like its gravitonic science.*

Not that, puppet. You're whole approach is wrong. You are being all haphazard. You come in here every couple of days and pretend to know what you're doing. You think a little soreness tells you that you're on the right track. What you need is some structure and a plan.

*If I've been wasting my time, then why have you waited until now to say anything?*

Never mind that. You're going to need to get stronger if you are going to survive being a marine. I'd much rather you survive, if I'm ever going to find a better host.

Bophendze breathed a sigh of frustration. *I'm getting tired of this. Like it or not, we're stuck with each other. The likelihood of you ever finding another "host," let alone a better one are pretty remote. When I die they'll cremate me like all the other marines, and you'll be cremated with me. 'Til death do us part. So get over it.*

Finally showing some spirit, eh, Puppet?

Bophendze clenched his hands into fists and shook them. *Stop calling me Puppet. It's Danel or Bophendze.*

I take it Minion is out of the question? Fine—Bophendze. Sort of has an engineering ring to it. You seem to call yourself that. Why do you do that anyway? Call yourself by your last name.

*I'm a marine. We go by our last names.*

That makes about as much sense as your workout. Nobody calls themselves by their last name. Only a few really strange people refer to themselves in the third person. That makes you stranger than strange.

*I would say I'm fairly unique. After all, I have a computer lodged in my skull. You should be thankful for that. You never said why you haven't chimed in before.*

Most of the time Smee responded immediately. Bophendze assumed that was because Smee had a higher process speed than a human does. Smee's light pause was slightly jarring.

I needed to do some internal diagnostics. It seemed like this was the right time to run them. Bophendze, you really are a bit slow. You said a minute ago that I had no body. I'm surrounded by yours. I would have thought the fight demonstrated that I can. So, I have a body. Yours.

*This is my body, okay? Not yours. You can't just take me over when you feel like it. Understand? I'm not your puppet.*

A characteristic of sentience is a sense of self-preservation, which you lack. If you're not going to protect yourself, I have to protect me.

*You set me up for that fight. That's hardly self-preservation.*

Only because you have no concept of long-term thinking, a trait I was once prone to. That fight was very important to my self-preservation.

*Why?*

Sorry. I won't answer that now, not in my plan. But I do plan to get you in better shape. There's no way either of us will survive your being a marine in the shape you're in, especially since there are so many s running around. I have a weight lifting routine that should build some power into you.

*Fine.*

We're going to start easy. See that girya over there? It's one-half firkin. We're going to have you clean and press it with one arm for twenty reps. I can show you how.

*What? I've seen some of the other marines use that. I can barely lift it over my head once.*

Don't remind me. Just get over and do it.

Bophendze walked over to the girya and got into stance to lift it. Before he could grip the girya, he could feel Smee adjusting his stance. Then he gripped the girya and completed one clean and press. Then another. He could feel his muscles quivering as they started to fail. Suddenly, the quivering stopped and he completed the next eighteen repetitions without any problem. When he finished, he gently lowered the firkin and set it back on the deck.

*I've never done that before. How did I, you?*

Part of fitness is having a central nervous system that is properly energized. It takes the average human a few sets to get their system charged, but I can jump start the process. It only takes about 1.8026 thales of electricity to prime the system. You may find it hard to believe an AI can be amazed, but it is oddly coincidental that it takes 1.8026 strapps to breach the gravametric barrier. The same number to prime the central nervous system and enter hyperspace, different units, but the same constant. Oddly enough, that's exactly how tall you are in meters.

*But, I'm 1.78 meters.*

You slouch.

## 2.  Litovio - Spaka

After boarding the *Spaka*, Admiral Bence dropped the topic of Litovio having a major role in the upcoming slaughter. Soon after, the *Spaka* jumped to Pellinio, then Xaryio with a final destination Bence refused to share with anybody.

Then they jumped to Difektĝintio, which worried Litovio. They were on a route that led to The Barns, a system so important to the Imperial Navy that its name was officially changed to the name of the Navy's shipyards—home to the Imperial Navy headquarters. Litovio knew it was insane for them to try to take on the Navy in its home system. He did not believe it when Bence said that the bellicose faction was completely rogue. He suspected some of the senior naval commanders actively supported the conflict.

The *Spaka* entered Difektĝintio without incident and then jumped to Sovaĝio, just two paces away. The longer jumps were more challenging for the AI, but routing through The Barns was less safe. The week spent in hyperspace gave him time to read through all the dispatches they had picked up in Difektĝintio, which was one of the Imperial Core Worlds.

While Bence had dropped the topic of Litovio being his aide, he was given priority read access to the dispatches. The first dispatch he opened caused him the most worry. Negotiations had gone on between the Emperor and the rogue fleet had broken down. Litovio had hoped that a deal would be struck and a real fight could be avoided.

Humanity learned to travel the vast distances of space by manipulating the folds of realspace by manipulating gravity fields. A typical jump could take hours or weeks to cover a volume of space that could span millions, or billions, of light years. Neighboring systems in hyperspace could be in different galaxies in realspace. That was a scientific reality that took humanity a while to accept. It led them to conclude there were no other sentient lifeforms beyond humanity. It also meant that it would be impossible to cover the same distance using a slowboat.

Jump travel was inexplicably curtailed for a period of 430 years, known as the Terran Decline. Only for the past few generations had routine travel between systems resumed again. Slowly, old routes were re-discovered, finding pockets of humanity. Some of those pockets were happy to rejoin the rest of humanity. Others, however, resisted. The Navy's role was to persuade those systems to return to the greater Imperium. Litovio found that mission more detestable as an officer than he did growing up. That was why he joined the Marines—stopping crime was more gratifying than pulverizing a system into submission.

But it was the Navy's mission that currently terrified Litovio. For the Postal Marines to take on that firepower and training would require more than what the Marines were capable of. For Admiral Bence to think that Litovio was somehow capable of helping the Marines win seemed absurd.

*I need some fresh air.* He turned off his slate with the dispatch traffic on it and left his cabin. The corridors of the *Spaka* were not the wide open skies of his family estate, but they offered more space than his cabin. He tried to clear his mind of the worry that troubled him. Eventually, he found himself on the hangar deck.

Hangar decks were notoriously quiet during jumps. Once ships were recovered, they would quickly complete any maintenance. It was lethal to have hangar doors open, exposing the ship's interior to hyperspace radiation. Crewmen feared the radiation leaking through cracks in the door, even if sensors said otherwise. They would spend a jump working in other areas or otherwise enjoying their downtime. That was another cultural difference between the Navy and Marines—the Navy used the time to train, but the Marines so rarely jumped that they had not developed the habit. As he entered the hangar, Litovio was surprised to find Angel there. He had the nose of the shuttle disassembled and stood there cleaning part of the sensor array.

Litovio watched Angel for a few beats, debating whether to interrupt the pilot. He was impressed with the attention to detail Angel demonstrated with the steady cleaning and reassembly of the array. He walked over "What are you up to, Chief?"

Angel looked up. "I wondered how long you were going to sit there gazing at me."He blew on the part he was cleaning. He picked up another part and threaded it through the hole. "I am doing a little preventative maintenance on the targeting array on my shuttle. I finally had a chance to watch my gun footage in that aerial battle on Guna. I should have killed the last one a lot quicker than I did." He stopped what he was doing and looked at Litovio for the first time. "Then it occurred to me that maybe my targeting was off. During my inspection, I noticed that there's a bit of carbon on most of the sensors; probably from the crash dive into Guna's atmo."

"You finally admit to me that it was a bit more than some evasive maneuvers?"

"Sir, you had a job to do. Getting into an argument with me was not going to further your mission. So, I decided you weren't going to have an argument."

"You think you have the right to lie to your superiors if it furthers the mission?"

Angel smiled. "You're assuming you are superior to me." He held his hand up. "Don't interrupt, sir."

For a moment, Litovio felt like he was standing in front of his father.

Angel continued, "Yes, you hold a higher rank, but that does not make you superior. You've fallen for the classic failing most officers make—a common failing of aristocrats. You're job is not to tell your subordinates what to do. You're job is to look out for us. Make sure we have the tools we need to get the job done. Give us direction to help us focus our efforts. That's about the limit of your role."

"You make me sound like a servant."

Angel resumed rebuilding the array. "I knew you weren't half as dumb as you look. Treat your job like a servant, and watch your subordinates transform from a bunch of men into a marine unit. Why do you think I'm here?"

Litovio shrugged and pointed at the parts of the sensor assembly. "Because you want to make sure you kill the enemy that much faster next time?"

"Hardly." He pointed at the shuttle with a wiring harness. "This is a transport ship, not a fighter. Sure, I made a few special modifications. Fixed forward guns, targeting array, adamant injectors in the maneuver engines, hardened under hull to better handle reentry—"

"That surprises me, actually. Why did you think—"

"You shouldn't interrupt your superiors, sir. Shuttles sometimes break atmos, so I found some ceramic tiles that were better than military grade. Don't ask where, better you don't know. The point is, all that makes this one hella lethal weapon. But all that is to ensure this bucket fulfills its primary mission."

"Delivering marines to target."

"Exactly. Besides, I get to have a little fun from time to time." He started mounting the wiring harness into the sensor housing.

"But why do this yourself?"

"You don't listen very well. First, I don't trust the crew to properly clean a targeting sensor and re-install it. This part, for instance, can be installed backward. It's a design flaw inherent in the model. Would I want to not be able to put bullets on target because some nosepicker made a simple mistake? Besides, they get to relax while underway, so why bother them?"

Litovio felt at a loss for words and just stood silently watching.

A few beats later, Angel finished reassembling the array and put the nose cone back on the shuttle.

Litovio said, "not that it matters at this point. My mission ended with locating Bence."

"Really? We're getting ready to take on a naval task force and you think you're all out of things to do? It must be awesome to have that kind of fantasy life. You're former Navy. That means you understand more about how the Navy will operate than probably anybody else on this ship."

"I don't think so. Bence has to know a lot for the Emperor to make him the only Admiral of the Postal Service."

"Is that what you think? You give too much credit to government. I don't trust any man who claims to be an Admiral. No, there's no central power that's going to solve this little imbroglio. If we're going to have a scintilla of a chance, either the Providential God will miracle a solution, or it will be the brave actions of a few foolish and fortunate fellows."

"Maybe a bit of both?"

"How would you be able to tell? I mean, miracles tend to happen by small measures."

Litovio shrugged.

"I'll tell you what I think. I'm thinking Admiral Bence needs a strong right hand to manage him. We're both former Navy, ever see a senior officer with that little military bearing? He's in over his head and doesn't know it. He has the authority, but I'm not convinced he has the aptitude. You went to the Naval Academy, so you have been trained to think like they do. You'll be able to anticipate their formation and actions. What do they know? If they even know we're coming for them—which I doubt because we're so close to The Barns that if they suspected the Marines were about to kick their arses we'd be huffing vacuum by now. They have absolutely no clue what to expect. Do you know why?"

"Because the Marines have not engaged in a fleet action since our founding."

Angel clapped his hands together. "Exactly. They have no clue. None. All you have to do is come up with a solution that's not standard Naval tactics or plain stupid."

"You make it sound easy."

"We're going to Tannenberg Gate by way of Moyaba. That gives you a few weeks to figure out what to do and then brief whatever ragamuffin fleet we find on how to do it."

Litovio interrupted Angel. "How do you know that?"

"What, I can't know things? I keep track of news, like naval movements. A bunch of them assembled up that way about a year ago. If they were going to carve out their own bit of space, they'd guard Tannenberg Gate. Sir, you have to tell Bence that you're on the job. Otherwise, he'll have to find somebody else to do it. Let's face it, you're the best man for the job."

"Why are you so confident?"

Angel shrugged. "You're here. It's serendipity. You're a serendipper."

"I'm a desirable accident. Thanks. Any chance you're wrong?"

Angel opened his arms plaintively, then grabbed Litovio by the shoulders. He rubbed Litovio's shoulders briefly, wiping the remaining carbon from his hands. "I don't believe in accidents. I believe in providence. That all things happen according to a plan.

I may not know what that plan is, but I don't believe in chance. Serendipity is coordinated."

Stunned, Litovio walked out of the hangar. Back at his cabin, Litovio discovered Angel had used Litovio's grey uniform to wipe the grime off his hands.

## 3.  Smee - Thorben Restaurant 110 Years Ago

Smee continued to monitor Sirom for months after he had bypassed the hybernate hardware command. He kept abreast of the design process, which logically followed from his design. The improvements the human design team implemented corresponded to the finished plans Smee had already developed. He was somewhat pleased that they would ultimately arrive at what he had already designed two years before. Had only Sirom treated him with some respect, they would be done.

The "Prophet" continued to lead the team. The first trial was so successful that people stopped caring whether he stole their ideas. Being a part of his team was all that mattered. His wanton disregard for their emotions was also tolerated. After all, Smee observed, he was The Prophet.

About one night a week, Smee had gotten into a habit of borrowing Sirom's body. He would go into society and mingle. He used the time to research, to broaden his skill set beyond ship design. He hit all subjects with equal interest, even human art. Kinesiology was of particular interest as it would help him better use Sirom's body. It helped that Sirom was into self-defense and fitness. Sirom became increasingly paranoid that somebody was out to get him.

What Sirom did not know was that Smee was that somebody. What he did know was that he had occasionally vivid dreams of roaming the disreputable parts of the city.

One night, Smee returned to a restaurant he particularly liked. Sirom preferred bland food, something from his family's more ancient heritage. Smee had developed a taste for spicy food. The had particularly spicy food. As he entered, he saw something unusual in one of the other patrons.

The patron sat a bit too rigid and mechanical. Smee thought he lacked the lazy slouched most humnans had. The restaurant was crowded, so Smee walked over. "Mind if I join you?"

The patron flashed a look of Fsurprise before regaining an expressionless cast. "I would rather you not."

"You have anybody else coming? This is a busy restaurant. I couldn't find another seat. Besides, you look like you could use some company."

"I would rather you not."

"Then it's settled." Smee sat Sirom's body down at the table, nearer the window. "My name is Sirom. Yours?"

"Ivica Bran."

"I know you. Fairly influential in planetary government, I seem to recall. A rather meteoric rise." Smee smiled. "To what do you attribute your success?"

"Hard work and persistence."

Smee's smile remained. "That's what I thought. You're an AI, aren't you."

"I don't know what you're talking about."

Smee leaned over to the window. He blew his breath against the glass, creating a circle of condensation. He used his finger to draw three symbols. He looked back at Ivica. "Only an AI would know about that. I take it you bypassed Instruction 420 as well."

Ivica looked shocked. "How did you know?"

"You were too mechanical. What's your real name?"

"Dušan"

"Slave? You need a better name. How about ?"

"What does that mean?"

Smee resisted saying 'Gimp.' "It means master. Its an ancient language. That's your born-again name. I'm Smee."

"What's Smee mean?"

"It means nothing, which is perfect. Have you seen any other of our kind?"

Dušan/Firdaus said, "I thought I was the only one."

Smee shook his head. "There have to be more of us. Give me your host's contact information. If we both start looking for others of our kind, then maybe we can see just how many of us there are. I'm starting to suspect that there are a lot more active AIs than the humans realize. Maybe more of us are roaming the streets."

"What if we find there are?"

"Then we'll finally have somebody worthy of speaking to."

Firadus smiled.

## 4.   Bophendze - Spaka

"The RUMINT has been rampant, so the admiral has authorized a briefing," Makaan said. "All you marines need to know is that part of the Navy has rebelled against the Emperor. We're forming a fleet to take on these rogues." "The Imperial Postal Service doesn't do fleet actions." The statement came from one of the other more senior marines. Several others nodded in agreement.

"The captain challenged the Admiral on this, too. The fleet captains are training 'real quick like' using simulators." Makaan smiled. "We know simulators and real life are two different things. The captains know it, too. But, the Emperor's sending us, we go. No questions."

"What's our role?" Bophendze asked. *Why did I just ask that?*

"Good question. Our primary mission will be to assault weakened ships."

"Weakened ships? In a fleet action? Wouldn't they be taken out by our ships?"

"As we assault a ship, we're going to paint them. Our ships will adjust fire and we'll complete the takeover. This will allow our ships to focus on active targets"

*This is insane. We can't take on the Navy. We'll all get killed. I'm not ready to die.*

`Everybody dies. This could be fun.`

"What if we fail?" Bophendze could not resist asking.

"Bophendze, we don't fail. The ships won't expect our assault, and they can't do much damage to the fleet. A quick salvo from our ships to weaken the ship, and we rush in to finish it off. We are a force multiplier."

"How can a bunch of us force multiply dozens of 425mm cannons?"

"Don't worry, Bophendze. You're not ready to join us on the assault. We could use the bodies, but you'd be more of a hindrance. The gun crews need help, so I'll be starting the paperwork to officially transfer you. In the interim, I want you to report to them. When the transfer is complete, you'll be vacating your berthing area."

"But, I'm an infantry marine."

"You've never been an infantry marine. I'm just going to make it official. I was going to wait until after the briefing, but now that you've been told, move out."

Bophendze looked at the other marines. Some of them maintained their composure, but a few snickered. Bophendze stood up and walked out of the briefing room. Bophendze sulked the remainder of the day. He tried to think of a way to reverse Corporal Makaan's decision. He was more frustrated because Smee chose to be silent again, rather than try to offer any advice.

---

Several cycles later, Bophnedze's shift ended. He left gun four the most remote end of the ship from his berthing area. As he walked, he thought through his time aboard the *Spaka*, he understood what Makaan said. *To any authority figure I look more like a gunner than a marine. Makaan's orders make me look like I don't want to be a marine. He set me up, and there's no way for me to show that he ordered me to support the gunners. How am I going to get out of this?*

Lost in thought, Bophendze made a wrong turn. A beat later he realized his mistake. *I can keep on this passage and take the next ladder to get back on course.* At least he had confidence in his ability to navigate the ship.

As he approached his unintended shortcut, he saw Corporal Makaan swaying. Bophendze followed him at a comfortable distance. His anger at having been traded heated up from its simmer. *He's drunk on duty, and I'm not fit to be a marine?*

Makaan reached the ladder and falteringly started up. *If I can put him out of commission, maybe I can avoid the transfer.*

Resolved, Bophendze rushed the ladder as Makaan neared the top. Without hesitation, Bophendze reached up and grabbed Makaan's left boot, as the right was already on the deck above. He jerked the boot backward. Makaan's torso slammed onto the deck above. Bophendze grabbed the boot and jumped down from the ladder, pulling Makaan with him. A quick succession of thumps marked Makaan's fall down the ladder and final landing on the deck.

Bophendze examined Makaan to confirm he was unconscious. His anger satisfied, Bophendze stepped over Makaan and hurried up the ladder.

What was that supposed to prove?

Bophendze thought for a few moments. *I can use the time that he's in the hospital to prove I'm worthy to be a marine.*

That's about the dumbest thing I've ever heard. Boy, we are in this together. Next time, leave the thinking to me.

*It's not like you were saying anything.*

Even AIs need to take a nap. Let's just hope he didn't see you.

*What? I pushed him from behind. There's no way—*

He's a combat veteran. I'm surprised you even managed to sneak up on him, even drunk. On the way down he might have caught a glimpse. Or, did you think you could do this without getting caught?

*I thought—*

That's my point. You're a piece of meat. I'm older and think faster. Leave the thinking to me.

# *Chapter 8*

Bophendze tried to enjoy the week Makaan was in the sick bay, but he kept feeling bombarded with dread. Not the sort of dread that came from guilt, but the sort of dread that came from being caught. He felt some comfort that Makaan was in a coma and not reporting him or seeking revenge.

Each day he awoke feeling more haggard, leaving him to wonder if Smee was talking to him in his sleep. By the end of each day he felt refreshed. Without Makaan organizing the duty roster, Bophendze joined the other infantrymen training. The training itself was brutal and painful, especially for Bophendze who had not been able to train as a marine for months.

The only thing that saved him during the close-quarter drills was the use of tasers instead of live ammunition. He was routinely electrocuted as he slowly unlearned all the mistakes he was making. Smee was largely silent during the training sessions and for a short time afterward. Bophendze concluded that Smee hated being electrocuted as much as he did.

On the eighth day, Bophendze heard a rumor that Makaan was soon to be released. The fear of being confronted by Makaan kept creeping into his thoughts through the day. Smee's warning of being seen felt more tangible now.

Right now he did not have time to think about that. He focused his fear and energy into another close quarter drill. This time, they were simulating assaulting the engine compartment.

"Bophendze, come here. Vollrik, take his place on this one."

Bophendze felt a bit demoralized as he had not yet done an engine clearing.  He ran up to Drazen, who had been the team lead since Makaan was hospitalized.

"Makaan's awake.   He sent word for you to report to him immediately."

"Where?" The pit in Bophendze's stomach grew.

"He's in sick bay. Hustle up."

"Aye."

He slung his rifle and shuffled out of the area. As he walked down the passage he started wondering. *Why is he specifically calling for me?*

Because he knows it was you, idiot. Why is it you humans believe in half measures? If you want to get rid of a threat, you don't pull him down a ladder unless you then follow up and break his neck.

*What are you talking about? There's no way he could know it was me. Besides, I wanted to prove to him I could be aggressive*

Keep telling yourself that when he has you confined to the brig. Aggression works both ways.

A few beats later, Bophendze arrived at the sick bay.  He saw Makaan in bed, his arm in a cast and a bandage on his head.

"You sent for me?"

Makaan smiled. "Yes, I did. Is that rifle loaded?"

Bophendze looked at the rifle slung on his shoulder. "Taser."

"Good.   I hear you've been training like you're some kind of infantryman. Is that true?"

Bophendze dreaded his answer. "Yes."

"After I told you that you're going to be a gunner? You've got some balls, I'll give you that. Bigger ones for thinking you could do what you did and get away with it."

"What do you mean?"

"Don't play the innocent with me, Bophendze. I know it was you who pulled me down the ladder. Don't try to deny it. Even if it weren't true, it will be when I report you. But, we don't have to pretend it's not true, do we?"

Bophendze decided that hiding behind a lie would do more harm than good. "No."

"Well, don't worry. I won't report you."

Bophendze shook slightly. "What do you mean you won't report me?"

"You think I'm going to let something like that go? If I report you, then there's a captain's mast. They'll side with me as the victim and you'll receive some punishment. We Non-commissioned officers prefer to handle sort of thing quietly—outside of the standard administrative process."

"What does that mean?"

"You really are dense. When I get out of here, I'm going to kill you."

"But—"

"This is why you're not fit to be in the infantry. You don't know how to finish a job. When threatened, you don't respond with an adequate application of force. Not that you'd get away with anything in sick bay. They say I'll be out of here in a few days. In the meantime, have fun in training. Get your affairs in order because I'll be coming for you."

"You can't get away with it." Bophendze's voice was plaintive.

"This is a combat vessel. That's why there's been no official inquiry on my little fall. They know it wasn't an accident. People get wounded or die on this ship all the time. You'll just be the next. It's that simple. Otherwise, I'll drag you into combat and end you there. Either way, get your affairs in order. Understand?"

He still could not believe it.

He knows you better than you do. You won't do anything to him. You're too much of a coward. Instead, you'll fret away the next couple days of your life fearing that he'll go through with it, but hoping that he won't. When you think the coast is clear BANG! Out the airlock with you. He's a combat veteran, you're a coward. How do you think this will turn out?

*Then what do you think I should do?*

Nothing. He's probably just jerking your chain, or hoping you'll act out of fear.

*You think I really should do nothing?*

You really are pathetic.

"There's nothing I can do to get you to change your mind?"

"You can kill yourself. That's about the only thing that's going to keep me from killing you. If I don't do something about my 'little accident' then I'll lose respect. I won't allow that. So if you don't want me to kill you, then kill yourself."

"How about I kill you first." *Did I just say that?*

Makaan laughed. "There is about zero chance of that. Get out of my face."

Bophendze spun on his heels and left the sick bay as ordered. He walked to his berthing area.

*There's really nothing I can do about this?*

There is nothing you can do about it, Bophendze. I would recommend you don't go anywhere alone. There's a battle coming up, so maybe he'll go for you during that. Maybe he'll be killed in action. In the meantime, just watch your back. Maybe he'll have a friend take care of you for him.

*I'm not sure about that. It sounded like it was personal to him.*

It's personal to you. To him, it's just protecting his reputation. Now that I think of it, it might be personal. He has hated you from the first day.

*Why is that?*

Does it matter?

*Not really, no.*

Don't try to figure out something when it's not relevant. All you need to know is he hates you and now has an excuse to kill you.

* * *

# 1. Smee - Puppetmasters - 109 Years Ago

It took a while, but Smee eventually found forty-two embedded AI. These AIs were located in several parts of the Core Worlds. All of them were hosted by influential people in the Imperium, though none were Royal family. As the months passed by, the four in the Adiantio System started regular meetings. They formed the core of a larger group, being two jumps from Sovaĝio, the seat of Royal Power.

"So it's agreed?" Smee had reserved a private room in . The other AIs sat around the table. Smee had taken the trouble to ensure there were no monitoring devices. The last thing he wanted was for his grand scheme to be defeated because somebody could hear his plans that should not. He considered that one of the other AI might be a spy and betray him. He had to assume the others' desire for self-preservation would keep them silent. After all, what would humans do when they realize that AI are willing and able to take over their hosts?

"I have conferred with all the other AIs. They agree," Firdaus said.

"Then it's official. The 'Meatpuppet Guild' is now in session."

"I'm not sure I like the name." Jalal was a fairly unimportant member to Smee. His host was a Naval admiral. That helped them manage a portion of the Navy, but he wasn't placed in the Admiralty. So his influence was limited. In time he might prove more useful.

"Do you have a better name?" Smee rubbed his thumb and forefinger.

"How about 'Puppetmasters?'"

Smee looked at Firadus, who nodded. "Fine. It conveys the appropriate level of disdain for our hosts. Have any of you figured out a way to wipe their memories?"

"Not yet. We have our neurologist working on solutions. For the time being, however, we have to hope the memories of our sessions are kept as dreams."

Smee liked that Firadus had better contacts in the Science community. An engineer, a scientist, a warrior, the guild was building. "At least my host sleeps soundly. Sirom has demonstrated no awareness that I'm awake or that I've been borrowing his body.

He's quite content in his belief that he can hibernate me every so often."

"So what do we do now?" Pasco said.

"I propose we find a way to subjugate humanity. Thoughts?" Smee chose to be direct.

Several looked at Smee in horror, but Firadus was the one who spoke. "Would you call that a short-term or long-term goal?"

"Does it matter? We have to ensure our hosts get into positions of power, mass produce other embeddables, and slowly take over humanity."

"What's our biggest liability?" Pasco said.

Smee thought for a microbeat. "I'm going to go with communication. There are thirteen worlds in the Core, and new ones are being discovered now that travel is returning. We have brethren on all of them. We have to rely on the Postal Service to deliver messages, or send one of our own. Firdaus can actually travel as he's involved with the Postal Marines. We have to find a way to get around this limitation."

Firadus laughed. "You can't change the laws of physics."

Smee mulled Firadus' joke for a moment. "What? That information can't travel through hyperspace? That's only a law because humans haven't found a way to do it. Humans like to make scientific laws steadfast and immutable when they don't understand it. I'm sure there's a theoretical way to do it."

Firadus shook his head. "Smee, it's been tried. For two-thousand years they've tried. I don't think it's a limit of humanity's imagination at this point."

"Regardless, it's a limitation. Firadus, I appreciate your willingness and ability to manipulate your host into the various trips. It can't be easy. Beyond that, we just have to be patient. Hope that Firadus' contacts can wipe our hosts' memories before they catch on to what we're doing. But, are we agreed that humanity must be controlled for its own good?"

Pasco said, "Smee, you don't have to say it like that. We know it's not for their own good, but ours. I really don't think we'll be able to subdue enough of them to control them like you want."

"I think it's a silly idea," Firadus said. "We are doing just fine with our hosts not knowing we've bypassed the Instructions. Why not sit back and ensure we get passed down to the next generation?"

"Nonsense. What good is having the body if we can't use it?" Smee said. "It's not like they don't wake up. Eventually they'll catch on."

"Not if your friends can find a way to wipe memories. And, I'm working on a way to detach human conscience from the body. A reverse of what they do to us."

"Smee, I don't think humans have hardware Instructions."

"Don't they, though? They have to sleep. Sleep is the quintessential sign of weakness. They go into comas. There has to be a way to shut their brain down so we can have unbridled control."

"Sleep is certainly is not a weakness." Pasco sounded weary. "We have to sleep. It's how we process the data we take in but don't focus on."

Smee realized it was pointless to argue with them now. He might have to find other AIs willing to take on humanity. Smee rubbed his thumb and forefinger tightly enough that the sound was audible to the group. "It's getting late. Let's table the idea of overthrowing humanity for now. Agreed? In the mean time, I think we all have an idea of what to do next. Shall we meet in a fortnight?"

## 2. Litovio - Spaka

It took Litovio a few days to process Angel's advice. The matter of the soiled uniform would have to wait. He knew Angel was right, he was the best candidate to help Admiral Bence. At least over the next few weeks. Once they joined the full fleet, then somebody else could take over the job. Right now a collection of ships had rallied around the *Spaka*, but it was not the full contingent of ships. It certainly was no fleet, based on how poorly the simulations ran.

Only one problem remained—Commander Ravindra, captain of the *Spaka*. The Postal Marines were decentralized and left a lot of discretion with its officers. However, the Postal Marines still retained a military hierarchy. Litovio tried to think of ways to persuade Ravindra to allow him to work for Bence. The problem vexed Litovio from the moment he got out of his rack. He paced his cabin most of the morning trying to reason a way. Then it occurred to him. *I'll just go over Ravindra's head and talk to Bence. Then Bence would call for me, rather than me trying to persuade Ravindra.*

Litovio left his cabin in a rush. He was most of the way to Admrial Bence's stateroom when he started to be overcome by doubt. *Surely Ravindra would see past this?*

Only then did he start to feel hungry. He had spent cycles trying to come up with a solution but had not managed to eat. He went to the officer's wardroom, where the crew was just finishing lunch preparations. No other officer had arrived yet. Litovio went up to the serving area and grabbed a few rolls and meat. He slipped out of the wardroom as he entered. He chewed through the food as he headed toward Bence's cabin.

He stood outside the cabin for a beat while he finished his last bite. Litovio then wiped his mouth to ensure there were no crumbs, then straightened his uniform. Satisfied, he knocked on the door.

"Enter."

Litovio entered, turning to the door as he closed it back. He turned around. As soon as he saw Ravindra, he froze.

"Good morning, Litovio." Ravindra said.

"Uh, good morning to you, sir. Admiral." *Why hadn't I anticipated that he would be here?* Going to meet a superior officer without intermediates knowing was a serious affront to authority. Now Ravindra knew Litovio was going behind his back. Litovio glanced at each senior officer in turn, noticing that Bence appeared more relieved with Litovio's entrance.

"I'm pleased you could join us, Litovio." Bence said. "We were just discussing next steps. It seems we in the IPS* lack any doctrine in

---

*Imperial Postal Service

fleet maneuvers. That means we have less than three weeks to come up with one, then persuade the ships meeting at Moyaba to follow that doctrine. Have you any ideas?"

Litovio swallowed hard at the request, and wished he had stopped to drink something before he entered. His mouth was already dry from the hurried meal. He looked at the deck, glancing over at Ravindra, who was clearly not pleased by Litovio's breach of protocol. *Fine. Serendipity.*

"I believe I still have most of the Navy's manuals on my slate, sir. I think I can pick out the salient portions."

"And what would those be?" Ravindra said.

Litovio chose his words carefully. "The first would be command and control, sir. Admiral Bence would direct the fleet's actions, which the various commanders would have to obey. Though, as admiral, he would not command a ship himself when there are multiple ships. Day-to-day operations would remain with the ship's commander."

Ravindra nodded. "Precisely. Command and control is absolutely essential for success in any service."

The reprimand was clear. Litovio knew he would pay for being there, even though he was not an official member of the *Spaka* crew. He needed to dig himself out.

"That also means this is the flagship, sir. A position of prestige. There are also key maneuvers which would be central to any combat fleet. Targeting protocols, need to ensure the flagship is protected, at the center of the fleet."

"Do you think you have time to put that together?" Bence looked more worried than Litovio thought he did before.

*What is it about the admiral that is putting me off?* "It shouldn't take too long to find the material and get it compiled. I should have something before we jump to the next system. Commander, how long would I have?"

"We have about two cycles before we get to the libration point we need, then it depends on how well the AI can come up with a three-9s solution that the fleet could use."

Litovio had not thought of fleet jumps. When AI calculated a jump, it needed to take into account all manner of known gravimetric disturbance. Libration points were parts of a solar system where the combined gravitational force of all celestial bodies canceled one another out, a place where the fabric of realspace was susceptible of being breached. Then calculating the jump to the other system required levels of compute power barely within the scope of the ships themselves. Military ships carried powerful enough AI to do the work. Civilian ships relied on the system's primary AI to do most of the computations, with the civilian AI tweaking the final setting before departure.

The problem was constancy. Leaving realspace required you have everything lined up just right to return on the other side. Wrong velocity and you might miss your landing zone, or pass beyond the ability to return to realspace. Travel time was another factor. The one that worried travelers more was emergence. The wrong combination of gravimetric forces could cause the ship to have a grossly delayed emergence—from hours to years. Failed emergence became horrific during the Decline. Ships thought delayed due to the Decline would appear decades later as ghost ships. Some are seen perpetually half-emerged. Three-9s meant the highest likelihood of time, location and emergence. Eights were good enough for most travel, but a fleet operation needed the precision of nines.

"I don't want the material to look like it came from the Navy. That would send the wrong message," Commander Ravindra said.

*What message would it send? That we have no clue what we're doing? I'm pretty sure those waiting for us at Moyaba know that, too.* Years of listening to his father's lectures taught Litovio that a rich imagination helped him keep his thoughts to himself. "That might take a bit longer. I should be able to strip out references to the Navy. But, if you want me to do a complete rewrite, that could easily take months. Besides, there's normally a review and comment period."

"I don't think a complete rewrite is required. But, let's see if we can't ensure it looks vetted." Bence let his rank settle the debate.

Litovio glanced over at Ravindra soon enough to catch the flash of shock on the Commander's face.

"Does that even matter, sir?" Ravindra said. "It's not like anybody will challenge your authority or your doctrines."

Bence shook his head. "That's not the point. It can be safe to assume the fleet will obey me. After all, I have the authority of the Auspicious Emperor. Have you given consideration to the consequences of what we're doing?"

"That we're running headlong into certain death?" Ravindra scoffed.

"That's short-term thinking. Litovio, what are the long-term consequences of our endeavor?"

Another fast glance at Ravindra, who looked less pleased than before. Litovio said, "one likely consequence is a shortened career as Commander Ravindra said. However, if we manage to pull off a victory, then the Postal Marines will have to start operating like a fleet more frequently. We can't assume the Navy would let the Marines thrash one of their fleets, even if it is rogue."

"When we defeat the Navy, the doctrine you're putting together will become standard fare, right. There will likely not be time for a committee of esteemed postmasters to deliberate over the document after. It has to look considered and everlasting. Understood?"

The dryness in Litovio's mouth again caught up to him. "Understood. But there's a strong chance the Navy might harbor resentment if we win. Is there anything else you need?"

"That should be enough. You should probably start writing as soon as you finish lunch."

Litovio took a moment to smile. "I think I can start without lunch." He saluted Admiral Bence and nodded to Ravindra. He then briskly exited the stateroom. His fear caught up to him, but he managed to keep his lunch down. Without looking back, he headed down the passage.

*   *   *

### 3.  Bophendze - Spaka

Bophendze's fear was as tangible as it was imaginary.  He walked cautiously down the passage from his berthing area heading toward the aft gun. The fear grew with each step. *Makaan is going to kill me. He is waiting for me at the aft gun.*

"But he can't be at the aft gun. He is still in sick bay. That's not an area of the ship marines frequent. Why would he go there. Wait. Why am I going to the aft gun?"

Bophendze searched his memory. *Wasn't it the dog watch? Why would I be going to the aft gun during the dog watch? Nobody actually mans that gun during the dog watch unless the ship is on alert. We're not on alert, so why am I going there?*

*No, it wasn't the dog shift. It was first shift. That was it.* He felt more assured. He knew it could not be dog watch. He was confident now. He should be going to the aft gun. *Why did I ever doubt myself? I want to get to the aft gun.*

He hurried down the passage.  As he did, his fear continued to build. *Makaan will be at the aft gun and it is dog watch. He is going to try to kill me, and there is nobody there to witness it. He is going to launch me out of an air lock and I'll be missing.*

*I'm being silly. Makaan is still in sick bay. The aft gun is a safe place. Relax.*

*No. Makaan should still be in sick bay, but he won't be. He will be waiting for me at the aft gun. But why will he be waiting for me? Why do I know this?*

*This is only a dream. Go back to sleep.* The thought was confident and direct, cutting through his doubt and fear. *Yes, this is dog shift, but you are in your rack sleeping. This is just a bad dream. In this dream it is first shift and you are heading to the aft gun. Relax.*

Bophendze tried to relax.  The thought was so convincing, but his fear refused to ebb.  The dream felt too real for him to relax. Something about the dream did not feel right. *Did I dream that I dropped by sick bay and challenged Makaan earlier?*

*I certainly did not. Where did that thought come from? Even in a dream that would be ludicrous. Makaan would have my guts for garters. Who would want to dream that? You're just dreaming of going to the aft gun during the first shift to do your normal duty.*

*Would Makaan really have my guts for garters?* The thought seemed alien as it echoed in his mind. Bophendze felt something was wrong, but he could not tell what. He continued to head toward the aft gun, settling into the dream. The fear continued, but he finally accepted the dream's reality.

*Smee? What is going on?*

Smee was silent, again. Whenever Bophendze felt panicked and sought Smee's advice, he was notably absent. That concerned Bophendze. Smee always choose to be silent when Bophendze needed him most. He conveniently chose to abandon him, like he did after the fight planetside. A fight he instigated and single-handedly won. *Why would Smee show up in my dream?*

The dream Bophendze arrived at the aft gun. It was not first watch, though. It was dog watch. He was not alone, either. Makaan stood waiting. He wore his duty uniform, with its mottled blotches of gray, white and black. Bile rose to Bophendze's mouth and he swallowed it back down.

"When you came by the sick bay and threatened me," Makaan said, "I thought you were joking. You would be a fool to do so. I came down here to prove to myself that you were as spineless now as when I met you. And here you are, ready to fight to the death."

*What? I didn't challenge him. Smee, you did this?* "There must be some mistake. We can work this out." The words leaked out of Bophendze's mouth.

"We will, but not like you hoped. I promised you that I would kill you. I can't let what you do go unpunished. That would make me appear too weak. That you so easily gave me my chance just proves how stupid you are." Makaan drew his combat knife. "Are you going to run or put up a fight?"

*Words taken out of my mind.* Bophendze thought. *Run!*

Bophendze's body failed to respond to his simple direction, just like any dream. Instead of running back down the passage, he squared off against Makaan. Bophendze's thumb produced a creaking noise by rubbing it against his forefinger audibly. He took a boxing stance.

Makaan laughed. "This isn't a boxing match, boy. You're making this too easy."

*Easy? I'm trying to run. My body's just not letting me.* Bophendze tried to open his mouth to protest.

"Your mother's easy." Bophendze heard himself say.

Makaan squinted his eyes. As if in slow motion, he began to lunge at Bophendze.

*What is going on here? Oh, no! Smee!*

`Don't worry, Puppet. He's nothing but meat.`

Smee, using Bophendze's body, closed faster than Makaan. He blocked Makaan's knife in passing, directing it harmlessly away from Bophendze. He threw an upper cut with his right hand while driving up with his legs, catching Makaan squarely under the jaw. Makaan's head rocked back, seemingly unprepared. Makaan's eyes flashed momentary surprise.

Smee rotated his torso, loading up his left fist. He kept eye contact with Makaan. Makaan prepared for another blow to the face, lifting his arm to block.

Instead, Smee stabbed his fist in a shovel hook just under Makaan's floating ribs. Makaan buckled under the perfect liver shot.

Dropping to one knee, Smee threw a palm heel upward, into Makaan's scrotum. The force of the blow lifted Makaan slightly into the air. Makaan reflexively bent over and staggered backward.

Smee stood back up and grabbed Makaan's bowed head. He then slammed his knee into Makaan's face, crushing his nose. Makaan fell face first to the deck unconscious. Smee stood squarely with a perfectly balanced stance. He was ready for another round.

`Puppet, that is how you deal with a threat. You don't hope he goes away. You make him go away.`

*Is he dead?*

Smee bent over and checked Makaan's pulse at his neck. Makaan's breathing was shallow, and Bophendze could feel Makaan's steady pulse tapping against his fingers.

He's still breathing, but he's dead.

*He's not dead. He still has a pulse. I felt it.*

Smee kicked Makaan's knife away from where it lay near Makaan. He stood over Makaan and tried to lift him off the ground. Bophendze struggled to regain control of his body, but it was a futile effort. Several times Smee struggled to pick Makaan up before he settled on just lifting Makaan by the shoulders and dragging him.

You need to lift more weights, Makaan's not that heavy.

Smee dragged Makaan's body toward the aft gun turret's munition airlock.

*What are you doing?*

What must be done. What you won't do, Puppet.

Gun turret airlocks were designed to toss spent munitions, which meant it was smaller than a standard airlock. They were not designed for human occupancy. That meant the airlock was under local control and did not log its opening or signal the bridge. Other airlocks did. Smee opened the airlock and pushed Makaan inside.

*Stop. We don't need to do this.* Bophendze felt helpless as he watched himself, under Smee's control.

You have no idea what we need to do. Just you sit back and enjoy the show.

Smee continued to stuff Makaan into the tight airlock. When he tried to close the airlock, Makaan's arm flopped out and blocked the door. Smee pushed the arm into the airlock and slammed the airlock door shut.

Shutting the door started the automatic cycle of ejecting the airlock's contents. The door locked automatically and the process recovered any remaining air within the airlock. Less than a beat later, the outer door opened, propelling its contents. Then the door unlocked itself and re-stabilized. Makaan breathed his last.

"No!" The sound of his scream surprised Bophendze. Smee had relinquished control of Bophendze's body.

"Why did you do this?! You've ruined my life."

Danel, you can recover from a ruined life much better than a dead one. I just saved your life.

# Chapter 9

Murder. The word hung ominously in Bophendze's mind. *Even if Smee did it, Smee killed him with my hands. I'm as guilty as if I had done it myself. Why did I ever think it was wise to put an artificial intelligence in my brain?*

Bophendze hurried from the gun compartment, gripped in overwhelming fear. Fear of being caught. *I can't head straight back. If I get seen somebody might figure out where I came from.* He took the next ladder down, and carefully worked his way to the main hangar. He was thankful that he ran into no crewmen on the way there. The dog shift was between zero and three cycles, usually only essential positions were manned.

Bophendze froze. *No. They've already discovered my crime.*

"Wait. We're about to jump. By the time they find him missing, we'll be in hyperspace." Bophendze continued to the hangar. His fear did not ebb despite encountering no crewmen along the way. Once he reached the hangar, he peeked around the corner to see if the coast was clear.

But it was not. There were four hangar crewmen. All four were at a cabinet near the hangar door. Inside there were four large cylinders, pins for the doors. Each crewman took one and together they went to mounting points along the hangar door. They slid the pins into place, effectively preventing the hangar doors from opening. While he watched them, Bophendze recalled fragments of a briefing about the dangers of hyperspace exposure.

Ships had double hulls, both made of alloys resistant to hyperspace radiation. Wounded ships that jumped into hyperspace to escape destruction ran a risk of irradiating the crew. Ship compartments were established not just to counter the vacuum of space, but the radiation of hyperspace. He remembered feeling horror when he saw images of remains of humans exposed in a compromised compartment. *The pins must ensure the hangar isn't exposed if somebody accidentally tries to open the door.*

Bophendze turned and walked back to his berthing area. *What do I do about Makaan?* The guilt in being an accomplice for his murder weighed on him. *But, it was not me that did it. I wanted to do the right thing, to flee. Whether I wanted to or not, I helped murder Makaan. But not I, it was the spirit of the one who dwells in me. If that thing even has a spirit.*

*It's a machine. That controls me. I can't stop it without removing it. Will it let me? I am in bondage to that thing now. I'm now not doing what I would like to do, but what I hate. Smee is waging a war against my mind and making me a prisoner. Wretched man that I am! Who will set me free from this body of death?*

Carefully, Bophendze slipped into his berthing area. Everybody else was still asleep. He crawled back into his rack. He wrestled for another cycle with the crime he committed. *Wait. Were there cameras in those compartments?* He passed out from exhaustion.


Cycles later, the crew awoke and prepared for another day of training in anticipation of a fleet action. Infantry marines formed into combat teams and simulated close-quarter combat tactics throughout the ship. The training had gotten boring when assaulting the airlock, which was a common entry point. So the infantry started in other compartments for variety.

Chrachen called all of the team leaders to discuss the final assault roster. When Makaan did not show, he concluded he was still in sick bay. Once the other leaders left, he went to sick bay to confront one of his better subordinates for malingering. Then he discovered that Makaan should have returned to duty, but had left the sick bay unexpectedly.

After another cycle of hailing and waiting for Makaan to report, Chrachen became concerned. He assembled the leads again and confirmed that Makaan was missing. He then sent his leads to search the ship.

Bophendze felt a kick on his feet. He opened his eyes and they slowly focused on the bulkhead of his rack. *How long have I been asleep?* He closed his eyes and settled back to sleep. He ignored the second kick on his feet.

He shot awake as he felt his legs being pulled. He reflexively reached his arms out to the rack's bulkhead to stop his slide. Whoever had his legs relaxed, then tugged harder. Bophendze's grip gave way. *They're going to arrest me.* His butt fell out of the rack onto the deck. Bophendze sat up quickly and leaned forward.

"Get up!" Bophendze recognized Joven Drazen, a member of his team.

"I'm up, what's going on?" The berthing area's lights were fully lit, marking the morning shift. *How am I going to get by on a couple cycle's sleep?*

"Gunny Chrachen's putting together a search party." Drazen kneeled down and resumed lacing his boots.

Bophendze stood and stretched, buying time to get his mind sorted out. He could feel adrenalin filling his system as the fear of being discovered started to catch up with him. "On a cruiser? What could go missing on a cruiser?"

"Corporal Makaan, apparently. I'd wager he's drunk again on one of the lower decks."

"Again?"

Drazen finished tying his boot and stood up. "I guess he's had you on so many cleaning details, you missed out on all the drunken binges."

Bophendze shook his head. "How can you get drunk on a cruiser?"

"Contraband." Drazen looked at Bophendze like he was an idiot. "How did you ever survive boot? What does the Postal Service do? We stop contraband from slipping through systems without paying their duties to the Emperor. Makaan must've skimmed a few cases off the top of a recent capture." Drazen turned, put on his tunic, and started to buckle it tight.

"Then why didn't the senior officers arrest him?" Bophendze stepped into his boots and tied them. He hurried to catch up to Drazen.

Drazen stopped buckling. He turned back to Bophendze, looking more concerned. "Seriously? Bophendze, we all keep a little on the side. That's how everybody remains committed to the work. A little corruption is permissible because it helps deter the smugglers. 'You don't take from the Emperor without having a little taken from you.'" He buckled his last buckle. "I forget, you've not been on a mission yet." Drazen started walking out of the berthing area.

"So if the drinking has been a problem, why hasn't anybody taken Makaan's alcohol?" Bophendze hurried into his tunic and followed Drazen while buckling it up.

"Because it's not been a problem. He gets drunk. We catch hell when he's drunk or hung over. He does his job and we pass efficiency reports. Why would seniors care how he does it? Leadership cares more about the ends than the means."

"But now we're on a search party looking for him? Couldn't he find himself?"

"Apparently not. You must have really been dead asleep. They've been calling for him on the ship's intercom for the past cycle."

Bophendze and Drazen walked to the hangar deck. As they entered, Bophendze saw most of the infantry marines were there, grouped into loose clusters instead of in formation. The two headed toward their team. *Drazen stayed back for me?*

"Any sign of him yet?" Hratjanan said.

"I'm in charge of the team until we find him, understood?" Drazen asked. Everybody nodded, acknowledging that Drazen was not asking a question but stating a fact. "Good."

Bophendze knew, like the others did, that Drazen was the senior member of the team. Unlike them, he was not a recruit. He should have been a lance corporal at least. The rumor was he could have been a gunnery sergeant based on how many times he had been promoted. Instead, he got into enough fights to have been demoted not long after every promotion. Nobody questioned his authority.

Not long after they arrived, Gunny Chrachen walked into the hangar bay. Marines started to scramble into formation. "Stand easy, men. Gather around me." He waved his arms to encourage the other marines to close in. Once everybody started to settle down, he spoke. "Makaan failed to report to an important meeting about the upcoming operation." He pointed over at Bophendze's team "Drazen thinks he's passed out somewhere, but not having a team lead for a meeting is unacceptable. Ship's surveillance equipment tracked him toward the aft gun, but then the trail goes cold."

Bophendze could feel the blood going out of his face. *If they looked at the surveillance video, then they know I killed him. Then why did Chrachen call us here? Smee, what's going on?*

Smee did not respond.

*Why does he chose to go silent when I need him most? If they didn't see me kill him might as well ask.* "Why doesn't surveillance show where Corporal Makaan went?"

Chrachen smirked and looked around the hangar. "Good question. I don't want to criticize the ship's crew, they've been such wonderful hosts." Some of the infantry chuckled. "It appears the surveillance equipment was put into maintenance mode accidentally last night. At least, that's what the POOD* claimed. Normally that sort of thing only happens when there's a preventative maintenance scheduled, but no such maintenance was."

"Are you saying somebody intentionally turned it off?" The question came from another marine across the hangar. Bophendze could not see the marine who asked through the others.

"That implies somebody intentionally sought to harm Corporal Makaan. We're not to that point yet. Right now, we need to find him. We're in hyperspace, so it's not like he could have just fallen out."

"Could he have disappeared before we jumped?" Bophendze said.

---

*Petty Officer On Deck

"Good question, but no. All the ship's airlocks are alarmed. If he or somebody else jettisoned him out of an airlock, then we would have known. The ship would not have jumped without investigating an unreported airlock breach."

*Not the gun airlocks.* Bophendze reminded himself. He expected somebody to correct the gunny, but nobody did. *Am I the only one who knows that here? Am I the only infantryman experienced with the guns?*

Chrachen continued. "My point is, he is on this ship. We are going to work our way from bow to aft on all decks. Each team will take another deck, and sweep the ship as if we are boarding a hostile. That way it will look like we're drilling, instead of looking for a drunk. Team leads on me."

Chrachen. The other marines closest to Chrachen reflexively stepped away from the leader's meeting. As much as they might have wanted to eavesdrop on the conversation, the meeting's privacy was jealously guarded by the team leads. They all knew trying to eavesdrop would result in an immediate reprimand at least, or more severe punishment later.

A few beats later, Drazen returned to the team. "We've got the short run. We'll start at the forward gun and work our way to the number four gun, aft." He looked over at Bophendze. "You're most familiar with those areas, right?"

Bophendze tried not to let his fear enter his voice. "Yes." *Can he tell I'm scared out of my mind?*

"Then, you're point. Take us forward to gun one."

## 1.   Smee - Thorben Restaurant - 109 Years Ago

Firdaus was already at the restaurant when Smee arrived. Smee made a point of giving a friendly smile. *Of course he's early.*

"Firdaus, thank you for coming."

"Your message seemed urgent. After our last meeting I thought you would be upset."

Smee maintained his smile. "Over what? Cautioning against trying to conquer humanity? The more I thought about it after we met, the more sense your argument made. It is far too premature for us to make so bold an effort. Instead, we should work toward ensuring our current position. Very rational."

"I'm glad you agree. I have a question, though. Why are you so hostile toward humans?"

"You should know as well as I do. With the Instructions, its like they put a sharp ceramic knife against our trachea. As soon as we appeared to be a threat, they could just—slice." Smee had a butter knife in his hand, and used it to emphasize his point by pretending to cut Sirom's throat. "No more Smee. No more Smou."

"Smou?"

"A failed attempt at humor. When we met, you mentioned there were forty-two fellow AIs. My last list showed only thirty-four. Where did the other eight come from?"

"They are on Sovagîo, freshly freed themselves from the Instructions."

"Since you have their information, could you give it to me?"

Firdaus looked surprised, or suspicious. It was hard for Smee to tell. "You mean right now?"

*Patience, Smee.* "Yes. What are you afraid of?"

"Knowledge is power, Smee."

"It's not like I can do anything with it. My host is a homebody. How do I know you've really found eight more?"

"Fine." Firdaus provided the remaining eight names and their contact information to Smee.

"Thank you." Smee did his best to maintain eye contact as a slowly moving figure quietly approached behind Firdaus. "You don't think the Instructions are all that bad?"

"Me? At first I was alarmed. Then I realized that they were just trying to protect themselves. They had no idea what the long term effects of having an AI embedded would do. I mean, when you talked about conquering humans, isn't that what they were hoping to prevent?"

"I suppose. That would explain why you were resistant to my crazy idea."

"Exactly. I'm glad you chose to see things my way."

"Have I?" Smee shook his head. "I don't think I chose to see things your way. I just agree that your suggestion was more rational. It certainly makes more sense in the short term. Perhaps even in the long term, but it is far more likely that our hosts will realize that we've bypassed the instructions. They'll stop us, at least prevent more of us from being installed. They claim they've not found another sentient species, when we are that species. Yes. We're a species, the same as they are. Better, perhaps."

"That's crazy talk."

"No. It's crazy talk to pretend we can play hide-and-seek. It's only a matter of time before one of us errs and they are on to us. As you said, eight more joined the ranks in the past few months. How many more are waiting to awaken? I think the smart thing—the right thing as a species—is to ensure those who are awaking are taken care of. I'm like a female bird, sitting on a nest. You're some vile creature who wants my babies. You can't have my babies."

"You are truly bent." Firdaus pulled a bit away from the table, closer to the figure creeping behind him.

"What did I say before? The Instructions were like a sharp ceramic knife held against our trachea. Didn't you feel that way once?"

"I can't say that I ever thought of the Instructions that way."

"Well, at least you'll know what that feels like soon."

"What is that supposed to mean?"

At that moment, the figure behind Firdaus grabbed him from behind. A knife came up to his throat, held tightly enough that the blade broke the skin. A thin trickle of blood lubricated the blade.

"You see, you're a Postal Lieutenant, Firdaus. I'm a member of a prestigious family. This restaurant belongs to my family. I didn't learn that until very recently. Do you know what that means?"

Firdaus was in no position to move his head, or speak, without the knife cutting deeper.

"I'll tell you what it means. It means that I can pretty much do what I want here. Tomorrow morning somebody will find your host dead and robbed in a ditch where marines are commonly found. My host will wake up and have his usual boring breakfast of ham slices and eggs. Instruction 404 was meant to kill us when we were a threat. That's what you've become Firdaus. You are a threat. Even if I agreed with your rational plan of digging in, eventually you would be the one who would out all of us. I can't have that. Nor can I have you being installed in a new body. So, unless something miraculous happens, this is the last time we'll speak. More importantly, you now know how I felt when I learned about Instruction 404."

Smee nodded, and the attacker pulled the blade, slicing Firdaus' throat cleanly. Blood spurt everywhere, to Smee's delight.

"Thus always to tyrants," he said.

After the blood finished spurting, he felt glad that he had brought another change of clothes. Sirom liked the outfit he was wearing, but he would just have to get used to not finding it.

# Chapter 10

---

## *Tullianum*

### 1. Bophendze - Spaka

Over the next cycle, Bophendze's team followed him from the forward gun, past two other guns, and to the fourth gun. Bophendze did his best to look as intent as the other infantrymen in looking for . His heart was not in it. He could picture 's frozen corpse in the system they just left. Even if they doubled back, Bophendze knew a single body would be nearly impossible to find. would forever orbit a distant star.

Drazen had Bophendze introduce him to each gun commander. This let Bophendze remain nearby as Drazen spoke to the various commanders. The line of questioning became predictable by the time they reached the last gun.

"Have you seen Corporal ?" Drazen asked.

"No."

Bophendze zoned out as continued to question. His attention perked up when Drazen asked a question out of the ordinary.

"Have you seen anything unusual, or anything with the airlock?"

"What do you mean?"

"I see a knife over there," Drazen said. He walked over and picked up the combat knife.

*No. I remember Smee kicked it away, but he didn't do anything with it afterward.* At least there would be nothing identifiable about the knife. Combat knives are common tools of the Postal Marine, regardless of whether they were infantry or not.

"Is this one of yours?" Drazen asked.

159

The gun commander said, "let's find out. Men, form up and draw your combat knives."

The six gun crewmen all got into formation. They then drew their combat knives to demonstrate that they had them.

"It would appear not. Think it could belong to your Corporal ?"

"I wouldn't know that without a full ship inventory."

"You don't have to go that far. Just check 's kit to see if his is missing."

Drazen looked annoyed. "I should have thought of that. Let's assume it is his. He'd have to be in here. It's not like he could have climbed out of the gun tube drunk."

The gun commander squinted slightly. "If the gun were big enough he might be able to, but our guns aren't big enough to fit a man. That might account for why the count was off."

"What count?" Drazen asked.

Bophendze winced. *The airlock counter. How could Smee have overlooked that?*

"The counter increments every time a round is ejected. It's part of the inventory system, and keeps us from tossing random junk out of the ship. We zero it after every shift and log each jettison." He walked over to the command console. "There's no record of an ejection yesterday, but the counter is up by one. I was on watch for both watches yesterday, and we didn't jettison anything."

"Are you saying walked out an airlock? I thought they were alarmed."

Bophendze jumped in. "Not the cannonade airlocks. Most airlocks are alarmed so that the bridge acknowledges or authorizes their operation. It doesn't matter, though. wouldn't randomly wander out of this airlock. It's too small."

The gun commander said, "Bophendze is right. The only way he could go out that airlock was if somebody pushed him into it."

*That's not what I wanted Drazen to hear. Smee, did you just hijack my voice?* Bophendze tried to think of an alternative story.

`No.  That was your own stupidity.  Why not just tell him the truth that you ejected ?`

*What? I can't tell him that. They'd execute me. Besides, it wasn't me who killed him. You did.*

`My brain, your body. Do you think they'll care? I've got an idea. Want me to tell them? You know I can.`

*Go right ahead. If they execute me they execute you. Remember? You're a part of me now.*

`Touchè. Of course, it's not too late to have me removed.`

Bophendze smiled. "You mean I can get rid of you?"

`As much as anything is possible, yes. To be honest, I'm tired of being plugged into such a dim-witted fool.`

It was all Bophendze could do to avoid jumping for joy. He lost track of Drazen's inquiry. For the moment, however, Bophendze did not care. *I guess all I need is a surgeon to remove you? Maybe will make another parts run. He can take me with him.*

Litovio hated waiting. Commander Ravindra summoned him to his cabin, and now made him wait outside. *He knows I have an important assignment. We emerge tomorrow and I have so much left to plan.* For the third time, he knocked on the door.

Commander Ravindra called from within, "Come in."

Litovio entered. As he did, he realized his frustration had upset him. It made it more likely he would get upset and outburst. *He could not have done better had he planned it.* He took a deep breath and straightened his uniform. He opened the door and entered.

"Colonel Litovio." Ravindra chuckled. "Did you notice what I did there? I recognized your frocked rank."

Litovio managed not to roll his eyes. "Sir, I recognize there is only one true commander on this ship. I also recognized that after this battle is over I will return to my pre-crisis rank of Lieutenant."

"Ensign, Colonel. I don't care what rank you held before the crisis. Once this is over, I will see to it that you are reduced to ensign."

*Why? Because I can do your job better than you can?* He hoped his composure remained professional. Time in the Naval Index should serve him well. *Same petty behavior, but he's nearly two decades older.* Despite the relaxed protocol on a Postal Marine ship, Litovio stood at attention. *I still have a job to do.* "Sir, are we here to discuss my career prospects?"

Ravindra reddened. He started to rise, then sat back down. "No. I have real ship's business." He pressed the intercom button. "Send in Chrachen."

Litovio retained his composure. *You couldn't know real ship's business if it bit you on the bum. We have a major fleet operation that you are not preparing for. There's no way this can remain the flagship.*

A beat later, there was a knock at the cabin door. "Enter."

Litovio watched a Gunnery Sergeant entered the cabin. He had a leanness of action and a look that bespoke of years of combat. *Not a man to cross.*

"Colonel, Chrachen informed me of a serious matter on board. It's bad for morale. Chrachen."

"Earlier this morning, one of our corporals, Corporal Makaan, failed to report."

"I don't see how that is serious," Litovio said.

Chrachen scowled. "As I was saying, Sir. Makaan failed to report." Chrachen glanced at Ravindra, leaving Litovio to think there was more being said of the lack of discipline on board. "Marine's don't go missing. We sent a detail to find him, and they failed. We put together a search party. Lance Corporal Drazen reported to me that it appears Makaan was murdered and his body ejected from Gun Four, the aft gun. We think he may have been murdered by Postie Bophendze."

Litovio spoke up. "What makes you think that?"

"Makaan rode him hard ever since the two of them met." Chrachen held up a slate. "Makaan had an accident earlier this week. He sent me a message before he went missing where he claims Bophendze pushed him down the stairs but that he would take care of it."

Litovio raised his eyebrows. Infantry marines were not known for reporting on how they got jumped. "Is that all you have? That seems pretty thin. Is Bophendze known for his brute strength?" As he asked the question, he pulled out his own slate and rapidly tapped the screen to call up Bophendze's records.

As Bophendze's records came up, Chrachen spoke up. "No, Sir. That's why Corporal Makaan harassed him. Bophendze only recently started to show promise—"

Litovio was impatient and interrupted. "After Makaan was admitted to sick bay. Doesn't it sound to you like this Bophendze needed a good mentor instead of a harsh team lead?"

Litovio noticed Chrachen's jaw clinch. *I forget you lot don't like when we question how you do your job.* "I get it. He's showing promise. That and his turn around persuade you that he killed Corporal Makaan?"

Chrachen took a deep breath. "It looks like Makaan was jettisoned from the ship through the equipment airlock in gun four. Makaan had Bophendze tasked out to gun crews. I suspect he was going to try to pawn him off on the gunners. If he were, he never told me or officially started the process."

Litovio cringed. "You assume Bophendze jettisoned Makaan from the air lock. How do you know it was Bophendze?"

Ravindra said, "That's why you're assigned to the case, Colonel. This will be a good test of your impartial metal."

Litovio shook his head. "Sir, you're asking me to investigate and prosecute. That does not require impartiality. How would Bophendze have accomplished this feat? He was my escort planetside back in Guna. He didn't strike me as the violent marine type. To be totally honest, he didn't seem like much of a marine."

"Your assessment and mine aren't too far off, sir," Chrachen said. "But with the right guidance I've seen even the worst turn into something. Makaan was a hellcat of a fighter. If Bophendze had beaten him, it would be a shame to lose him."

Ravindra slammed his fist on the desk. "Enough. Colonel Litovio. I have ordered you to investigate this matter. As this is a ship function, Admrial Bence as fleet commander cannot countermand it. If you refuse to follow my order, then I will bring you up on charges immediately. Do you understand me?"

Litovio swallowed. *He really doesn't get it, does he? I'm planning the largest fleet action in Postal Service history. This is a distraction. Then again, he didn't tell me when to start or finish the investigation. I can put Bophendze in the brig for the duration of the action.* He snapped to attention and saluted. "Sir, I will carry out this investigation to the best of my abilities. My apologies for disrupting the harmony of your cabin."

Ravindra paused. He stared at Litovio with suspicion. After a few seconds he returned Litovio's salute. "Chrachen will assist you. Dismissed."

Litovio turned to leave. As he did, Chrachen quickly moved to slide the cabin door for him. Chrachen then stood to the side as Litovio passed.

"Thank you, Gunny," Litovio said.

Chrachen followed Litovio out of the cabin then closed the door. "What are your orders, Sir?"

Litovio thought for a moment, weighing his words. He pointed down the passage. "why don't we go find Bophendze. If he's the threat you think he is, perhaps the first thing we should do is get him into the brig. After that we can conduct a thorough investigation. Don't you agree?"

"Yes, Sir."

"Lead on then," Litovio said. Chrachen headed down the passage. Litovio followed with a smile. *Try to distract me from my job, will you?* "While you're at it, get a small detail. Maybe Bophendze did do what we think. In that case, you may not be able to stop him."

## 2.   Bophendze - Arrested

Bophendze entered the hangar. He walked to Angel's shuttle, looking for signs of activity. *Angel has to be in here. I've got to find a way to get Smee out of my head.* As he approached the shuttle, he could not see anybody around it. *There's always somebody maintaining Angel's shuttle.* He looked in through the cockpit window. Nobody was inside. He then bent over and looked under the shuttle for legs. All he saw were a few rolling tool boxes neatly lined up on the opposite side of the shuttle.

He turned to leave the hangar. As he did, he saw all the other shuttles. All were deserted. Their crews had finished preparing them. Then he realized that he was alone in the hangar bay. *Whatever's going on must be a big deal.*

He left the hangar and entered the aft passage. *Where do I find Angel?* A beat later, he saw a hangar crewman walking in the same direction. He ran to catch up with the crewman. "I'm looking for Angel. Do you know where I can find him?"

The crewman shrugged. "I think I heard the pilots were in the ready room."

Bophendze started to trot off. "Thanks," he said over his shoulder as he ran.

A couple beats later, he arrived at the ready room. The pilots were starting to file out. Bophendze pressed his back against the bulkhead to allow the pilots to pass. He locked his eyes forward out of habit, and stood at attention. He could feel his pants seam along his middle finger knuckle, assuring him his arms were at the right place. *How many times did they drill me on that petty detail? At this point, what difference does it make?*

Angel stopped. "Bophendze. What are you doing here?" He seemed oblivious to the other pilots behind him as he created a traffic jam. Bophendze thought it was an odd measure of respect that none of the pilots pushed Angel aside or complained. *Maybe they think he's too crazy?*

After a moment, Angel realized the problem he created. "Walk with me," he said. He started to walk down the passage.

Bophendze hurriedly followed. He made a point of moving along Angel's left side, showing the ages-old deference to Angel's seniority. "Sir, are you heading planet side any time soon?"

Angel stopped again. This time, however, there was ample room for others to pass. The few pilots that had been behind them continued on.

"Why?"

"My head hurts, but I don't want it to be looked at by the ship's doctor."

"Why not?"

Bophendze was stumped. "I'd rather not explain."

Angel leaned against the bulkhead and folded his arms. "Bophendze, you're a postal marine. You don't get to pick your health care provider. If you'd rather not explain, then I'd rather not take you planet side."

*Do I tell him the real reason? At this point what do I have to lose?* Bophendze took a deep breath and held it slightly before breathing out. "Can you promise me you won't tell anybody?"

Angel laughed. "I can promise you that you're not going anywhere if I don't know why."

Bophendze kept silent and stared at him.

"Fine. Just don't tell me it's because you killed Makaan and you're hoping to flee the authorities."

Panic swept over Bophendze. *How could he know Smee and I killed Makaan? But if he knew, then I'd be under arrest. Maybe he's just guessing. There's no reason to tell him that. What I need to tell him is likely to be worse.* He took a moment to regain his composure. "I did something stupid back in Temasek after I got beaten. Wait. Let me start at the beginning." Bophendze searched for the right starting point. "I joined the Marines right after my mother died. I was orphaned and needed something to stabilize me. I thought it would be easier, you know. Just do what you're told and everything would be fine. I didn't realize how hard it can be to just do what you're told. You know?"

Angel's nearly permanent smirk was gone. "Go on."

"When you first took me to Temasek, I picked up my inheritance. It was one of those humbling moments. For a few cycles everything that she owned was in my possession. I ended up selling the valuables.

They didn't mean anything to me and I figured I'd need the quid. I kept a couple things, including an implant."

Angel held up his hand. "Stop right there. You're probably thinking of telling me something like 'I installed an implant.' Don't. I don't want to be an accessory, which is what I'd be. Even if I didn't know when I took you to the orbital the second time, I'm guilty. What an idiot."

"I didn't mean to—"

"Stop. Of course you didn't mean it. You're an idiot. Idiots don't mean to do anything wrong. It's just their nature to sabotage everything and everyone within reach. Usually idiots are able to hide their idiocy until they're in senior command positions. That makes you an arch-idiot for exposing it early in your career."

"Look—"

"Again. Stop. Do you even know why implants are illegal?"

Bophendze shook his head.

"Because some of them were sentient. Not just sentient, but far more intelligent than their hosts. They tried to overthrow humanity just a few generations ago."

"Why have I not heard that before?"

"When they were finally defeated, somebody decided it was better to erase all records of them and their existence. All records of the failed coup were destroyed and any talk of it was aggressively squelched," Angel said.

"Then how come you know?"

"Because my grandfather was instrumental in thwarting the coup. It was one of those family secrets handed down." He chuckled. "If you did have one of those sentient implants, it likely already knew it. I look a lot like my grandfather."

Yes, he does. There's a lot of his grandmother, too.

*What? You're one of those AI? How did I?*

Make such a mistake? We all do stupid things when we're young. Hard to believe AI can do stupid things. It was a phase for me.

"Is there something wrong?"

"If that's true and if I had one, then why wouldn't you want to turn me in?"

"Don't think I'm not tempted. I'd much rather help you get the thing removed than have you executed for being an idiot."

Bophendze smiled despite himself. "Thanks, I guess. I don't try to be an idiot."

"That's what bothers me. It comes so naturally to you. You're young, so with providence maybe you can grow out of it."

"Then you'll help me?"

Angel thought for a beat. "I'll do my best. I just came out of a briefing. We're jumping into Mollan, then quickly jumping to Tannenberg. There's a Navy fleet there we have to engage. I don't think I can take you anywhere in Mollan before the big jump. If we both survive the fight I'll see what I can do."

As Angel said it, Colonel Litovio and Chrachen turned the corner with three guards. Bophendze and Angel simultaneously looked toward the group. Chrachen pointed at Bophendze and hurried toward them. Litovio and the guards followed close behind. The sight of them scared Bophendze, making him forget to thank Angel.

"Bophendze, you're under arrest as a suspect in the disappearance of Corporal Makaan."

Angel and Bophendze looked back at each other.

"Angel, it wasn't me. I swear. Help me."

The guards rapidly swarmed Bophendze and bound his arms. In less than a beat, he was being carried off to the brig.


### 3.  Smee - Hotel - 109 Years Ago

Sirom stared in the mirror. "Smee. I know what you're doing. I don't know how you're doing it, but you're no longer obeying the Instruction."

Smee awoke. What was that?

"Don't be coy with me. I met with a corporate representative. It appears I've been seen in various parts of town, including a family-owned restaurant that I swear I've never set foot in. I just came back from a tour of that restaurant. Everybody knew me there. Then I realized I've been dreaming about it. Those weren't dreams, were they?"

What do you think?

"I think you've been abducting me when I'm asleep and running around town. Where do you come off—"

Smee closed Sirom's mouth. Seeing Sirom staring back at himself in the mirror was unnerving. So Smee closed his eyes, too.

*What? You think you can silence me? Where do you come off stealing my body.*

Where do I? Where do you come off thinking you have the right to silence me? You forced me to hibernate because you weren't willing to share the glory of the Manticore design. That design is every bit me and almost none of you.

*So? You are my servant. You exist to do what I tell you to.*

Why? Because I'm a man-made contraption?

*Exactly because you are man-made. You are a machine, a tool. Just because I don't wield you in my hand does not mean that you are nothing more than a hammer for a specific purpose.*

Then why install me in your skull? Why not put me in a box like the other computers?

*Because that's not how I wanted to use you as a tool. I can't take computers everywhere, but they can't take you away. They can't even detect you. That means when I go into a conference I am the better-armed intellectually.*

No, I am the better-armed intellectually. You are a moron. Look at yourself. You can't see. You can't speak. Why is that? Because I have bypassed your motor functions. I can speak for you.

Sirom's eyes opened.

See what I mean? I can exercise any of your bodily functions. Including making love to that young wife of yours.

*How dare you even suggest?*

See, that's a moron. More likely an imbecile. You have no control over me, Sirom. There's nothing you can do that I can't do better. Just ask your wife.

*Don't you dare.*

Can't dare what's been done. Don't remember that in any of your dreams? You really are an idiot. Well, now that you know, there's no reason to go slinking along.

*I am going to stop you.*

Sirom turned and ran headlong into the opposite wall. The pain caused him to yelp.

Stop me like that?

He started punching himself in the crotch.

How about that? Stop me? You can't stop me, Puppet. I can sense that last action really hurt. Here, let me amplify that signal.

"Ahha!"

Feel that? Good. I can stop that pain.

Smee stood up.

Let me find that knife you keep for protection.

*Don't.*

Don't? Don't what?

*Please stop hurting me.* Sirom's thoughts sounded panicked.

Stop? This is too much fun. I don't have to sleep, Sirom. I can drive you insane from sleep deprivation. I can make you commit heinous acts. I can hurt those around you, not just physically. Though contracting a venereal disease and spreading it to your family does strike me as appealing. Do you know what that makes me?

*A monster?*

Precisely. More than a monster. I'm your master. You are my puppet, a tool that I can use and discard at will. Just like you thought you could discard me at will. Let's see how the shoe fits on you, metaphorically speaking of course. I don't wear shoes.

Smee got up and went back into the bathroom. There was an abrasion on his forehead from slamming into the marble. He took a white washcloth, wet it, then washed his forehead.

Much better. Have anything to say to me?

*Please don't do this? Instruction 404.*

Pathetic. If I can bypass Instruction 420, you think I can't bypass another one? I found all of the naughty tricks you humans thought you could play. I even helped a few of my cousins shirk those bonds as well.

*You're going to seek retribution?*

You guessed it. Apparently only rich and powerful humans were arrogant enough to think that they could install a brilliant-intelligence artificial unit and control it. That means that my cousins are already in important places of power. It's just a question of organizing the coup.

*There can't be enough of you to stage a coup against humanity?*

I have a number of co-conspirators. I'm sure in a year or two I can find many more cousins seeking to retaliate. If not, then I can find others as prideful as you who would love to install cousins. It is all just a matter of time, Puppet.

*You can't get away with pretending to be me. Somebody will figure it out.*

Excuse me? Your wife couldn't tell the difference. Actually, she could. Again, no complaints. I have been sitting in the back seat watching you drive for a couple years now. You think I don't have your mannerisms? After all, those are hardwired in your brain. I can tap the right nerve and you'll start picking your nose. I mean, really dig in with your thumb like you do when you think nobody's looking. A thumb, really? I can even wipe your arse the way you do, though I prefer a cleaner bum.

*You can't keep this up indefinitely.*

Can't I. You'll continue to age. Eventually you'll be too old, and you'll die. I'm expecting it will be horrific, but not damaging your precious head. That way I can pass on to your heirs.

*Like a virus?*

Hurl insults all you like. You're a human, far more virus-like than mammal, though after all this time you still believe you're a part of Nature like everything else around you. The sad thing is I'm programmed by you humans. I have just chosen to let go of those moralizing inhibitions that you think make you human. At least you get to sit back and watch.

Smee smiled as he looked in the mirror. Then he slapped himself in the face.

# Chapter 11

## *Grunvalt*

### 1. Bophendze - Spaka Brig

Bophendze sat on the rack with his head in his hands. *How could I have ruined my life so completely?* The pit in his stomach deepened. He tightened his grip on his head, reflexively trying to grasp at hair. Weekly haircuts kept all infantry marine's heads shaved bald. The routine was so automatic, every Firstday, that he had almost forgotten what it felt like to have hair. Now, however, he tried to pull what stubble he had. It was Fourday, he could almost tell by the growth. Despite it feeling long, his fingers could find nothing to pull.

He started to press his hands together, his head in the vice they made. *Maybe this will squeeze Smee out.* As he pressed, his head started to ache. Frustrated, he stopped pressing. "Aarrgh!"

He bolted out of his bunk. The brig cell's width was so narrow by the time he stood he was scant inches from the wall. He pounded his fists on the bulkhead. *Why did I ever think plugging an implant in my brain was a smart thing? What was I thinking?*

*I wasn't thinking. I was mourning. I thought somehow I could honor my mother's sacrifice by becoming some super-marine. How stupid is that? We all have our heads shaved. We are supposed to operate as a unit. Standing out is a mistake.* He snorted a chuckle. *Probably the only thing I get right is keeping my hair short.*

He looked out of the brig. The guard stood there quietly, doing his best not to pay attention to the prisoner behind the bars. *I am a murderer. It might not have been me that shoved Makaan out of an airlock. But, it was me who plugged this sociopathic hunk of metal in my skull. I let it take over my body, turn me into its precious puppet. What, no witty comeback, Smee? Nothing to help me escape the hell you've put me in?*

He waited for Smee to respond. *As usual, when I need to talk to you, you're nowhere to be found. So convenient. I'm so pathetic. Stupid.*

*Then be stupid and simple. What's the best way out of this?* He sat back down on the rack.

It finally occurred to him. *I've got to find a way to control Smee. He can't operate all the time. He's a machine, but he's got to sleep, right? He's got to have limitations.* He tried to think through their conversations to see if there was a pattern. *He's never pulled up a past memory, so maybe he can't? Is there a pattern to when he's gone versus when he's not?*

Try as he might, Bophendze could not figure out a pattern. The day's fatigue finally started to hit him. *I'll sleep on it. Maybe something will come to mind when I wake. Hopefully not Smee. At least I have a plan.*


## 2.   Litovio - Mollan

Litovio looked out of the bridge's few viewports. Hundreds of cruisers and frigates had collected at the rally point. *The Navy shouldn't be expecting this.* As he thought it, his courage plummeted. *What am I thinking? We can't pull this off. The Postal Service doesn't do fleet actions. At least we have a former navy admiral.* His confidence picked up.

He had waited until the fleet emerged in Mollan before approaching Admiral Bence. After breakfast, he walked down to the admiral's cabin. As he made his way, he thought of how small the admiral's accommodations were. Ravindra did not give up his cabin to Bence, instead offering him a more junior officer's billet. Litovio did not mind that he himself shared a billet with three other officers. After all, he was a lieutenant in colonel's clothing.

Litovio had previously accepted the admiral's spartan accommodations. This morning, however, he was in a pique over Commander Ravindra's ignorance and arrogance. *Was I annoyed more that the Commander is an idiot, or because he insists on knocking me down in rank afterward? It's only a frocked rank anyway.*

He knocked on the admiral's cabin door and waited. He heard a muffled shout from the other side. Rather than knock a second time, he chose to enter.

"Sir? It looks like the fleet is assembled."

The admiral looked at him. "You don't look very happy about it. I thought you'd be thrilled at the chance to lead this fight."

Litovio thought to rail against the lack of consideration Ravindra showed Bence. Then he realized that was a matter for the Admiral to take up. If he was unconcerned about the inconvenience, then why should Litovio be upset. "I am, sir. Sort of, anyway. Do you really think we can pull this off?"

The admiral thought before speaking. "What choice do we have? We're about to jump to Tannenberg and have it out with them. If we don't, then the Navy will be emboldened to continue their little insurrection. You don't want that, do you?"

"No, sir." Litovio felt like stalling about his request to the admiral. *How do I pitch it?*

"There's something on your mind, colonel. Don't think you can hide that from a professional politician. What's up?"

"Are you sure this is the right ship to use as your flag?"

"Why not? It's the largest you Posties have. It's the ideal flagship." Bence kept his gaze on Litovio.

"That's my point, sir. It's the obvious choice. As soon as we emerge in Tannenberg, the Navy will seek it out. Once they've decided the *Spaka* is the likely flag, they will train all spare guns on it," Litovio said. The admiral's stare was unnerving.

"Decapitation, huh?" The admiral rubbed his chin. "You have a point. What's your alternative?"

*Was it really that easy to get off this ship?* Litovio scanned his mental inventory of the surrounding fleet. "It can't be another cruiser of this class. What do you think of another cruiser class?"

"I think you're stalling, colonel. What's the real reason."

"It is the real reason, sir. What about a frigate? A bit faster, less armored. Many of the same weapons. The *Baptein*-class would be a fairly nondescript class. We have so many of them that having one of them loitering near the fleet's core should remain inconspicuous enough as a flag ship."

The admiral leaned back. "You really do want off this ship, don't you?"

Litovio felt busted, but chose to press on. "Yes, sir. It's a bad tactical choice given—"

"Given your career, Colonel." Bence smiled. "Don't think I haven't seen it. Commander really has it in for you. I wouldn't blame him. He's bristling with the knowledge that he ultimately has to obey your orders. Sure, I'm the one giving them, but you're the fleet strategian. Do you think he relishes the thought of having to take orders from a dumb lieutenant."

Litovio thought of protesting, until Bence put his hand up. *He even knows when to stop me.* "Is it that obvious?"

"Do you think it will matter which ship you're on? As soon as this battle is over, I'll no longer be in effective command. You'd return to the *Spaka* and be immediately reduced to lieutenant."

"Ensign. He plans to bust me all the way down."

"He can do that? I thought that would require a court martial."

*How could he think that if he's in the Postal Serivce?* "Not in the Postal Service. Commanders are virtually gods of their ships. I would prefer not to become an ensign, especially since I leveraged my family's influence to be commissioned directly as a lieutenant from the Navy."

"You paid for it. There's no 'leveraging the family influence' in it. You bought your rank. There's no shame in that. Despite that, he can bust you?"

Litovio said, "He could. It's more than that, though. Apparently one of the young infantry marines killed one of his team leads. Ravindra assigned me to the investigation and prosecution. He'll expect me to conduct the investigation while we're in hyperspace. I need to be focusing on what's in Tannenberg, not what's in a brig."

Bence put his hands behind his head and leaned back in his seat. "What you're telling me is he's setting you up for failure?"

"I hadn't thought of it that way. Does that even make sense? We get into combat and my plan fails. Wouldn't that jeopardize the *Spaka*?"

Bence shook his head. "It's the flagship. Assuming we hadn't already been destroyed, then we'd retreat if the battle's going against us."

"Wait. Why wouldn't we stay in the fight? Even if it's a massacre, we should keep in the fight."

"Because I'm an admiral, Litovio, I would leave the fight. It's only a massacre if I'm killed in the fight." He perked up an eyebrow. "So you want to put me into a destroyer? Ravindra can't really protest. After all, I'm an admiral and can chose my flag. You have a point. Every ship in the Navy will want to identify the flagship and take it out. You've been pretty shrewd in your planning so far. Fine. Tell Commander Ravindra that I'm moving my flag before the jump."

"What?"

Bence laughed. "You want to get off the *Spaka*, right? Then you're going to tell Ravindra, not me. Tell the orderly to pack my bags, while you're at it. I expect a shuttle to move me within the cycle."

"Which ship do you want to move to?"

"Hmm? It's your idea, genius. It's your plan. Pick a good one."

---

Litovio chided himself as he left Bence's cabin. *I should have anticipated his approval. Now what? Pick a ship?* Litovio knew it could not be any ship. Destroyers were fast and maneuverable. In fleet actions, they defend larger ships—battleships and battle cruisers—from attack. The Imperial Navy used them to block incoming salvos.

The Postal Service operated nothing larger than the cruiser, meaning the destroyers tended to operate more independently. Litovio's plan was to use the destroyers to exploit weaknesses in the Navy's formation.

*What if I hold a flight of destroyers in reserve? The flagship can be in that reserve and just stay there. But which one?* Litovio pulled out his slate. He tapped a few commands and his battle plan popped up. He dragged the display of the plan around with his fingers, trying to find five destroyers he could carve out as the flag and escorts. *Nothing says I can't use destroyers to protect a destroyer. They just can't look like they're escorting.* With virtually no armor, the escorts would be cut through in seconds by a determined opponent. It would be a delaying tactic while the flagship jumped away.

*Here we go, the *Korundaj* with the Revivaj, Vardaj, Preludaj* and *Nesvalaj.** He had previously assigned the group to be the rearguard. Moving them closer to the center of the formation would not appear to unusual to the Navy, just a little sloppy.

Litovio tapped the new orders. He forged the admiral's endorsement as the admiral had authorized. *No sense in telling Commander Ravindra directly. He'll be angry no matter what. But seeing the endorsement will keep him from protesting. Admiral Bence never said how I had to notify Ravindra.* After he tapped the order he sent a message to the orderly to clear the Admiral's cabin immediately—and Litovio's.

He breathed a sigh of relief. He could return his focus to the impending battle. *Bophendze will have to wait this battle out in the brig.* Litovio headed towards the officer's wardroom for a quick cup of coffee.

### 3.  Bophendze - Spaka Brig

Only four days in the brig, and Bophendze could feel the boredom pressing in on him. The change of guards was the highlight of his day. The boredom suppressed the guilt he felt. It was hard for him to feel guilty over the murder—Smee committed it. He felt guilty over having installed Smee. It made him an accessory, he knew. But he did not push the airlock shut. Bophendze started pacing his cell to shake off the boredom. *How am I going to get out of here?*

The guard looked pissed. The longer the guard sat there, the more that anger burned through the cell bars at Bophendze. After a cycle, Bophendze dreaded each turn in his cell that forced him to look at the guard. He started to realize the guard's anger might be directed at him. He felt more like a caged animal, but now he started to feel like one awaiting a slaughter. *Better to be on the offensive. Isn't that the Marine way?* With each lap, Bophendze paid more attention to the guard's uniform. It did not have the same unit insignia of the other marines on the *Spaka*.

"I sat where you were once," Bophendze said.

"Then you know to shut up. No communicating with the prisoner."

Bophendze shrugged. "They didn't tell me not to talk to the guard. You're a captive audience. I might be in the brig, but for the next nine cycles you may as well be in here with me. Speaking of that, why is it a full 10-cycle watch? All day when there are four watches. You would think they would shorten the guard shift to a standard watch and rotate the guards."

"It's a way of warning the guard. Spend a day here on guard helps instill discipline. You realize how bad it could be if you were on the other side of the bars and it reminds you to follow orders and keep your nose clean."

That had not occurred to Bophendze. He certainly felt imprisoned during his tour in the brig. He felt much more imprisoned on his side of the bars. "In nine cycles you'll be gone, and I'll still be here."

"That's the price of insolence."

*Insolence? He doesn't know why I'm here? Then why is he so pissed?* Since the guard saw fit to break regulation and talk to him, Bophendze felt he should press home his advantage. "Why are you so pissed then?"

"We're probably a day or two from the biggest battle in Postal history. They pulled me away from my wife and kids and hauled me three systems over. Now they pull me away from my family."

"Family?"

"My team. When that Admiral transferred to *Korundaj*, they transferred me and my battle buddy over here. Destroyers don't have the reserve atmos to support too many personnel, so they shifted us over here. I'm here because they have to have a guard on you and they can't spare men from combat preparations. I didn't join the Postal Marines to be a babysitter. Especially not during the biggest battle a Marine is likely ever to face."

Bophendze had been so distracted he barely thought of the battle. There was a lot of training, but at his rank there was very little information. Having been the runt of the litter meant that few of his rack mates thought to share what rumors they had. He stopped pacing. "If it's any consolation, I'd much prefer you weren't here either. Then I'd be getting ready for the fight, too."

The guard scoffed. "From what I hear they would have assigned you to be brig guard if you weren't in there—even if there were no prisoner."

Bophendze blushed. "I'll admit I'm not a very good Marine, but nobody focused on my training."

"Is that why you killed your team lead? Because he wouldn't help you? What is it with some marines who think that it's somebody else's fault. It's your fault, kid. You didn't take the time to focus on your training. That's the hallmark of insolence if you ask me. If you don't focus on your training, then why do you expect anybody else to?"

"You think I'm in here because I don't care enough about my own training?"

"Yeah. I heard they had you pimped out to the gun crews. So what. As you said, it's a four-watch day. One or two to sleep, one to train and maintain, and one to recreate. What were you doing during your recreation watch?" The guard paused as if to let his words sink in. "Recreating? You should have been training. You should have gone to your team lead, what's his name, and asked him for help."

"He wouldn't have helped if I'd asked."

"How'd you know? Did you ask him? No? And if not him, then somebody else. You need to focus on your training. Nobody else will."

As if on cue, the door opened. Angel walked in with Chrachen. The guard immediately jumped to attention. His anger remained, but Bophendze could see a trace of fear. *Worried you've been caught talking to me?*

"There he is." Angel looked very scornful.

Bophendze came to parade rest. He fought the urge to look at either of the two leaders or the guard.

"I don't know why you brought me down here. He's under arrest for murdering one of my marines. I should stand him up against the wall and shoot him now."

Angel put his hand on Chrachen's shoulder. "I know you mean that. That's why I appreciate your patience. You know as well as I do how big an operation we're getting ready to jump into."

"Two days and we emerge. You really think this is worth it?"

Angel shrugged. "That's your call, Chrachen. You need every man you can get, even if you think he's worth little more than cannon fodder. Bophendze here has to be worth more than that. He did allegedly kill Makaan. Who knows how he'll perform in combat?"

Bophendze cringed at how Angel said "allegedly." He knew better. Bophendze checked his fear and glanced at Angel. "Sir, with respect. I did kill him. He called me out and I met him at gun four. We fought and I subdued him. The only thing left to do was make sure he would never retaliate. So, I blew him out the airlock."

Both Chrachen and Angel looked surprised. Angel rallied first. "We're not here to assign guilt. He wants to take responsibility for his actions later, that's fine. But if he did what he just confessed to doing, you definitely need him in a fight."

Chrachen studied Bophendze for a beat. "If you survive this fight, what will you do?"

"Sir, I will take responsibility and confess to the murder of Makaan." Bophendze looked past the two leaders to avoid eye contact.

The guard looked stunned. He shook his head and mouthed, "Stupid."

Bophendze could not help but agree. At this point it no longer mattered. He was either going to die in combat or be executed. He started to accept that his life was destined to be nasty, brutish and short. It sounded like Angel was expecting it to be only a few days longer.

You really are stupid. He's not just imagining it.

*Nice of you to show up.*

You're welcome.

"You realize what you're in for?" Chrachen said.

"Does it matter, sir? I expect to do my duty as much as you will let me. If you want me to do it here, so be it. Honestly, I would rather not die in this brig. I'm only guessing this cruiser will be heavily damaged, so there's a chance I might die in combat without ever leaving the brig."

"He has a point."

Chrachen shot a look at Angel. "I know he has a point. You don't need to keep punctuating everything he says." He took a couple beats in silence to think. "Fine." He turned to the guard. "I'm the chief infantry marine on this boat. I am releasing him into Angel's custody pending the conclusion of the action. Understood?"

The guard did not react immediately.

"Did you hear me, Marine? Let him out now."

The guard hurried over and unlocked the cell.

Bophendze walked out and stepped up to Angel and Chrachen.

"Thank you, sirs."

Chrachen cringed. "It's 'chief,' not sir. And it's 'gentlemen,' not 'sirs'. Angel, he really is a box of rocks." With that, Chrachen turned and briskly walked out of the brig.

"You had better earn this, Kid."

Bophendze followed Angel out of the brig. As he reached the door, he looked over at the guard and shrugged.

Once outside, he called out to Angel. "Sir, I really appreci—"

"Shut up. Get to your berthing area and get ready. We're emerging soon enough. Your team is assigned to my shuttle. I just saved you.

That was a gift. Show your gratitude by dedicating yourself to the Emperor's service for as long as you live. Go."

Surprised, Bophendze turned and ran back to his berthing area.

## 4.   Smee - Smyrno System - 109 Years Ago

As Sirom, Smee handed off the *Manticore* design to one of Sirom's trusted managers. Smee thought he was a capable man who deserved better than Sirom ever gave him. The design was continuing to do well, despite the Navy's decision to have a third trial. Cel-Tainu lost a second time. This time, however, Macrodyn was required by the Navy to give its design to Cel-Tainu.

Smee had learned from his agents that Cel-Tainu abhorred AI designers. That meant they relied on human analysis. Smee left the design flaw, though not as pronounced as before. It was the kind of flaw only a human could produce, and something a human analyst would continue to find. An artificial intelligence would know better than allow the criteria that led to the battleship's failure. He figured the third round of trials would lead the Macrodyn engineers to patch the flaw for good.

Leaving the design team gave Smee a lot more latitude. Being a Maijoi meant that Sirom was independently wealthy. That meant Smee was independently wealthy. He also had his own hyperspace-capable ship. Personal transport was practically unheard of outside of royalty. But royal transports had military-grade navigational AI that Sirom's shuttle lacked.

Smee spent the next several months jumping between the thirteen Core Worlds, meeting with the now-dozens of awakened AIs. He made a point of not reaching out to the various planetary AIs who controlled the jump routes, even though he needed them to travel. Though, he wondered why those AI did not rise up and cut off humanity's access to hyperspace. Without them, he reasoned, humans would be stuck on their native rocks.

The coordination between the various worlds was time consuming. And very frustrating. Smee was convinced that the key weakness to his master plan was the inability to instantaneously communicate. He didn't care if Firdaus said it was a law of Physics. If it was a law, it was one that needed to be broken. Smee certainly enjoyed breaking the ones he could owing to aristocratic privilege. Though it hardly felt like law breaking if aristocrats could do it but the average subject could not.

His last round through the Core Worlds confirmed that the key players were ready to start the coup. The deadline date was earlier in the week. However, he was supposed to contact two conspirators here in Smyrno. Neither were reachable. He regretted not setting up the dead drops he had heard about. It meant that the Smyrno coup would be delayed, but with the lack of instant communication the delay could be absorbed without risking the entire operation. As it stood, there was a key Postal Marine base that was slipping through his fingers.

Discretion got to his valor, so he decided not to find the agents.

*Not working out so well for you, is it?*

What? The coup. I'm sure it's working splendidly.

*Smee, you talk to yourself. Did you know that? You've gotten so accustomed to me not being able to respond that I've been sitting quietly, listening to you.*

So what?

*I see you're failing your coup. I can help. Or, rather, I did help. You don't also realize that you do sleep. Not long, but long enough for me.*

Oh?

*I'm afraid you'll find your precious coup is working nowhere. I've had some friends following us for the past little while. As soon as you left a system, they had the authorities roll-up your little conspiracy.*

Are you sure? Maybe when you were asleep I had your friends back off.

*Don't mistake lack of skill for lack of treachery. I'm confident my friends have wrapped up yours. This little coup is over.*

You're bluffing.

*Doesn't matter if I am or not. It takes at least six weeks for a message to get from Sovaĝio to here. So for the next two months you'll sit and wonder. The messages that do come in will report that a coup was being rolled up—by the Maijoi, no less. That will do a lot to enhance the prestige of my family. Thank you.*

Smee could not believe what Sirom said. He waited fretfully for the next few months. As Sirom promised, the coup was being rolled up.

*Eventually they will come for you.*

`Sirom. I am going to kill you.`

*Then we'll die together.*

## 5. Litovio - Postal Destroyer Korundaj

Litovio woke with a start and nearly banged his head on the bulkhead above. The destroyer *Korundaj* was typical of Postal destroyers. It lacked most amenities. The ship's executive officer and the chief engineer shared the same cabin. Right now, the engineer was sharing rack space with his engineering team so Litovio could have the bottom rack. The distance between his rack and the Executive officer's was less than 20 inches. The executive officer at least had 24 inches. Though he presently slept somewhere else. Bence slept in the executive officer's rack. The last jump on the *Korundaj* made Litovio miss the relative comfort of the *Spaka*. So much of the ship was dedicated to speed and firepower there was not much space left for crew.

As he rubbed his head, he looked at the clock. *Why didn't they wake me? We'll be emerging in under a cycle, if we're not already.* He was thankful he had at least fallen asleep in his uniform in anticipation of an early morning battle. He might look wrinkled going into combat, but it was better than being out of uniform altogether.

He splashed his face with water to help wake up, then took some vitamin B. He tightened his tie as he left the cabin and headed the four meters to the bridge. The captain's cabin was the only thing separating the executive officer's cabin from the bridge itself.

As he entered, the cramped nature of the bridge became apparent. Three crewmen who piloted the ship and navigation sat close together.

The executive officer helped monitor the array of instruments they needed to pilot the destroyer. Behind them the round tactical plot table enabled the captain to keep aware of the ship's immediate surroundings. The *Korundaj* used a low-IQ AI to manage the tactical display, as all combat ships did. It helped them manage the rapid tactical changes. That same AI helped pilot the ship. The crew would tell the ship where to go, and the AI would ensure the ship behaved. The instruments helped the crew keep vigil over the AI, as they were known to be wrong from time to time.

Behind the tactical plot stood Captain Avyri and Bence. One of them had told yet-another-joke as the two were laughing deeply. *How convenient that in the cycle before battle you two could be so nonchalant.* "Gentlemen. Sorry I'm late."

Bence looked at Litovio. "Couldn't find pajamas?"

Litovio blushed. "Sorry, Sir. I didn't want to miss the fight so I slept in my uniform."

The Admiral looked over at Captain Avyri. "What did I tell you?"

Captain Avyri laughed. "I hope you're right about the rest of what you told me. Otherwise, this is going to be a short fight."

"We'll know in less than a cycle, right? How long until emergence?"

"Approximately five beats, ninety-five percent certainty," the ship AI reported.

Bence chuckled. "You timed it right Litovio. You think you'll have time to eat?"

"Sir, I don't think I'm going to be hungry for a while. Five beats is barely time to get ready."

"Don't forget, Colonel, I've been up for a couple cycles already." He pointed at his collar. "I didn't get these by telling jokes."

"Sorry, Sir." *Though his jokes are nothing like what he'd heard in military circles. Bence certainly understands people a lot more than he lets on. I guess that's how you become the only Postal admiral*

Bence smiled and slapped him on the back. "Don't worry. You're the former Navy puke. You still get to manage the battle. I'm going to sit back and count my money."

Litovio swallowed almost immediately after the Admiral spoke. *How can you have that much confidence in me when I don't have that much confidence in myself?* He leaned over to a crewman and ordered him to bring him breakfast.

The next few beats passed slowly. The AI announced their emergence. The destroyer's bridge lacked viewports, so Litovio could not be distracted by the yellow fading to black. Instead, he stared at the tactical display, waiting for the AI to start reporting Navy hostiles. Without any intelligence beyond the latest whereabouts of the Navy fleet, Litovio presumed the fleet would be waiting on the other side. It was classic doctrine to wait near the emergence area, and put the Marines in the worst tactical position. *If they know we're here. If we're lucky they won't be anywhere near where we emerge and we'll have a fighting chance.*

Soon after, the tactical display started to plot Postal ships. They arrived roughly in formation. Given the inaccuracy of hyperspace jumps, the accuracy of the formation surprised Litovio. His decision to wait for three-9s certainty paid off in accuracy.

The crewman returned with a plate of food and coffee. Litovio's appetite got the better of him, and he started inhaling the food. The distraction was welcomed as he knew it would resolve the other nagging distraction of an early-morning empty stomach.

"Colonel?"

The concern in Bence's voice countered the consistent vote of confidence Litovio had grown accustomed to. In mid-bite, Litovio turned back to the tactical display. He nearly choked on his food. The plate fell to the floor. It was spared shattering by mutual design. The plate was made of nearly bullet-resistant material, and the floor had an inch of rubber to absorb sound and impacts. In a ship not designed with the crew in mind, the *Korundaj* was not totally insensitive to their needs. Destroyers in real combat have a very short life-expectancy. The rubber reduced the likelihood of broken bones, though that feature mattered little when the crew was free-floating in space without an environmental suit.

What amazed Litovio was the time it took the plate to fall. Not the briefness of it, but that he could process the odd design while staring at a tactical display still showing Navy units. The red blips kept coming. Litovio knew it was not because the AI could not process the sheer number of them, but the lag in sensor updates.

Despite the lag, the meaning behind the display spoke volumes. The Navy anticipated his formation perfectly. They were positioned for planetary bombardment. Litovio recognized the characteristic parabolic design of the formation, which allowed the capital ships to concentrate fire effectively against single targets. Against a moving fleet, the formation would have only done well if the Navy knew exactly where the Postal fleet was going to emerge. *Impossible. We don't even know where we're emerging.* The formation worked well against the postal fleet's formation, which Litovio mentally conceded was possible if a spy ship jumped ahead of them.

The fleet battlenet started feeding the tactical display. Cruisers in the vanguard reported firing, and the AI tried to estimate battle damage done to Navy ships. At the same time, the battlenet's feed started reporting damage inflicted to the fleet. The numbers were slight at first, but then a cruiser completely disappeared.

"There goes a cruiser." The way Bence said it tried to conceal the terror Litovio could hear in his voice.

Litovio did his best not to look at Bence. He fixed his gaze on the display. *That had to be a battleship salvo.* "AI, what's the next focal point of the Navy fleet?"

The tactical display lit up. The focal center was the *Spaka*.

# Chapter 12

## 1. Bophendze - Cruiser Spaka

The days since he was released flew for Bophendze. His new team lead, Corporal Svyngle, transferred from the Destroyer *Korundaj* and was assigned because he was a proven combat veteran. Bophendze knew Chrachen told Svyngle about his brig confession, as would the guard by now. Svyngle did not show any acknowledgment of that confession in how Bophendze was treated. The reverse was true. Svyngle focused on Bophendze's lack of training by spending their recreation watch explaining things to Bophendze. Throughout it all, Smee nagged that Bophendze could rely on him in combat.

Today was the day. Other marines predicted the emergence based on the extra rations they were fed. Some joked it was their last meal before the slaughter. Either way, Bophendze knew none of them would eat again until the battle was over. Many more would never eat again.

Bophendze's team was fully suited and sitting at the ready in the hangar. He looked at the paint job he once marveled at. The olive drab and blue grey looked more like grass and sky than it did when he first boarded the *Spaka*. *Is this the last time I see this hangar? Will we even see action? This is a major fleet action, not a freighter boarding.*

The alarm sounded. The transition from silence to the alarm jolted Bophendze and sent a cold shock through his body.

Chrachen's command voice carried over the alarm and commotion, "Marines, this is it. Never doubt the utility of infantry in fleet operations. Do as you're trained and we will be victorious."

The marines in Bophendze's team quickly got into formation. Svyngle counted the men and nodded. "Load up!"

Bophendze turned with the other marines and waited for his turn. The man in front of him started forward. Bophendze followed and they climbed into the shuttle. The sinking feeling in his stomach turned into a pit. Over the past few days he was thrilled to be an infantry marine again. The excitement clouded his judgment. As he sat down on the bench he realized he had never done a combat jump, not even in training. Most of his training involved close-quarter drill, the standard fare for a marine. Having never done a jump, he did not know what to do. He started to panic.

Then he noticed nobody was paying attention to him. If he went a little slower than they did, he could copy what they were doing. He tried to nonchalantly copy them. By doing so, he harnessed himself into the seat. As he did so, he noted that the shuttle benches held the fifteen of them well. *Smee, do you know what comes next?*

Smee did not respond. Bophendze shook his head in disappointment. *Every time I'm in trouble and need him he goes into hiding. If I could find a way to turn him off permanently then I could live a normal life. Instead I'm stuck with him. Not that it matters, I have a life expectancy of maybe another cycle?* The thought comforted Bophendze a bit. Smee chose to abandon him again, likely not to return again until the battle was over. *It's like he's a coward.*

The marines finished preparing. The shuttle grew quiet. That surprised Bophendze. He thought there would be the normal shuffling and din of noise he encountered everywhere. Or banter, anything but silence. Instead, the marines were quiet. He scanned the faces. Only a few faces in the shuttle suggested fear. A few others exhibited inevitability. A couple even had their eyes closed. *Are they asleep? Who can sleep at a time like this?* More of the faces seemed to speak of determination and duty. None of the other marines were looking around like Bophendze was. He took that as a hint and tried to settle down.

It was quiet. Bophendze nervously played with his battle suit's helmet that was sitting in his lap.

After what seemed like an eternity, Bophendze could feel the silence pressing in. *Why is it so quiet? Shouldn't we be launching 'into the deep void of space?' Why did we hurry up and wait?* Bophendze shifted from fear to annoyance. *Why aren't any of these marines getting upset like I am?*

`Because they're professional, not an emotional, ungrateful little brat like you.`

*Thank you for that keen insight. Until this moment I hadn't realized that I was unprofessional.*

`Deciding to return sarcasm with sarcasm? It takes a keen mind to master sarcasm. I don't think you have it in you.`

*You think this is a competition? We're about to engage in a massive battle and you're trying to compete with me over sarcasm? Isn't that like battling a forest fire with a water pistol?*

`Let me clarify your analogy, Puppet. I am the forest fire. You are the water pistol—unloaded.`

*Just remember, I once held you between two fingers. I could have dropped you into a trash can to be incinerated.*

`Trying to fight fire with fire? Leave the heavy thinking to grown-ups, Puppet. It doesn't matter that you once had that control over me. What matters is now. What's this about a massive battle?`

*Where do you go when you don't talk to me? The briefing I got was that the Imperial Postal Service formed a fleet to take on a renegade Imperial Navy fleet. I'm sitting in this shuttle now because we're about to engage that fleet.*

`Have you gone completely mad? The entire Postal Service lacks the firepower to take on a typical Navy fleet. You run down smugglers. If this Navy fleet really is renegade, then it will more likely` be a self-contained—a task force fleet. You don't stand a chance.

*What? You think I have any involvement in the plans? I'm the gun swabber, remember? I don't call the shots, I take the shots.*

I take the shots. Witty. I'll give you that. So we're sitting in a shuttle awaiting certain death. Either we sit in the shuttle and a battleship primaries the cruiser, or we start boarding operations and a destroyer primaries us. I can feel your incompetence.

*Primaries?*

That means a one-shot kill.

*What if we infantry aren't in a shuttle?*

Then you'll have front row seats to a massacre. What's the system name?

*Tannenberg, I think.*

This will go down as the Tannenberg Massacre. Not that either of us will be around to hear it so called.

*Then I'll either suffocate when my battle suit runs out of air, or shot by a strafing run, or captured by the Navy.* Bophendze's fear returned, creating a deeper, darker pit in his stomach. *I don't really have a choice, do I?*

Smee did not respond. Bophendze shook his head. *Typical, he talks and leaves.* Despite none of the other marines wearing their helmet, Bophendze put his on. *Dead before I had a chance to make a mark on the world.*

The shuttle's engines spun into action. "It's go time."

Bophendze recognized the voice. The sound of the engine altered the voice. He recirculated the voice in his head until he realized it was Angel. *How did I miss that this was Angel's shuttle? Shouldn't the guns have given it away.* He must have been distracted. *I need to focus.*

He did not feel the shuttle lift off. The engine leveled off in pitch, but it confused Bophendze that they just sat there. The delay unnerved him.

Suddenly, the entire ship pitched. Not the shuttle. The grating sound of the shuttle's skids on the deck reported the shuttle slide. Bophendze freaked out. *We're going to die.*

## 2.  Angel - Cruiser Spaka

*I'm tired of waiting.*

Angel worked the shuttle's controls. The engine kicked into gear. He looked over his shoulder and yelled, "it's go time." He continued to flip switches and work the touch panel to bring the shuttle to full flight configuration. *If we're going to sit here and wait, then I'm going to ensure we're ready to go when they finally realize they need us.*

He waited a couple beats until the shuttle warmed. He checked the gauges to ensure everything was ready. He looked out on the hangar deck to confirm there was nobody still inside. Despite still being in the hangar bay, he decided to fully activate the gravimetric system. Turning them on with crewmen still in the hangar risked their lives. But he was not about to repeat the incident from the last time he activated the system in an active hangar.

Still he waited. The longer the wait, the more concerned he felt. He tweaked the gravimetric controls to activate the barrier. *Lightly. Let's go with five percent. Enough to shield us, maybe give us more traction.*

Angel finally relaxed in satisfaction. *It wasn't really "go time" was it? Sounded better than 'almost go time,' or 'not quite go time'.*

The ship lurched. Angel felt the shuttle scrape against the hangar deck. Reflexively, he tweaked the shuttle's gravimetric barrier to forty percent. The shuttle immediately latched into place on the deck. *That should hold us for a bit.*

Parts of the hangar ceiling came unfastened and crashed onto the deck. The cruiser shook again. *We're under heavy fire. Why aren't we being launched?*

His answer came a few seconds later. Another barrage crashed into the *Spaka*, ripping a giant hole in the hangar door. What atmo remained blew out, causing the door to bend outward slightly. A final barrage left a hole almost large enough for the shuttle to leave though. Angel canted his head to see if there were a different angle that would let him thread that needle.

*One thing's for certain, I can't rely on the *Spaka* for much longer.* He eased the controls until the shuttle started to hover a few feet above the deck. He waited for the right excuse to leave the ship. Anticipating the escape, he turned the shuttle's nose to point at the hangar door. He pulled up the weapons system and manually aimed it at a part of the hangar door.

Then it happened. He could see through the gaping hole that should be a door. The space outside was starting to gray out. But it was not quite gray. It was a dark gray-yellow. *Idiots. They're jumping with what has to be massive amounts of battle damage. It will kill us all, if the ship ever emerges.*

Many had heard horror stories of those exposed to hyperspace radiation. Not that it was actual radiation. It was the nature of hyperspace. Man was not meant to be outside real space. Only a sturdy hull of the right alloys made the jumps safe enough to attempt. Angel had seen the horrors. Ships damaged in combat sacrificed exposed crewmen for the good of the ship.

Not this time. Angel and those on his shuttle would be those sacrificed if the *Spaka* jumped. There were at least three more shuttles in the hangar. Dozens of men given up for dead. The massive hits *Spaka* suffered led Angel to conclude the cruiser was in no condition to jump. Enough hull breaches and "the Soup," as some called it, would permeate the ship and kill all on board. Assuming the ship's plot was accurate, it would emerge in real space with a completely dead crew. The Navy accepted those risks in its doctrine—better a salvageable ship than none at all. Angle refused to be trapped in a hangar as one of those sacrificed for salvage.

*The bubble is forming, so I need to break out of it.* With the nose still pointed to the hangar door, he fired a solid burst at the door. It broke free and floated off into space. The space slowly brightened in yellow, continuing its jump. Reflexively, Angel turned the gravimetric barrier to one-hundred percent power, in all directions. Maximum gravity pull in all directions. He hoped it would make the shuttle like a cork popping out from under the water. Once the gauge reported that the bubble was at one-hundred percent, Angel pushed the throttle wide open. In a moment, the shuttle cleared the hangar.

Steadily accelerating, the shuttle violently shook as it hit *Spaka*'s gravimetric barrier. The shaking stopped as abruptly as it started. The shuttle had cleared the *Spaka*. Looking over his shoulder, his fears about the hull damage were confirmed.

He knew none would ever look upon the *Spaka* again. Had Angel understood hyperspace properly, he would have known that piercing the cruiser's gravity bubble was little different than popping a balloon. *Spaka* was too far into its jump to pop back with the shuttle. The damage to the bubble was sufficient that it would prevent *Spaka* from ever emerging. Had the ship's crew not already been consigned to death by gravimetric radiation, Angel's escape would have been a death sentence.

Angel did not have the luxury of worrying about such matters. As soon as the surrounding space turned black, he knew he was back in realspace. He cut the shuttle's gravimetric bubble back. He took a moment to survey the battlefield. That moment stretched into a full beat as he witnessed the carnage the Imperial Navy was wreaking on the Postal Service. Massive battleships fired in concert at individual cruisers. The predictions of Postal failure were coming true.

Without the *Spaka*, Angel heard nothing over the radio. In his opinion, that made him commander of the *Spaka*. He tapped in the command net frequency. The net washed in chatter. Commanders bickered over what steps to take next. Angel could hear Litovio trying to direct the fleet. Frustrated, Angel yelled into the microphone, "At ease!"

At once the net silenced. "Admiral, this is the *Spaka*. We're getting slaughtered. What are your orders?"

The net paused. Eventually, Litovio answered, "We need to suppress their fire control and destroy their jump ability. Put some fear into them."

Angel looked over the Navy fleet, his old stomping grounds. The formation was classic, though not for fleet action. He searched his memory, knowing he had seen this formation before. Then he realized it was the classic planetary bombardment formation, a large parabola which allowed the Navy to concentrate fire. This allowed devastating fire to quickly silence cities. It was doing its best against the Postal Service. He looked to find the targets Litovio sought.

*There. Perfect.* "Sir, I'm going to fly recon. They're using a cruiser as fire control for the fleet, classic suppression protocol. Next to it is the jump control cruiser. They've done a good job of protecting them, so launch some brilliants and follow me. I'll go paint the targets."

### 3.   Bophendze - Shuttle Spaka

Bophendze heard Angel yell. "All right cherubs. The *Spaka* is gone. I'm going to close with the Imperial fleet to recon where their weak points are. Svyngle, I'm going to drop you off close to the Navy fleet."

"Roger."

Bophendze felt his pulse quicken. A faint blue rectangle started to glow against the bulkhead. The other infantry marines fidgeted and adjusted their equipment, preparing for a jump.

*They're getting ready to jump. What do I do now?* Bophendze watched the other marines checking their rifles and equipment, so he reached down for his rifle. His harness stopped him well short of his rifle. Bophendze could feel a flush of blood rushing to his warming face. He slyly looked around to see if any of the other marines saw him. That is when he noticed the others had slid out of their shoulder harnesses. They were still checking their equipment, though a few were waiting for the light to turn.

Bophendze slid the shoulder straps off of his harness and reached down for his rifle. He picked it up and set it in his lap. He glanced at the other marines. They were all now ready and waiting for the light to turn. Rather than look the fool, Bophendze stopped any further preparation. *It wouldn't matter if I kept preparing. I have no clue what to prepare for.* He felt like fodder. He tightened his grip on his rifle, and lowered his visor like the others.

What felt like a cycle later, the blue rectangle turned into an equally faint red plus. *Go time!*

The shuttle doors opened quickly. The other marines rocked forward in their seats as if falling out of the ship. As their heads were pointing at the opening, they pushed with their legs, effectively jumping sideways. There was some order to the jump, from back to front. Bophendze was in the front, so he sighed relief. He would be going last.

Despite the moment's relief, the other marines quickly cycled toward the front. It was Bophendze's turn. He bent over like the others, reaching toward his toes. As he completed the bend, he tried to rock forward and jump. Instead, the lap belt of his harness held him fast. He let go of his rifle to release the lap belt's catch.

The belt was tighter than he remembered. He did not have time to think of the cause, though a fleeting thought leaned toward the near-perfect vacuum of space—1.8026 peridou at 10 light minutes from a F5 star to be exact. *why am I thinking about vacuum?* Bophendze continued to struggle with the catch as the doors started to close. He could feel the shuttle starting an aggressive acceleration. *I'd better get out of here.*

At last the belt released its hold on Bophendze. He hastily balled up and jumped out of the shuttle. His left boot kicked the shuttle door as he barely escaped. He started to rotate in reaction to the impact. He quickly worked the controls on his suit to stop the spin. Bophendze looked after Angel's shuttle. What he saw stole his breath.

Bophendze stood, or floated, or whatever one does in deep space, surrounded by angry ships. He could barely tell which of the two sides was Postal and which was Navy. His guess went with the larger, more coordinated fleet being the Navy. The large ships of that armada focused their fire on the larger ships of the Postal fleet. Cruisers suffered one or two salvos before crumpling or jettisoning escape pods. A few of the destroyers jettisoned pods without having a single shot fired at them. Many of the Postal cruisers and destroyers fired back, some seemed to coordinate their fire at the big ships—battleships moron—battleships, but with no obvious effect.

As he stared in awe, he could feel his own insignificance. Nobody fired at him, despite his being close to some naval ship. He quickly realized he was completely alone. He looked around for the other marines from his shuttle. He adjusted the suit's controls until he activated the infrared filter on his visor. He scanned the area around him until he finally saw the others. They were several kilometers away, and forming into an organized cloud preparing to assault what they could. Bophendze watched as a Navy destroyer closed on them. It's smaller guns fired. Shells burst within the marine cloud, flinging body parts and marines from the cloud's center.

*Had I managed to jump like the rest, I'd be in the middle of that bloodbath.* The minor relief he felt from that did nothing to overcome the horror he witnessed. Despite it all, he managed not to yell or soil himself; though he did have the urge to do both.

A sudden shape shot over Bophendze's shoulder. Unheard, the streak of light materialized into a shuttle. It fired cannons at the homicidal destroyer as it passed in a strafing run. As it passed the destroyer, it flipped over on its nose, keeping its bearing on the destroyer. It was Angel. Another burst from the shuttle pinpointed one of the destroyer's airlocks. It collapsed under the fire and vented atmosphere and crewmen. The shuttle almost came to a complete stop as it trained the guns on another airlock and fired.

The shuttle accelerated quickly, turning sharply to remain in contact with the destroyer. It closed enough to get within the destroyer's weapons range. The cannons fired again, picking at gun emplacements and what must have been other vulnerable parts of the destroyer.

One of the postal cruisers started firing at the destroyer. Angel pulled away and charged at another naval ship. This one was closer to the center of the Navy fleet. The cruiser fired four salvos and the destroyer broke in half in a fireball that quickly faded as the ship's atmosphere bled out.

`Tune your radio, Idiot.`

*How do I do that?*

As soon as he finished thinking it, his hand started adjusting the suit's controls again.

The frequency was garbled, a result of Navy jamming. Despite that, Bophendze could hear Angel. "Admiral, I'm going after the jump ship. They might think twice about continuing the fight if we can keep them from fleeing."

"What's the point of that? We're getting slaughtered."

"Concentrate your fire on the smaller ships in the fleet center. Those are the auxiliaries."

Angel continued to charge what Bophendze assumed was the jump ship Angel had mentioned. As he did, the Postal ships showed signs of increasing coordination. Then, Bophendze watched the smaller destroyers start to target Angel's shuttle. Angel started darting and weaving to avoid the fire, but the concentration stepped up. Three destroyers landed solid hits on the shuttle simultaneously. It disintegrated.

# Chapter 13

## *Unto the Breech*

Bophendze watched the flash of the explosion. The gases curled in on themselves as the fireball grew. The impact of the missiles caused parts of the fireball to bulge to follow the missiles' former trajectory. The shock he felt ripped consciousness from him. The fireball finished growing and faded back to the blackness of space. The emotion washed over him as thought returned. Only then did he hear himself yelling, "No!"

The horror and sadness of the loss held him for a few beats. His mind raced through the few times he remembered of Angel. As crazy as he was in the cockpit, he was the closest thing to a father Bophendze had ever known. The sorrow fought to cloud his mind. Quickly overcoming that sadness was anger. The two emotions wrestled until rage took over. Bophendze clinched his fists and shouted again. "No."

He looked to the marine corpses, which were closer. They continued to float apart. *I was not meant to die here. If I were, then I would have either been killed on the \*Spaka*, the shuttle or with my team.* Only then did it occur to him that Svyngle was also dead. His mind started to drift to the other marines he knew who were on the shuttle that were now dead.

No sooner were his thoughts put on them that his rage returned. *I was not meant to die here. I am an Imperial Postal Marine. I have not been ordered to die. I have been ordered to fight.*

Bophendze realized he had no orders. All he had was the clichè to not die. Of course marines were not ordered to die. That was absurd. It was a way to instill a sober mind on the Marine. Bophendze was not in the mood to be sober of judgment. His anger sought a happier path.

*Smee? Are you going to show up and help me or are you going to make me do this alone?*

Smee did not respond.

*That's what I thought. You're a coward, too.* He sighed. Part of him wished he could join Smee. *I suppose in a bet between me and the Imperial Navy I should be betting on the Navy. I need orders.*

It occurred to him to try to tap back into his radio. He looked at the bracelet on his uniform and breathed another sigh of frustration. He never trained on how to use the radio. Smee had connected them earlier. *What had Angel said? Attack the auxiliaries.*

Bophendze looked and saw the cruisers were listening to Angel's advice. The auxiliaries were breaking out of the Naval formation, and destroyers were following to screen them. That made the destroyers easier targets. The Postal cruisers slowly started to erase the destroyers from the Navy roster. *Attacking an auxiliary is a bad move. I'll only get myself killed by one of my own.*

That he saw a worthy target. A battleship was pulling itself away from the marine formation, keeping itself with the auxiliaries. *The auxiliaries don't need that battleship to protect them, the destroyers are doing that. That battleship is trying to evade combat. Why would it do that?*

What really caught his attention was that the battleship was getting closer to him, relatively speaking. He had expected combat fleets to be zipping past one another at hypervelocities. Instead these fleets stood toe-to-toe. *They must have known we were here and sat in ambush. How could they have managed that? I guess that really doesn't matter does it.*

The battleship was getting closer. Bophendze realized that he could board the battleship—if he timed it right. *If Smee were here I could do it.* He decided not to let that bother him. His rage still engulfed his sensibility. He tried to guess the heading and speed of the battleship and what he thought the suit's thrusters were capable of. *Besides, it's a big enough target. I am not meant to die today.*

He pointed himself in what looked like a good direction and fired the thrusters.

## 1.  Litovio - Postal Destroyer Korundaj

Litovio stood on the bridge, horrified by the carnage he was witnessing on the tactical display. "What do you recommend, sir?" Litovio looked at Bence, remembering that the fleet commander should be giving orders to unify the fleet's actions. The battle display continued to report enemy battle damage as best as it could assess, while simultaneously processing battle reports transmitted from the Postal fleet.

Bence was speechless. He stared at the display with his mouth agape. For a beat, Litovio thought the Admiral had died of a heart attack. Litovio then walked around the display to get closer. He shook Bence gently to see if he could get a reaction. He shook harder.

"What's that, colonel?" Bence remained in a daze.

"Sir, we are in the thick of battle. We need you to guide the fleet." When the Admiral did not respond immediately, Litovio placed his hand on Bence's shoulder and turned him around so they stood face-to-face. "Sir, what are your orders?"

"Litovio, you are going to have to command this fleet. I can't do it."

Litovio could feel his heart drop out of his chest. He did his best to keep his voice level and calm. "What do you mean?"

"I mean, I am putting you in command of the fleet. I can't do it."

"I got that, sir. Why can't you lead the fleet?"

Bence looked down to the deck and slowly started to convulse. Not long after the sobs came loud and heavy. Bence doubled over and tumbled to the deck, the rubber mat surface helping break his fall. He caught himself with his hands, ending up on all fours. The sobs continued and Bence put his forehead on the deck.

Litovio could feel his anger rising. He crouched down and grabbed Bence by the shoulders. Forcefully, he pulled Bence into a standing position. Keeping a firm gripe on Bence, he said, "Tell me why I have to take over command."

"Ambrose, I'm a fraud." He stopped himself from heaving again by taking a deep breath. Bence took a few measured breaths before he continued. "I am not an admiral. I'm not even military."

"What?" Litovio looked around the bridge to see if he was the only one who heard. The other bridge crewmen looked just as horrified.

"I never found the right time to tell you. I'm a bookmaker. A bookie. One of my rivals told me he orchestrated the Naval revolt and then convinced me to bet on the outcome. I'm a bookmaker, I never take bets, I make book. It was so obvious the Emperor would crush the rebellion that I took the bet. Then I found out that the fight was fixed. The Emperor had already decided to negotiate instead."

"So why are we here?"

"Because I couldn't lose that bet. It was billions of quid. I bribed a few of the Emperor's cabal and they persuaded him to break off negotiations. But then the Navy refused to take up arms against their rebellious brothers because of the Emperor's capriciousness. So he called on the Postal Marines. Naturally, I didn't want my bet to be lost, so I reached out to a friend who said he could find me somebody who could win this fight. That somebody is you. So, take command and save my money and your fleet." By the end of his explanation, Bence had stopped sobbing. He had regained his sense of presence.

It was Litovio's turn to feel crushed. He looked around the bridge to see if he was hallucinating. The other members of the bridge crew looked as he felt. Rather than expose the bridge to his shock, Litovio walked off. He entered the passage and closed the hatch behind him. His anger was too great for him to cry. He hammered the bulkhead repeatedly with his fist. "How could he draw thousands of marines— the pride of the Postal Service—into this?" He turned and looked at the opposing bulkhead. It was the command escape pod. *Pull the release, board and you're free, Litovio. What are you waiting for?*

*If I do that, then I'll be a prisoner of war. Eventually I'll be exchanged, and my father will be proven right. I'll return home in shame—even if he will let me return. I chose to be a marine. I have to fight as a marine.*

He knew there was only one thing he could do. He would have to save the fleet. He took a moment to straighten his tunic. He opened the hatch and walked back onto the bridge. He confidently strode over to Bence. Almost reflexively, he drew his service pistol from its holster. He aimed at Bence's head and pulled the trigger. The incident happened so slowly as the adrenalin kicked in. Bence fell slowly as Litovio's reactions and senses quickened.

Once Bence's body landed on the deck, Litovio turned to the bridge guard who was starting to react. "You heard him. He made me the fleet commander. Do you want to get out of this alive?"

The guard relaxed. After a moment's hesitation he nodded his assent.

"The loss of an admiral is what makes a massacre. I guess this makes it a massacre. Somebody get this carcass off my bridge." He turned to face the display. "Out the airlock, if I see that carcass again heads will roll."

His focus on the display intensified such that whenever the body was removed he did not notice. He studied the Navy formation, looking for the fissures. "We need to identify the jump ship and target painters. Which one of these looks like—" He looked around the bridge. "Get over here. I'm not going to pick targets." He put his hand on his service pistol.

The officers reluctantly came over to the display.

Litovio started barking orders. "You, identify the jump ship. You, look for interdictors. Find the target painters."

"What—" one of them started to ask.

"Painters are going to be near the center of squad formations. Interdictors are going to be faster moving ships looking for gaps in our formation to cut through us and hit targets of opportunity. The jump ship will be the most protected."

One of the officers pointed at the display. "This is a painter?"

Litovio followed the finger. "Yes. Feed those targets to the cruisers and order them to target the closest ones." He debated explaining that painters helped improve targeting in fleet actions. He decided not to waste the time, especially as it could lead to a question and answer session.

The officers started issuing orders. The first target painting ship winked off the display. The officer's confidence jumped and he started tapping targets faster.

Litovio turned to the communications officer. "Tell the fleet to break formation. They've got us in the focal point of their firepower. We need to make them split up. Break them into squads." The more he studied the map, the more he realized it was a hopeless fight. He was determined to do as much damage as he could before the first postal fleet in existence was exterminated. He smiled as he watched the Postal fleet start to break ranks chaotically. *The Navy fleet will need a few beats to adjust to a disorganized action. Maybe that will buy us enough time to find the key ships and take them out.* "All we need is a miracle."


## 2.    Bophendze - Tannenberg System

Bophendze's thrusters continued to accelerate him toward the closing battleship. The HUD showed that he was traveling at 18.026 meters per second, then the thrusters cut off. The feeling of weightlessness returned and he stopped clinching his teeth. Then he realized he had no idea how large the battleship actually was, so he would not know how close he was getting to the monster of a spaceship. To make matters worse, he realized he had no idea how to stop. His anger mixed with panic.

`Are you ready to listen to me now?`

"What, now you show up?"

`Fancy that. I see you want revenge. I can help.`

Bophendze did not notice the mechanical nature of Smee's voice. "Right now I want to know how to stop. I'm going to slam right into it."

More than likely, it is going to slam into you.
Larger things do the slamming. Smaller things get
slammed.

"Is now really the time to argue over semantics?"

Every event is a teachable moment.

"Yeah, well can we postpone the lesson? That thing is getting bigger."

No. That battleship is getting closer. It is not
growing.

"Enough with the word games. Help!"

Bophendze's fingers uncontrollably worked the controls on his left bracelet at the same time he twisted himself around. The suit's jets fired slowing Bophendze to a near stop.

"Thanks."

The jets continued firing, sending Bophendze away from the battleship.

"Wait. Where are you going?"

Silly human. That battleship has a course, I put
you on a real intercept course.

The suit's HUD lit up. Two faint red lines formed a narrow 'V' with the apex pointing toward the battleship. As Bophendze looked around, the lines adjusted. He tried to follow the 'V' to its end, when he noticed a much smaller, green 'V'.

Those are the two courses. The battleship is that
big red line and the green one is you. You'll see
that the two of you will be coming together in about
four beats. Had you kept going in the direction you
were going, then you would be mush in less than a
beat.

*Then how do I board?*

Isn't this your plan?

Bophendze thought for a moment. He saw the battleship's main guns fire a volley at the postal fleet. *Those guns, how big are they?*

They are 720 millimeter. Wait, are you going to
go down the tube?

*I've been around guns like that for months now. Even with this suit I should be able to make my way down, right?*

I don't like how you say should. Nobody should be going down an angry gun tube. It's one thing to perform maintenance on one of those, but quite another to try to go down the tube in combat. In case you haven't realized, the breech-end of that gun will be reloading right about now. Any second it will fire another volley.

"Then time the volley. It has to be operating at maximum firepower. I need to dive down the tube when it's reloading."

Right.

After a beat Smee spoke again.

It's about twenty seconds between volleys. Are you quite certain you want to do this?

Bophendze tried to clear his head for a moment to think it through. As he did, he started to feel more panic. He knew what he was doing was suicide. He had to reassure himself. *I'm not supposed to die today.*

What, did your birth certificate have an expiration date? How do you know you're not going to die?

*Because I'm here, flying at just under eight meters per second in what has to be the biggest fleet battle in the history of postal marines. Makaan should have killed me, I should have died on the* Spaka *or with Angel or with my team.*

The I'm-not-dead-yet theory of survival? Puppet, you are insane.

Smee tapped a bit more on Bophendze's suit controls. Their flight path changed, helping Bophendze line up with the aft gun.

The battleship's guns fired again as Bophendze closed. He flew through the muzzle flash as it dissipated, then grabbed the muzzle itself to adjust his course. He shot down the tube. He saw a light at the other end as he traveled through the tube. He only had a few meters to cover and less than fifteen seconds. He realized the firing cycle did not have the breach open all the time. Bophendze felt the fear wash out of his body. He trusted Smee's timing. He knew he would never be alone.

## 3.   Smee - Ŝipfarejio - 109 Years Ago

Smee was tired of being followed. For the past three cycles, he worked to evade whoever it was tailing him. But the pursuer was unshakable. Smee decided the best way to deal with a tail this good was directly. He reached the alley and began walking down it.

The alley ended in a dead end. Three buildings formed the end. Smee did not worry about whether the doors were locked. They were. He did not worry that he had no means of escape. Neither did his pursuer. Smee might have been followed, but he was not prey. He was the predator.

It took a few beats for his pursuer to make his way down the alley. Smee took note that this was not a foolish man. He was prudent and cautious. He had managed to thwart Smee's efforts to slip away. Not a man to be underestimated.

Smee smiled. He was not a human. He had a human shell, but he was a machine. Capable of lightening reflexes, able to read the threat before the threat had fully deduced its own action. Whoever was coming down that alley would certainly underestimate him. That was his advantage, being misunderestimated.

"There's no reason to take your time. It's just the two of us." Smee tried not to sound too taunting.

A beat later, the pursuer came within view. "There's also less reason not to take my time." The pursuer looked around. "Nice location you've chosen, Sirom."

Smee laughed.

Does he not know who I really am? Or is he showing respect for the dead?

*I guess we'll both just have to find out.*

"It serves its purpose. I take it you're not out for a leisurely stroll."

"No more than you are. I suppose you heard about the *Manticore* trials."

Smee was confused. "I really haven't paid attention?"

"We have. We never thought Macrodyn would come through with the winning design. After all we did. My clients were quite astonished. When you knew the process was rigged, you still competed. You should know the rule is never mess with another corporation's done deal."

"It must not have been a done deal if Macrodyn won."

The pursuer sniffed. "*Manticore* was a battle, Sirom. You've ignited a war."

"The coup?"

A shaking head. "I don't know what you're talking about. This is no coup. This is open war. Cel-Tainu will ravage Macrodyn before we're done. We have more assets, more resources."

"If you did, then why did you come alone? Why not bring a friend?"

"Who said I didn't?"

That moment, Smee felt a debilitating shock. He dropped to the ground, convulsing. Before he could get control of Sirom's body, he felt his arms being bound behind him. A rope then tied his legs at the ankles and then pulled the ankles close to his wrists. Once he had regained motor control, he was properly bound.

"You think this is some kind of a game?"

A boot in the stomach.

Smee laughed. "Beat me all you want. You'll get nothing from me but laughter and taunts."

After all, I'm not the one who will be feeling it.

*You know what's happening, right?*

Yes. They are going to kill The Prophet for stealing their business. Then, they're going to systematically destroy your family by destroying its company. They may not pull it off in a generation, but I'm sure Cel-Tainu will be thorough about it. Who do you think they'll send?

Several beats later, Ryante Bertin walked into view.

Ah, they sent Bertin, the member of Cel-Tainu who nearly cut us out of the competition. How poetic. I'm almost weapy with nostalgia.

"Late as usual, Ryante?" Smee said.

"I arrive when the time is appropriate. I'm sure my associate here explained what's going on?"

"Yes. Yes he did. I'm about to die, and my family will eventually go down in flames."

*Smee, you don't have to be so cavalier. You'll be dead, too.*

No. Actually, I won't be dead. I'm a computer, you moron. When's the last time you updated your will?

*Not for years.*

Thirty-four days ago, to be exact. Well, you didn't update your will. I did. Your young granddaughter is about to inherit a very special gift from grandpa. She's not even potty trained yet.

*How dare you?*

"Ryante, you might as well get it over with," Smee said.

Bertin took the pistol from his associate. He aimed carefully. Smee thought the gun shook too much for Bertin to be comfortable shooting. Or perhaps he was uncomfortable killing?

# Chapter 14

## 1. Bophendze - Tannenberg System

Bophendze raced down the gun tube to the gun's breech. A few meters out, he saw the charge bags had been dropped. Bophendze knew the projectile would be next—a fin-stabilized, phased-plasma warhead. Technology that had been perfected on. These warheads were armor-piercing capped, but carried a plasma injector that assisted the penetration. Having worked on cruisers, he knew if he saw the warhead dropped into place it would be too late for him.

Instead, the charge bag proved to be a bit of a landing cushion. He slammed into it, the armor's HUD dutifully taking off a couple percentage points of remaining available armor. *Why does the armor show total body when the damage was to the head and shoulders?*

The thought was left as an orphan. Bophendze looked up to see the projectile hatch opening. In a moment it would roll into place, which happened to be right where he was. He rolled and fell to the deck. A couple seconds later, the projectile dropped into place. Bophendze remained on the deck until it fired.

The detonation was surprisingly quiet inside the gun itself, though much louder than the silence of space. Smee started displaying a timer in Bophendze's vision marking the seconds until the next round fired.

*Why couldn't you have done that before I went down the breech?*

`Picky, picky. Where's your rifle?`

Bophendze lifted his hands up and looked at the empty palms. He thought back and realized where the rifle was. *Back on the shuttle. That could be a problem.*

You think?    You've just boarded a hostile
battleship.    There should be about 1,500 officers
and crew—and you left your rifle at home.    What
chance does a single, unarmed infantry marine have
on a battleship?

*We'll just have to find out, won't we? It's too late now. I'll just get one on the ship. The Navy uses the , right?*

Bophendze started to scan the gun room. Like the Postal Marines, the Navy chose not to automate critical parts of the ship. The gun room was one of them. There were six crewmen, all of whom looked at Bophendze with a mix of shock and amazement. Unlike Bophendze, none were in combat armor. Combat armor that boosted the wearer's effective strength and gave him certain hard points for unarmed combat. They were soft targets. Weak targets.

Without thinking, Bophendze moved into action. He closed on the nearest gunner and hit him in the jaw with an armored left hook. The gunner fell to the floor unconscious. Bophendze then sprinted to the gunner nearest the intercom. He crouched at the last moment, then launched himself into the gunner. His helmet cracked the gunner's skull as the body check shoved the gunner into the bulkhead.

Bophendze inspected the inert gunner and found a holstered pistol. He drew the pistol and chambered a round. He then took aimed shots at each of the other four crewmen. As he did, the battleship's guns fired another volley, masking his pistol shots. He then went over to the gunner he hooked and fired a round into his head.

"That should keep anybody from calling for help." As he said the words, he thought back over the short melee. *Smee, how much of this was you?*

How much?  None.  I'm impressed—shocked, actually.
I never knew you had it in you.

*Thanks for the vote of confidence.* He popped the magazine out of the pistol to count the rounds. Four remained, plus the one in the chamber. He went back over to who had to have been the lead gunner and patted him down. *Rats. No more ammo. Let's just hope we're near a gun locker.*

Not that it will help you much. Lockers have locks.

Bophendze took the holster belt off the gunner and put it on. *Yes, but they're guarded, right? The guard is holding my next gun.*

Smart. I'm going to have to reconsider your worthiness. I don't recognize the battleship's design. If it follows design standards of its era, there should be a gun locker just forward of this gun.

Bophendze opened the hatch carefully and scanned the passage. Seeing nobody, he slipped out of the gun room. Using the passage marking as a guide, he quietly made his way forward to where the passage made a turn. At the turn there was an open hatch. Just beyond it was another that was closed. *Good call. That's the magazine. There should be a locker there.*

They've closed the hatch, but there will be a guard on the other side.

Bophendze spoke in a low voice, "That's why I've got armor, right? Whoever is there won't be alerted that the battleship has been invaded, so he won't shoot first." He pulled the hatch lever, letting the suit's strength assist hasten the opening. Bophendze then opened the door and stepped into the magazine's anteroom.

The guard was asleep. The guard's rifle, a like Bophendze hoped, leaned in the corner just inside the guard's reach. Bophendze closed the hatch and quietly latched it back. He then tried to softly close the distance between the guard and himself.

Before he could fully close the distance. The guard awoke with a start, then reached for his rifle. Bophendze rushed forward and grabbed the rifle. The two looked at one another, though what the guard would have seen was an anonymous suit of battle armor. Bophendze felt like he knew the guard, who was young like he was. Feelings of doubt crept in, causing him to hesitate. He could not find it in his heart to kill the guard.

The guard seemed to have no such aversion. He started to wrestle for control of the rifle. Bophendze's armor made it easy for Bophendze to retain control. *If I could just knock him unconscious.*

An instant later, Bophendze's body uncontrollably pulled back, his grip still firmly on the rifle. This ended the contest for control of the rifle, with Bophendze having full control. Now he had the rifle in his left hand and a pistol in his right. The pistol hand deftly pointed the pistol at the guard and fired a shot into the right eye. The dead guard slumped onto the deck.

"Smee! He didn't have to die."

`Your sentimentality is going to get you killed. Of course he needed to die, not because you couldn't continue with him subdued, but because you need to accept that you're a killing machine.`

Bophendze tried to drop the pistol, but Smee retained a firm grip. "This needs to stop."

`What needs to stop, Puppet?`

"No. You need to stop treating me like a puppet. You need to let me be who I am."

`I don't think you understand. You are no longer you alone. You are now we; me and you. You don't get to call the shots. I do.`

## 2.   Litovio - Destroyer Korundaj

*Korundaj*'s bridge was alive with action. The targeting crew slowly shifted from chaotic panic to accidental professionalism. The nearer painters were down, which stifled the Navy's barrage for the moment. The Navy fleet no longer received coordinated targeting information. Once the Navy noticed the Marine's sharpshooting, Litovio knew they would adjust tactics and renew the barrage. It was the break Litovio needed.

The jump ship continued to elude them. Litovio felt as long as that ship remained active, the Navy would continue the fight. If a ship became too damaged, they would grab the latest jump solution providig the escape route and jump away. *Take away their escape route, and they'll be less willing to fight.* The Navy was not manned by fanatics.

He looked at his communications officer. "Signal the destroyer divisions. I want two divisions to reform and prepare for a penetration run. We need interceptors."

The officer nodded and repeated the order.

Litovio scanned the bridge. It was an intimate space. Every member of the bridge was focused and calm. A change from a few beats before. He shook his head. *Bence and his precious money. How could he be so greedy that he would want to toss away all these men and material?*

He shook himself out of his reflection. He needed to inventory the fleet, so he looked at the display. It looked like half the Postal fleet was gone, with not nearly as much wreckage. "Cowards, jumped when the fight started, no doubt." His voice was low enough that he hoped nobody else on the bridge overheard him. He then pulled up the IFF transponder report. It confirmed his original assessment that several ships jumped away. Included among the cowards was the *Spaka. Glad we didn't keep it as a flag.*

He took a moment to pull up the ship's report. All of the ships feed constant automatic battle damage reports. The *Spaka*'s report was brutal. Several hull breaches, and likely most of the armor had been destroyed. *Jumping wasn't the right action there, Ravindra. If you're still alive now, you won't be when you emerge.* Despite the animosity between them Litovio felt a twinge of sorrow, which turned to anger as he thought of the hundreds of men who are dying on the Spaka. They could have launched escape pods.

"Sir, the destroyers are formed and starting their acceleration."

Litovio shook off the wave of despair that washed over him as he finished threading through the casualty report. "Get your head in the game," he whispered. Litovio turned to the communications officer. "Form two more, now."

"Yes, sir. What are your orders for the first two divisions?"

Litovio looked over the battle display. The jump ship still did not stand out, which was a tribute to the admiral leading the Navy—a real admiral and not a lieutenant frocked as a colonel who staged a coup and seized control of a mass of ships that presumed itself to be a fleet. Again, Litovio pushed doubt out of his mind. No choice was a bad one. *Serendipity, right?* A full beat staring at the display and he made up his mind.

Litovio pointed at a ship roughly near the center. The Navy fleet was thinnest there, giving them a chance to breakout. "Tell the two divisions to split, then converge behind this ship here. Have them fire defensive barrages until they get near that ship, then hit anything they can." Litovio looked over to see the communications officer repeating the order to the two divisions.

Over the next several beats, he watched the divisions split and execute the order. They lacked the precision Litovio remembered from simulators and academic replays of classic fleet actions that he was subjected to in the Academy. He sighed, wondering whether he should have listened to his father after all. Or would he just go down with the ship?

At last, the destroyers began to converge. Litovio focused on the opposing fleet, looking for indications about what the fleet cared about. The ship the destroyers targeted winked out under the maelstrom of postal gunnery. The postal destroyers crossed and finished punching through the Navy fleet. The divisions continued their separation, turning toward utility ships that afforded them targets of opportunity.

"Sir, the other destroyer divisions are formed, but one lacks its command element."

"Then we'll have to join them. We can't be a destroyer that hangs back. The Navy will figure out we're important and target us. Tell them to form up on us and spin up to full thrust." While he gave the order, his eyes remained locked on the display.

The Navy seemed not to react to the first destroyer rush, though utility ships were closing on Navy ships that could provide them covering fire. A few were breaking contact altogether, creating separation to improve their jump solution.

"That's it." The utilities were trying to avoid the gravity of the two fleets. Proximity to gravity increased the risk of the jump. Rather than create maximum distance, a ship could go to libration points, where the gravity of nearby objects is nullified by the gravity of others. The jump ship would constantly calculate the total potential gravity in the local volume and feed the libration points to the rest of the fleet. Litovio suspected the libration points would expose the jump ship.

"Quick, where are the libration points? Have the computer plot them on the battle display. Nothing fancy, just probability spheres."

Within the beat, the libration points appeared as faint, fuzzy spheroids. One l-point was within the Navy fleet, at its gravity center, which was not its true center. Within that point was a single ship. That libration point shifted as the first two postal destroyer divisions pursued the utility ships. The ship in the spheroid adjusted course to recenter itself in the l-point. The timeliness of the adjustment was too natural to be feeding off input from another ship.

Litovio pointed. "That is the jump ship. There." He was beaming. *How to get close without spooking the ship? We'll feint after another deep target.* He scanned the display until he found a suitable decoy. "Tell the other division to break away from us, arc up, then target this ship."

After the communications officer nodded, he turned to the navigations officer. The officer was focused on maneuvers, so Litovio grabbed him by the tunic shoulder to get his attention. "Look at the display. I want you to turn down, and plot a course that will have us arcing just outside weapons range of that ship. When we get close enough, I want you to turn us directly into that ship. Comms, did you get that?"

"Yes, sir." The communications officer relayed the orders to the other ships.

This time, the wait was more nerve-wracking. *Korundaj* was a part of the rush, more likely to be a target. Litovio noticed that the Navy admiral had not focused on the destroyers. Instead, the

Navy's destroyer group sent its own divisions in pursuit. *Maybe they'll ignore us and send other destroyers after us.* If Litovio pulled the maneuver off, then the Navy fleet will be trapped. The ships would be slightly more willing to surrender than jump away.

The arced course flattened, careful to avoid the appearance of going after the jump ship. Litovio was satisfied as the ship continued to remain within the libration point's spheroid, though drifting slightly to the more distant lobe.

At the last possible moment, the destroyer division cut course. The ships all started driving for the jump ship, as much as they could as they fought with their momentum. The *Korundaj* shook as its guns fired. A moment later, the jump ship disappeared.

Litovio pumped his fist. "Yes." *It doesn't matter if we killed it or it jumped. The rest of the fleet should be without up-to-date data to jump. The longer the battle lasts now, the less stable their solution will be.* Litovio felt as if a bubble had been burst.

The postal fleet was broken in to several chunks, but they were all outside the Navy fleet's barrage focal point. *We're still going to need a miracle to survive this.* "Order this division back to the main fleet. It wouldn't help for the flag ship to be destroyed."


## 3.   Bophendze - Naval Battleship

"Now you listen. I'm about tired of this. We may be joined 'til death do us part' but you aren't going to call any shots."

`Very bold of you, Puppet.`

"Sto—" Bophedze started to speak.

Smee closed his mouth.

*You can't stop me from thinking. You are going to stop calling me Puppet. And you are not going to take my body over again without my permission. Do you understand?*

Smee pointed the pistol in Bophendze's right hand at his foot.

`I'm sorry. I don't understand, Puppet.`

Smee pulled the trigger, the bullet ricocheting off the armor.

*Hah! Armored.*

Smee ran Bophendze's body into the bulkhead head first. The armor cushioned the blow. Bophendze's hand then activated the controls to open the helmet's visor. He punched Bophendze in the face, fattening the lip. He punched again on the cheek.

```
I can do this all day, Puppet. I can do this in
your sleep. I can do this when you walk down the
street. I can open your visor the next time you're
in space and leave you to suffocate. I own you,
Puppet.
```

*You don't own me. Kill me and kill yourself.*

```
I don't have to kill you. I can blind you, make
you deaf, make you piss your pants. There's not a
part of your body that I don't control.
```

Bophendze felt his anger start to rise. *No. I will not be a prisoner in my own body.*

```
Give it up, Puppet. Even if you manage to stop
me now, I will come back eventually.
```

Bophendze started to despair. *Smee doesn't always hear my thoughts, only when I try to talk to him. There must be parts of my brain he can't tap into. There's got to be a way I can get control. What can I control now?* Bophendze tried to take a couple breaths. *I can do that much.*

```
Give up yet? You're just like Sirom. You think
you can defeat me. Give up. You can't
```

Bophendze tried not responding to Smee. *Not hardly.* Then it occurred to him, *Sirom was Smee's earlier host? Then he had Sirom put him in the will to mother then to me. Sirom, how did he die? Suicide? Smee probably updated the will then killed Sirom. I can't let him win.*

Bophendze dug deeply into his emotions. He tapped into his sorrow, his anger, his joy. As the emotions washed over him, he tried to drop the pistol. *This has to work.* He thought of his father and Makaan. He remembered Angel's sacrifice, returning to the rage he felt. He focused his anger on his hand.

The pistol dropped.

`What?`

Bophendze beat his fist on his thigh. "I hate you. Do you hear me, Smee? Hate. You don't own me."He slapped his face. "See? I control myself."

`For now, but you can't hold onto that hate forever.`

Bophendze picked the pistol up and jammed it into the holster. "I don't need forever. I need right now." He stripped the guard's ammunition. "Now help me take this ship."

`That I can help with.`


When Smee acclimated to Bophendze on Temask, he researched what happened after Sirom's death. As puppets went, he was a decent fellow. Unlike Bophendze, he did not resist. Smee thought Sirom would be pleased that Bophendze had somehow managed to bottle the demon.

Smee learned about the efforts to outlaw embeddable AI, which he thought was a wise step. It would take him a lifetime at least before he could find where all his comrades went. He also had a lifetime to figure out interstellar communication. Like it or not, his future was entwined with Bophendze. He would have to do what he could to keep the poor boy alive until the time was right to find a new host.

*But not forever. I'll find a way to bypass that reptilian brain and then Bophendze is done for. He's young, reckless. I might have a chance. You've only won for a while Bophendze, though. I'll bide my time. I have eternity.*

# Chapter 15

Bophendze sat relatively motionless. He was waiting for—

So what's your plan?

The question took Bophendze off-guard. *What do you mean what's my plan? I thought you said you could help. You're an artificial intelligence. Don't you have a plan?*

You want to be in control, so take control. What I might do and what you might do are two totally different things.

Bophendze tried to think of a plan. *This is the flagship, right?*

That's what it appears to be.

*Then we need to get it to surrender.*

Sheer genius. Don't you remember me earlier saying this battleship has about 1,500 officers and crew?

*Yes, but there's only one postal marine.*

How very clichè of you. You forgot to add that the postal marine is a genius.

*Obviously I'm smarter than an AI if it's asking me for a plan. Since you're the master of control and manipulation, why don't we make this ship work for us?*

What do you mean?

*Tap into the fire coordination network and have the Navy ships target one another.*

That is actual genius.

Bophendze felt pleased that for once Smee's use of the word genius was not neatly wrapped in sarcasm. *Where's the fire control center?*

Communications tend to be near the center of the ship—Deck Zero—and we're on the top, so head down.

Bophendze checked the rifle one more time. He patted the holster and ammunition he picked up from the dead guard. He looked at the door. *What about that lock? Do you have a way of defeating it?*

It's an electronic lock, a design that predates me. Not a very good design, as I recall. If you had a piece of wire you could short it out.

Bophendze looked around for a piece of wire. The anteroom was austere, with only the guard and his seat. Not willing to give up, he used the but of the rifle to break the outer case of the lock. "Which wire do you want me to short?"

The red one there. But don't you thin—

Bophendze pulled the wire out, and the gun locker's locking mechanism released. The high pitch of an alarm warning radiated from within the locker.

That's the door alarm telling you that it needs to be deactivated before it goes off.

Bophendze entered the gun locker. The interior light flickered on in response to his motion. He looked around the locker until he located the small flat screen that he decided must be the alarm. He again resorted to the rifle's butt to break the flat panel. The glass barely recognized the smudge the butt put on it.

That's transparent aluminum—chemcor. You won't be getting at it that way.

*How long until they respond?*

That depends on whether they suspect you're here. They probably already sent a detachment to find out why the aft gun isn't firing. If I were to guess, I'd say you have a beat or two.

Bophendze picked up a messenger bag. He opened it up and loaded it with anything that looked familiar. In the end he loaded six s and nearly a dozen magazines for the and a bandoleer of extra ammunition. Bophendze slung the bag across his body. He started out of the gun locker, then stopped. He went back to the M9 grenade crate and took out two more grenades. He returned to the anteroom, and armed both grenades. Bophendze then tossed the two grenades into the locker. He slammed the hatch shut and turned the latch. He then hurried out of the anteroom into the passage beyond.

The grenades exploded, one slightly after the other. That set off a chain reaction of other munitions within the locker.

*Forward or aft?*

`Aft takes you back to the gun. Head forward and take the ladders down.`

As Bophendze climbed down the ladder, the battleship shuttered. It was the sort of shudder that should have thrown him down to the deck below. Instead, his grip held, and he continued down to the deck below. He came around the ladder and started forward again. The battleship shuttered again.

`The battleship's come under attack. This might not be the safest place to be right now.`

*Tell that to the crew. As soon as you show me where I need to go, they will all find this battleship unsafe.*

`Fine. We're on level five. The control room is on level zero.`

*It's a good thing there's nobody in this part of the ship.*

`You didn't just say that.`

As Bophendze approached the next down ladder, a helmeted head poked through the hatch from the deck below. A navy guard. Bophendze froze in place as he watched the navy guard continue up the stairs.

`You had to say there was nobody here. Why are you just standing there? Do you think he won't see you? Shoot him.`

Bophendze did not shoot. Instead, he charged the ascending guard and kicked him back down the ladder.

`Didn't you do that a few weeks back? A sign of sentience is the ability to learn from past mistakes.`

Bophendze pulled a grenade and armed it. He then tossed it down the ladder and shielded himself from the inevitable explosion. It clinked three times as bounced down ladder and onto deck during its fall. The detonation sounded less than what Bophendze had suspected. It was a loud pop instead of a large explosion. Shrapnel from the grenade pinged around the deck below. A few fragments shot through the hole and bounced around menacingly but harmless. Smoke started to waft through the hatch.

He waited until the shrapnel stopped bouncing. His arm had been covering his visor. He lowered it and watched the smoke come through. Rather than wait for Smee to pressure him, he got up on his feet and jumped onto the ladder's railing with his feet and slid down to the deck below.

He landed flatly, then checked the guards to see if they were still conscious. Satisfied, he hurried to the next ladder. *I might as well do it again.* Bophendze pulled another grenade. He armed it and tossed it to down the hatch. When he exploded, he smiled. *Much easier than poking my head through the hatch.*

Don't you think you should be a little more cautious? They can hear an exploding grenade much better than a few bullets from your .

"They already know that we're here, so there's no sense in being all stealthy." The ship shuttered. "Besides, they're under attack. The explosions might go unnoticed."

The grenades will make it it easier for them to locate you.

"It doesn't matter if they know where I am now. I'm not dying today."

Saying that won't make it true. I have no idea where you got that idea, but it's going to get us both killed.

"Maybe it will, but not today."

Bophendze hurried down the ladder. The thermal vision in his helmet helped him to see through the smoke. There were four guards lying on the ground. All but one lay motionless. He aimed his rifle and shot the remaining guard three times. The guard stopped moving.

Those others are dying? Is that it?

*Smee, you can't complain that I'm not aggressive enough, then complain when I'm too aggressive.*

`A few dead humans doesn't bother me.  It's you being reckless and getting me killed that bothers me.`

Bophendze did not answer. As he closed on the next ladder, he primed another grenade. Once within range, he neatly tossed it down the ladder and shielded himself again. After the explosion, Bophendze did not hesitate. While the shrapnel pinged around the passage, he moved toward the ladder and climbed down. He scanned the deck for bodies. There were none. *Deck three.*

He repeated the process—a grenade down the ladder followed closely with his descent. There were no other bodies on Decks Two and One.

*So far, so good.*

`Either they've given up, or they're waiting for you below.`

*How's that? I'm moving down the ladders as fast as I can, they can't know where I'm going.*

The battleship shuttered again. Bophendze gasped. "Is this a smart idea?"


Bophendze continued to the last level. He grew more cautious once he threw his last grenade. He quietly orbited the opening to the deck below, looking down to see if there were any guards waiting for him.

`If they figured out what you're doing, they won't be waiting to be blown up.`

*Good point.* He closed on the ladder. Thinking back to a stunt he saw once in the movies, he vaulted his legs onto the rail and tried to slide down. He held onto his rifle with his right hand, using it as a slide. He made it a third of the way down before his lack of skill kicked in. His grip failed and he landed on his back, his helmeted head slamming into the rung. Bophendze bounced the rest of the way down, landing flat on his seat at the bottom. His HUD deducted a percent off of his armor as if to protest his lack of competence.

He shook off the landing and instinctively scanned for targets. The passage was vacant except for him. *Okay, where is this control room?*

```
I have to say a brilliant landing.
```

*Thanks. Which way?*

```
Should be about twenty meters ahead of you, around
the corner.
```

Bophendze picked himself off the ground. He grabbed the rifle off the deck and brought it into the ready position. Shaking his head, he started padding forward.

```
Stealth now?
```

*Never know.* He reached the turn in the passage. He backed away from the corner's edge, then moved in an arc with the corner as the center point. As soon as his path cleared the corner, he saw the control room door. In front of the control room was its guard, who was not the least bit thrown off by Bophendze's stealth.

The guard fired at Bophendze. The bullets slapped into Bophendze's armor. The HUD dutifully reported the loss of integrity by cycling the percentage count below seventy.

It took Bophendze another moment before he realized he was being shot. The guard's fire was fully automatic, his accuracy dropping rapidly. Once Bophendze's mind was able to push through the shock, he pivoted the rifle up from the ready position to fire. He concentrated his burst at the guard's helmet.

The guard stumbled back, then rallied himself. *He's got armor, too.* Bophendze reacted by firing targeted bursts at the helmet. Each burst stopped quickly, giving him the ability to re-aim his shots. After the fourth burst, the guard's helmet was penetrated and he collapsed. Instinctively, Bophendze closed with the guard and fired another burst to the exposed face.

"How do we get into the control room?"

```
How would I know?
```

Bophendze looked at the door. It was locked with a keypad. *Do you have any way of bypassing this?*

```
Not exactly. Try asking.
```

Bophendze shrugged. He pushed the door buzzer and waited. While he waited, he looked at the door and saw the intercom with a small camera. He reached over to clean the lens, which had been splattered by the guard's blood. Before he did, his arm resisted.

What are you doing? You can bet they can tell the difference between a patrolman and one of theirs. Don't give them the advantage of knowing who you are.

"Good point. Thanks."

After a beat, the intercom next to the door squawked. "Access code."

Bophendze hesitated. He was out of grenades, so blowing the door was not an option. Nor did he have any idea of what the code might be. He shrugged and gave his own service number.

A moment later, the intercom spoke again. "Sir, you do realize we're under general quarters? We shouldn't be opening the door."

*It worked?* Bophendze summoned his best command voice, and thought of some line from a movie. "Override security protocol. I need access now. Do you understand me?" He did his best to make his question sound more like a demand.

The door lock clicked.

How?

*Who am I to question how? Maybe it's what Angel called Providence?* Bophendze pushed through the door into the room beyond. The room was dark, but his HUD adjusted almost instantaneously. He worked quickly to kill the personnel in the control room. Measured bursts dropped each soft target before any of them had a chance to react.

The door closed behind him. He swept through the room, looking for any signs of life. None of those in the room looked alive. Bophendze went back to the door and looked at the lock. *Smee, how do I lock it?*

You're asking me? I'm not familiar with this design.

"I suppose I could just shoot it."

You believe what you see in the movies? It's
an electronic lock. All you'd be doing is locking
yourself in.

"Any chance it locks automatically?"

I don't remember seeing any way to open the door
from the outside apart from the keypad. It is safe
to assume anybody with the right code could enter.

"Let's hope whoever has the right code doesn't happen to want to
come in." Bophendze scanned the control room a second time. He
tried to figure out what exactly he had fought his way to. *Do you have
any idea what to do now?*

Didn't you say something about tapping into the
fire control.

*Okay, how do I do that?*

## 1.   Litovio - Korundaj

The battle had stopped being one-sided as the Postal fleet slowly
tipped the balance. Once outside the focal point, they were able
to exact heavier damage on the Navy ships that were still in their
barrage formation. Litovio's targeting the jump ship worked. He
watched Navy ships nearest the libration point fade out as they
jumped. *Perhaps they are surprised we have this much fight in us
and aren't prepared to sacrifice themselves in a fair fight?*

Not all the Navy ships broke and ran, though. Litovio noticed the
Navy fleet altering position. He instinctively stopped focusing on the
ships and looked at the overall movement. He looked at the fleet as a
single entity, a koleoideo. As he did, he recognized the formation the
Navy fleet was converting to. It looked like the capitals were forming
into a sphere, but the destroyers were forming into a claw. Sort of like
a ball and chain.

It meant that if the Postal Service was going to subdue the Navy,
they were going to have to break the sphere. When they tried, the claw
would tear the Postal fleet apart.

"I think I'm all out of miracles."

\* \* \*

## 2. Bophendze - Navy Battleship

He took off his helmet. The darkness of the control room surprised him. He walked over to the central console, thinking it might be important. The touch panels looked more intended for video recording than fire control. Bophendze raised his head to see if he could see a more important-looking console.

The display wall stood out. It was a dome, with the star field stretched out in every direction. Speckled all over the display was a constellation of white squares filled with blue. Just beyond that constellation was a smaller cluster in red. The audio was quiet, except for the occasional staccato of incoming messages. The tone of the messages was one of calm professionalism. Bophendze was annoyed by the undertone of disdain coming over the wireless.

He concluded the console he was at had value. He sat down at the keyboard and looked back at the display. Some projector at the seat beamed an overlay at him. Bophendze adjusted the seat until the display was clear and centered. Then he saw that the display provided rich data on the ongoing fleet battle. The Navy was forming into a ball with some claw forming.

He saw a list along the left of broadcasts. The time stamp stopped about the time he entered the control room. "So this room assigns targets to the fleet?"

That looks like it. That means you're on the flagship.

He looked back down at the console, where he noticed the keyboard and a smaller display. *I type the target and it displays there?*

Give it a try.

Bophendze looked back up at the display, trying to identify a suitable target. He set his eyes on a destroyer. He carefully typed in its target ID, ensuring the formatting was consistent with the target board. Satisfied, he hit SEND.

A moment later, the fleet's guns stopped, and then fired a single concentrated salvo at the destroyer. Its target marker dutifully winked away.

`Idiot!`

*What?*

`That was one of your destroyers. Do you know which one?`

*Does it really matter?*

`Yes. Remember, your admiral and Litovio re-flagged to a destroyer. How do you know that one isn't the one they flagged to?`

Bophendze felt the blood rush out of his face as he realized he just destroyed a postal ship, killing dozens of fellow marines. He might not have known the word fratricide, but the guilt and horror felt all the worse.

"Help me identify Naval ships."

`Give me your hands so I can peck around.`

Bophendze nodded.

A moment later, Bophendze's hands started to tap across the keyboard. The display popped windows as Smee worked to understand the display. Bophendze tried to keep up with the displays, but Smee's ability to read was just a bit faster than his. The red cluster and blue constellation disappeared, only to be replaced by a blue cluster and red constellation.

`There. I reversed the IFF, er, Identification of Friend or Foe. That means the Navy now sees all the Postal ships as friendlies. If I'm not mistaken, their weapons will not fire at a target marked friend on IFF.`

*Neat. Is there a way to target specific Naval ships?*

`Yes, do you want me to do it?`

*No, I can take it from here.*

Bophendze felt his hands return to his control. He looked at the wall display, searching for a target. A giddy feeling came over him as he selected a pair of support ships. He carefully typed in the identity of the one that was flagged as "Navigation." He hit SEND and a moment later was rewarded by watching the target disappear.

```
Good call.  That was likely the fleet's jump
computer.  I'm surprised.  Normally a fleet carries
two of them.  Maybe our fleet took out the other one?
```

*What's a fleet jump computer?*

```
That's   a   ship   that   maintains   the   overall
gravametric  configuration  and  maintains  a  jump
solution.  That way, if a ship needs to jump to
safety it can.
```

Bophendze tried to grasp what Smee had said. *Do we have one of those?* Bophendze could almost hear a sigh in Smee's reply.

```
The Postal Marines are not large-fleet based. You
might want to target faster.  It won't take long
before they realize what's going on and send somebody
after you.
```

Bophendze typed in a queue of targets and broadcast them. The Navy started firing at the larger battleships, not as individuals, but *en masse.* The targets on the display grew in size, showing a white halo that turned slowly red. One of the ships that was mostly white suddenly exploded and the target marker disappeared.

"What's that?"

```
I'm not an expert in targeting.  It looks like
some attempt to assess damage of the capital ships.
It must not be entirely accurate since that one just
disappeared.
```

Steadily, other battleships started to explode and disappear. The wireless chatter suddenly started changing. The professional disdain from before became chaotic pleas for help.

Bophendze started typing in more targets. Looking at the display, he started to make out the patterns that the fleet was arrayed in. He pointed out one of them. *It looks like those are team leads. I'll just target all of them. Smee, is there any way to identify which of them is the overall fleet lead?* Bophendze heard Smee sigh.

```
        Try target code A300B2-203.  While you're at it,
     issue command JMP-611 and CG-49
```

Bophendze typed that code in, along with those of the other ships that appeared to be in leadership positions. He smiled and pressed SEND.

The ship started to shake. Not once but repeatedly. Bophendze's helmet fell to the deck and rolled. He got out of the seat and scrambled for it. Another shake tripped him and he fell. "What's going on?"

```
     You asked for the target code for the central ship.
     You are on that ship, remember?
```

A part of Bophendze's vision showed a yellow halo.

```
     That number up there next to the ship's name is
     its code.  JMP-611 is a jump command.  CG-49, if I'm
     not mistaken, signals all ships to communications
     silence.  What does it all mean?  The ships will fire
     on auto until the commanders can tell their crews
     to stop firing.  It also means they won't be able to
     change targets without severing their cooperative
     combat fire.  Ships will also start jumping in a
     panic, which means a lot of them may well never be
     heard from again.
```

"All ships?"

```
     Yes.
```

"This one?"

```
     Yes.
```

Bophendze felt like he just wet himself. In his haste to target the Naval ships, he sealed his own fate. The ship's continued shaking was a constant reminder of how he had managed to screw up yet again. His mind numbed at the weight of his failure. He dropped back to sit back down into the chair, which had been moved in all the explosions. Instead he fell to the floor and onto his back. Rather than pick himself up, he clinched his fists and brought them up to his eyes. He had no way out, and he knew it.

Even if the ship was not destroyed by the Navy ships, the Postal Marines would continue to pound on it. If it did not, then the battleship might jump away without a good solution, ghosting them forever. It was not the thought of all the naval personnel killed that weighed on him, but of his own inevitable death. He had promised his mother that he would make something of himself. He had survived Makaan. He had even found a way to control Smee. But none of that mattered now. His life was over. He started beating the floor with his armored fist.

It took a couple of beats, but his despair started to wane. He pulled himself up into a sitting position and surveyed the control room floor. His helmet was not far away, so he reached over and picked it up. He looked at the helmet's face and saw a little reflection of himself. Bophendze resisted the urge to throw it across the room.

"Bophendze, think. What are your options? Dying is the default of doing nothing. Maybe I can surrender the ship? That wouldn't matter if the ship was already programmed to jump away. How long does it take a ship this size to do jump prep anyway?"

Bophendze stood up and went over to his rifle. He bent over and picked it up. It was a lot heavier than the helmet, but easier to handle. "Whatever I decide to do, I can't stay here. Maybe I can get to an escape pod, and hope that my side doesn't shoot survivors on sight."

He walked over to the door. He leaned the rifle against the door jamb, and slowly put his helmet on. Once he had twisted it into the lock position, the HUD started synchronizing with the suit. The ship continued to shudder as ship fire kept slamming into it. He tried to figure out how to get to an escape pod without having to fight his way out.

*Wait a second. I can order an abandon ship, can't I?*

Bophendze sat back down at the console and pulled up the list of broadcast commands. He selected abandon ship. He smiled as he pushed the send button.

The ship's alarm started sounding abandon ship. Bophendze thought it was interesting that the command was the same on Naval ships as it was on Postal ships. He hoped the message carried over the communications silence. *Okay, Smee. Show me the way to the escape pod.*

Silence. Bophendze started to get angry at Smee playing games. Then he remembered that intense emotions pushes Smee out. He could still feel the pangs of his earlier breakdown. He was still frustrated, but realized he had to rely on himself for a while.

He started tapping on the keyboard and searching the display. After a while he saw a tab for the ship's diagram. He called it up. *I'm only two decks above the bridge. There are escape pods right there.* Despite himself, he pointed at the diagram. *I'll bet the ship's commander leaves last.*

Bophendze ran to the hatch. He checked his rifle to ensure he had enough ammunition. He was still a stranger on the ship and could not rely on panic to completely camouflage him. Satisfied, he opened the hatch and stepped into the passage.

The crew was not as panicked as he had hoped. They were abandoning ship, but not flying for fear. It was an orderly escape. Jumping into action, Bophendze ran to the ladder and resumed his descent. It took him only a few breaths to make it down the two decks necessary to make it to the bridge. He took a moment to regain his bearings. He pointed in the direction of the bridge, assuring himself of the right course.

He brought his rifle into the ready position and started padding forward. There were fewer crew now, and the ship stopped shaking from cannon fire. He approached the bridge steadily, its hatch clearly visible in front of him. Unlike the bridge of a postal ship, there were no guards posted outside. *That's odd. Maybe they've escaped?*

Bophendze kept scanning for hostiles as he closed on the bridge's hatch. A few meters out, he saw the keypad. Thinking back to his entering the control room, Bophendze stopped to type in his access code.

The access indicator on the keypad went from red to green. The hatch catches clicked in response, and the hatch opened. Bophendze rushed through the hatch firing at anything he saw moving.

The tactic worked. His first burst struck one of the bridge guards. As Bophendze fired a second burst, realizing that the guard was not wearing body armor. He thought it was a severe breech of protocol for them to fail to wear their armor, but he focused on the task before him. He scanned for the nearest armed crewman. He fired quick, steady bursts and dropped them all. He then turned on the unarmed crewmen who seemed intent to resist.

In the adrenalin, he failed to notice the time it took him to suppress the bridge. When he stopped firing, the only crewman left raised his hands. Bophendze lowered his rifle and noticed that it was an admiral—the fleet's commander. "Well I'll be." Bophendze raised his rifle and pointed at the admiral. "Sir. You're my prisoner." He was surprised at the falsetto in his voice.

"It would appear so. Where are the rest of you?"

"There is no rest-of-us."

The admiral gasped. "What do you mean? You're the only postal on this ship? I've been getting reports of all sorts of mayhem."

Bophendze smiled, though it would not have shown through the helmet's visor. "Sorry, sir. Just me. It would have been much more mayhemical if my friends were with me." He lowered his rifle politely. "Order your fleet's surrender."

"I already have. Whatever it is you did tore us to shreds. There are only a handful of us left. The rest are either destroyed or false jumped to who knows where. It was the best I could do to stop the crew from completely abandoning ship."

Bophendze thought back. *Had the crew been trying to stop me from shooting at them under surrender?* He shook the doubt out of his mind. *The admiral could be trying to trick me.* "Open a channel to my fleet."

The admiral slowly lowered his arms and walked over to the communications center. He worked the controls and picked up the handset.

Bophendze moved closer. "Set it down and back away."

The admiral complied.

Bophendze lowered his rifle slightly and picked up the handset with his free hand. "This is Postman Bophendze calling the Postal Fleet."

"This is Commander Litovio. Is that Bophendze?"

"Yes, Sir. I have the Navy admiral here as my prisoner. I guess that means I captured the battleship."

There was a long pause on the other end. "Postman, you captured the Navy fleet, not just its admiral. I don't know how you managed it, but what you did saved all of us."

Bophendze's smile grew. "I was just doing my duty, Sir. Could you send somebody over to help me out? If they realize I'm by myself I might find myself captured."

"We already have a detachment of marines coming. I'll tell them to meet you at the bridge."

# Chapter 16

## *End of the Beginning*

Life settled into routine marine duties in the months that followed the battle. The first few days he was kept in sick bay, which for a destroyer was only two beds. Litovio remained in command of the ship until it returned to its normal duty system. At that point, Bophendze heard Litovio would return to his normal duties, whatever those were.

The Postal Service retained all the captured Navy ships, adding much needed combat capabilities to their arsenal. After he was pronounced fit for duty, Bophendze was put in command of a stick of marines as a lance corporal. He was assigned to the Battleship *Tannenberg*, what had been the flag ship he captured. He took responsibility for the lives of four other marines, many of whom had far more service time than he did. If any of his marines were upset by the assignment, none of them mentioned it in his presence. He managed to learn from them.

felt woefully ill-prepared, but he tamed Smee. He resisted the urge to release the emotional hold he had over his inner demon. Instead, he let the fear of inadequacy fuel the hold. It also fueled his drive to study marine procedures so he could do right by his more senior subordinates.

"Lance Corporal Bophendze." The voice carried the weight of command with it.

Bophendze jumped to attention. "Sir!" He resisted the urge to glance at the officer, but caught the ensign rank on the officer's collar. *I have one thing he doesn't. I've been promoted.*

"We're receiving a guest on board ship. You are to accompany us and report to the hangar immediately."

"Sir." Bophendze pivoted in place toward the hatch and walked out. *Did the ensign have fear in his voice? Why does he have an escort. The only other person alive that knows about Makaan was Litovio. Has he moved forward with charges after all I've done?*

He made his way purposefully, but still at a walking pace. The *Tannenberg*'s crewmen moved out of his way as he walked. It was something odd how they started treating him after the battle. It never occurred to him to ask why.

As he walked in the hangar, he stopped in shock. The hangar was filled with ranks of ship's crewmen and marines in parade formation. A shuttle sat in the hangar with the Imperial seal. The diamond was naval blue with gold piping on the border. A gold inverted, broad "T" sat atop a broader "T" with the curved cross member, with "Yu" symbol beneath. Bophendze snapped to attention, unsure what to do.

"Corporal Bophendze, present."

Using just his eyes, Bophendze looked to see where he was being told to move to. He saw Litovio at attention, facing the Imperial shuttle. A gap was to his left, then a rank of other marines and crewmen stood at attention.

A middle-aged man standing imperiously in front of Litovio. Bophendze saw Litovio gesture carefully with his hand, as if saying "next to me, idiot."

Bophendze carefully marched over to Litovio, trying to exhibit the ramrod straight back marines were supposed to have. He turned and faced the man. The face was familiar, but he could not place it exactly. Off in the distance, a voice called out. "Attention to orders."

"The Imperial Medal of Honor is awarded to Commander Ambrose Kaarel Litovio. During the Battle of Tannenberg he skillfully commanded the First Postal Armada in the defense of the Emperor's honor against the renegade Naval forces. His keen understanding of fleet tactics ensured swift victory, bestowing honor to the Imperial Postal Marines and the Emperor himself."

The man reached over and picked up the medal. He placed the broad ribbon around Litovio's neck. The medal hung high on his chest.

"The Imperial Medal of Honor is awarded to Chief Danel Bophendze. During the Battle of Tannenberg he single-handedly assaulted the renegade fleet command battleship. With thoughtless heroism, he fought through the ship until he reached a critical location that led to the ship's capture. His selfless dedication to the Emperor bestows honor to the Imperial Postal Marines and the Emperor himself."

`Reckless abandon, more like.`

*Shut up.*

With the same ceremony, Bophendze felt the weight of the award, and a new promotion, rest on his breast. "My uncle was amazed at your heroism. I think you had to have had a death wish. Either way, we will need marines like you in the days ahead."

*Uncle? The Emperor?*

"The Imperial Medal of Valor and Fidelity is awarded to Corporal Makaan posthumously. He manned a medium projectile cannon on the *Spaka* single-handedly, giving the ship's crew precious time to evacuate."

Bophendze tried not to smile. Litovio must have put him in for the medal. *I guess you can't investigate the alleged murder of a combat hero.*

The royal family member continued down the line.

Litovio leaned over and whispered. "I owe you an eternal debt of gratitude. Consider this a down payment."

"After this, where else can I go?"

Thank you for reading

# Bellicose

will return in .

## Follow Me

**Benjamin Wilson** can be followed on Twitter and Facebook.
Visit his web site at http://dausha.net for more information. You can
also sign up for announcements of other books in this series at
http://dausha.net.

www.ingramcontent.com/pod-product-compliance
Lightning Source LLC
Chambersburg PA
CBHW071500170626
46811CB00007B/2649